INFLECTION POINT

INFLECTION POINT

A QUINCY HARKER, DEMON HUNTER NOVEL

JOHN G. HARTNESS

Charlotte, NC

FALSTAFF
BOOKS
WWW.FALSTAFFBOOKS.COM

1

B ecks led me off the elevator and down the hall to an apartment we'd converted into a base of operations during our Great Archangel Pokémon Game of 2018. It had been a long, uncomfortable helicopter ride from Memphis, but at least the magic helicopter she commandeered to fetch me was fast. Of course, "fast" going from Memphis to Charlotte meant we made the trek in five hours of chilly silence rather than the eleven hours of chilly silence I would have endured in a car. Flynn rebuffed all my attempts at apologies, explanations, or tactical questions, answering everything with "we'll handle it when we're home."

I assumed that to mean when we weren't in the company of Homeland Security's Regional Director and tenuous ally Keya Pravesh, plus the grim-faced man and woman in the cockpit of the chopper. I tried to reach out gently across our mental link, but found a wall blocking me. Yeah, she was pretty pissed.

I couldn't blame her. After all, I did sneak out in the middle of the night leaving nothing but a note and cut off all contact for half a year. And I did shut her out of our link for that whole time, letting just enough through to make sure she knew I was still alive. It was a dick move, and ultimately useless, but like many stupid decisions I've made in the century and a quarter or so I've been alive, it seemed like a good idea at the time.

Now here we were, standing in the hallway of a building I owned, but felt like a complete stranger in, with the woman I loved more than oxygen and good whiskey. I was scared shitless of how this was going to go down, and underneath all the roil of emotions about my relationship, if I still had one, with Rebecca, there was a nasty, copper-tasting undercurrent of worry about Luke.

Luke. Lucas Card. That's what he was going by these days. He was coming to the end of the lifespan of that alias, though, which meant that in a few years Lucas Card was going to have to move away and be replaced by his younger nephew with similar features, a different haircut, and a new name. It was the haircut that Luke hated the most. I think he secretly liked the other parts: the playing dress up, the reinventing himself every couple of decades, the new names and histories. It had to be a little entertaining for a man whose real story had been told so often, so thoroughly, and so spectacularly incorrectly even since Abraham Van Helsing sat down with his friend Bram Stoker and helped create the "fictional" account of my uncle, Vlad Tepes. Count Dracula.

But now that uncle was missing, and for once, I was the one playing cavalry. It was a reversal of nearly a century of Luke bailing my ass out of bad situations, and while I kind of relished being the one riding in on the white horse for a change, I really, *really* didn't want Luke to have to be kidnapped and probably tortured because of it.

I reached in my pocket for the key to the apartment, then realized that I left those keys, along with every other remnant of my life here, in the drawer of a bedside table in a converted store room of a magical neutral zone dive bar on the Mississippi River. "Um, I don't have my keys," I said.

"It's probably open," Flynn said, reaching past me and turning the knob. Sure enough, the door swung open without a sound. I stepped through and caught it before it hit the wall. Heavy. Someone had upgraded the security since I'd been gone.

Becks caught my look and nodded. "We reinforced all the doors and windows, plus the frames. The ceiling was fine, since it's a helipad, but we added titanium sheeting under the carpet. Director Pravesh brought in some mages to ward everything. Nothing short of an Archangel is getting in here without an invitation. Too bad we didn't think of it until it was too late." Her jaw tightened, and I saw the anger and self-recrimination flash across her face.

I wanted to reach out, wanted to take her in my arms and tell her it wasn't her fault, that if someone was going to kidnap Count Friggin' Dracula, that she wouldn't have been able to stop them anyway. But I could feel the anger boiling through our link and let it go. We'd figure out our shit later, once Luke was safe. Because burying my feelings had worked so well for me the last six months. I just bit my tongue and stepped over the threshold.

The place looked just like I remembered it, only with fewer Archangels lounging about. There was a big conference table dominating the living room, with eight chairs around it. A monstrous TV hung on one wall, and the blinds were open to the balcony, letting in the first rays of sunlight. On a couch off to the side of the room, a tall African American woman with dreads and her foot in a walking boot snored quietly, stretched out with a hammer laying on the floor next to her. A little girl with her mother's nose sat on the floor by the couch playing on a tablet computer, and she grinned when she saw me walk in.

"Uncle Q!" she cried as she sprang to her feet and barreled over to me. "Mommy said we might not see you for a long time. Were you on the helicopter? I heard it, but Mommy was asleep. Do you want some breakfast? I can make Pop-Tarts, but I bet Gran will make you scrambled eggs if you want some."

I reached down and patted the girl on her head. She wore pink and purple pajamas with unicorns on them, and I felt a little pang looking at them, thinking of my pal Dennis, who was once a computer genius, then spent several years as a disembodied soul trapped in the internet, and was currently the Archangel Uriel. My life, it has the weird.

"Hey Ginny," I said. "Pop-Tarts sound great. Do you have the brown sugar and cinnamon ones? Those are my favorite."

"I don't know. I'll ask Gran." She turned and marched off to the kitchen where her grandmother was busy making coffee. I followed the girl, giving my best smile to Cassie as I walked behind the bar into the kitchen.

"Hey Cassie," I said.

Cassandra Harrison, Luke's current Renfield, turned from the coffeemaker and I gasped. Cassie was getting older, in her mid-sixties now, but she'd never looked her age until right that moment. She looked *old*. She looked old, and she looked frail. This was the woman I'd seen stare down Frankenstein's monster without blinking, but now she stood there in the kitchen with her arm in a sling and a split lower lip, and she looked like a stiff breeze would knock her over.

"Jesus Christ, Cassie, what did they do to you?" I held out my arms, and she rushed into them, pressing her face against my chest.

"I'm sorry, Quincy. I wasn't strong enough. They burst in the door like some kind of SWAT team in the movies, all dressed in black with guns and smoke grenades and gas masks. It was like the stuff I saw on the TV out of Alabama when I was a little girl. One of them grabbed me before I could hit the button to lock down Luke's panic room, and he threw me against the wall. I think I sprained my wrist."

"She's lucky she didn't break anything," Jo Henry said, limping over to the bar that separated the kitchen from the living room. She had a crutch under one arm and a big bruise under one eye. "Becks and I were in here watching Netflix when we heard the commotion. She grabbed Ginny and hid her in my room while I took my hammer and ran out to see what was going on. We didn't know…we thought… shit, Harker. We thought you were right and some of your shit had come down on us. I thought to myself if you pissing off Lucifer got my mama or my baby hurt, we were going to see how many places in you I could shove a nine-pound hammer."

"But they weren't after me," I said.

"No," Director Keya Pravesh of the Department of Homeland Security Paranormal Division said as she walked into the room and strode over to the conference table. It was still a couple hours before dawn, but Pravesh looked as put together as if it were ten in the morning. She had on a sleek black suit, her hair pulled back in a tight bun, and a jacket cut well enough that I could just see the bulge her pistol made. Her only concession to the action her job sometimes saw was the pair of black sneakers on her feet. No stylish heels for Director Pravesh. I was willing to bet my house that she had a backup pistol strapped to one ankle, too.

"They were after Luke, and they knew when and how to hit him. They came in mid-afternoon, when the building would have the least security and when Luke would be at his most vulnerable. It was only a fluke that Detective Flynn and Jo were home to attempt to fend off the attack."

"For all the good it did us," Becks said bitterly as she joined Pravesh at the conference table. I followed suit, yielding the head of the table to the leader of the off-the-books government agency in the room. Jo and Cassie flanked me at the opposite end of the table from Pravesh, who sat with Flynn at her right hand. There were a few empty chairs, but the last time we'd used this room, there were a lot more of us involved in the plan.

"They were good, Harker," Jo said. "I've fought a lot, and these guys were well trained. They kicked our asses, but they pulled their punches. If they wanted human casualties, we'd all be dead."

I opened my mouth to say something but caught movement out of the corner of my eye. It was Ginny, standing at my elbow with a plate of Pop-Tarts, her mouth a silent "O" as she processed what her mother said. "You mean those men that took Uncle Luke might have...killed you? Or Gran? Or Aunt Rebecca?"

"They might have, sweetie, but they didn't," Jo said, looking the frightened girl right in the eye. "I'm here, and I'm okay, and nothing bad is going to happen to me."

"That's the damn truth," I said. "Because you're not going anywhere near those bastards again."

"Fuck you, Harker," Jo said, giving me a snarl. "You don't get to run off and drink your problems away for half a year and come back up in here like you're running things. You gave up that right when you snuck out of here in the middle of the night like a chickenshit."

"What did you want me to do, Jo? Stay here until Lucifer just shows up on our doorstep one day and blasts us all to dust? I've seen that movie, and I don't have some fancy time-traveling glove to put everything back together. Yeah, I bailed. Yeah, it was a chickenshit move. Yeah, I regretted it the second I walked out the door, and every day for six fucking months, and I regret it even more now that I see how fucked everything got because I was gone."

I took a deep breath and looked around the table. "It was the worst fucking thing I've done in my life, and some of you have an idea exactly the kind of things that are on that list. It was the wrong call, but it's the call I made. So now that you've called me an asshole, and I've agreed with you, can we move the fuck on?"

"I never called you an asshole, Harker," Jo said.

"You want to?" I shot back.

"Yeah," she said. "You're an asshole."

"Feel better?"

"A little."

"Okay, then. That's settled. Anybody else want to yell at me?" I looked from person to person. Except Ginny. I figured the fifth grader would give me a pass. There were no takers, although I did get a little mental message from Flynn.

Don't worry. I have plenty to say. I just don't feel like saying it in front of everyone, she said over our mental link.

I didn't think we were through talking about it, I sent back.

Not even close. The mental wall slammed back down between us, but it didn't feel as solid this time, giving me a little hope that maybe the damage I'd done wasn't irreparable.

I turned my attention back to Pravesh. "Well, Director, would you like to tell us why your sister agency has gone apeshit and come after Luke? Are they on some kind of *Twilight*-hating kick? Because let me tell you, Luke hates that movie, too."

"They didn't take Luke as the end game, Harker," Pravesh said. "They know about vampires. They have decades of data on vampires at their fingertips. They took Luke so they could get their hands on something unlike any other creature they've ever seen."

"What's that?" I asked, then it hit me. "You gotta be fucking kidding me."

"Not even a little," Pravesh said. "They took Luke to get the attention of the only known living human-vampire hybrid. They took Luke so they could get to you."

_____

2

"What do we know?" I asked, looking around the table. "DEMON has decided they want to study me, and they kidnapped Luke to get my attention? Why didn't they just ask me for a blood sample?"

"Would you have given them one?" Pravesh asked.

"Well, no," I admitted. "I would have told them to shove their test tubes up their collective government asses. But I figured a federal agency would be a little more centered on following protocol than me."

"They were, until a few months ago," Pravesh said, opening up a tablet and tapping the screen. An image appeared on the TV behind her of a familiar woman. She was trim, African American, and pretty, with sharp features and intelligent eyes.

"I know her," I said.

"You do?" Flynn and Pravesh asked at the same time.

"Yeah, that's Agent Walston from DEMON. I met her in Memphis when I...accidentally wandered into one of the off-books containment facilities. Grumpy, and has a strong right arm."

"She hit you?" Becks asked.

"Yeah, I mouthed off and she slapped the shit out of me."

"Wish I could have seen that," Flynn said, but the way the corner of her mouth twitched up when she said it, I knew she only meant about half of it.

"I wish I could have sold tickets, or at the very least put the video up on YouTube. That shit would be worth a million views easy," Jo said.

"If you two are done?" Pravesh asked with a sigh. She looked at me. "They don't act like children when you're not here."

"What can I say? I bring out the best in people. Now what does a mid-level Special Agent with a hefty suit allowance have to do with DEMON going rogue?" I asked.

"Would it make more sense if I told you that everything she said to you was a lie?" Pravesh asked.

"She works for the government. I took that bit for granted. Is there something specific she lied about that you know of, or are we just working off general assumptions?" I was pretty sure DHS didn't have me bugged somehow, and I doubted they were eavesdropping on black sites of other government agencies, so I was about sixty percent sure she didn't know anything about my conversation with Walston. But that left forty percent.

"I don't know anything she said to you specifically, Harker," Pravesh replied. "But I know she's no mid-level agent. She reports directly to Adrienne McDonald Shaw, the new Director of DEMON. She was appointed with a mandate to clean up the agency and eliminate any working relationships with non-humans. She's gone about that with gusto, terminating any agents with any supernatural connections, and severing ties with all groups of cryptids. This Walston woman is one of her top lieutenants."

"I thought DEMON usually played well with others," I said.

"They did. Until Director Shaw took over."

"Can somebody explain to me why there's a Paranormal Division within Homeland Security and a whole separate agency to deal with what seems like the same stuff? Is it just typical government redundancy, or is there a real reason for it?" Jo asked.

"The agencies each have a slightly different focus," Pravesh said.

"While both are tasked with keeping an eye on supernatural creatures and paranormal activities within the boundaries of the United States, DEMON has historically been more focused on cryptids and their activities, while DHSPD has spent more of its time on mystical and religious-focused problems."

"DEMON hunts monsters, and Homeland Security hunts demons," I said.

"Oh, that makes *perfect* sense."

"It does when you take the federal government into account," I replied. "Look at it this way, Jo. DHS basically has a Paranormal Division because of the Shadow Council. Luke helped make it happen in the wake of World War II, when Wild Bill Donovan was setting up the CIA out of the remnants of the OSS. What is now the Homeland Security Paranormal Division started in Europe as the Supernatural Detail of the Office of Strategic Services."

"Wait, *Luke* founded the Paranormal Division?" Flynn asked.

"In a manner of speaking," I said. "That's what I heard, anyway. I was a little...indisposed during the time he worked with Donovan to make it happen."

"That's putting it mildly," Cassie chimed in. "Jo's granddaddy Alex told me some tales about Luke and the Council and Wild Bill and his bunch of misfits. He used to laugh and laugh whenever Julia Child would come on the TV, talking about how that woman was the deadliest spy he ever met. Said she had a way with poisons that would make a Borgia jealous."

"Julia Child?" Jo asked, disbelief written all over her face. "The cooking show lady? Now you're just pulling my leg."

"No, she's not," I said. "I met her a few times in the fifties, after I came back to myself. Nice lady. Helluva cook. She was ecstatic when she found out Luke wasn't allergic to garlic. Said even for the dead, life without spice wouldn't be worth living. Luke and the Council worked with Donovan to set up the Paranormal Division after the war, to be a longer arm of the Council. As we all know far too well, with government money comes government oversight, and it wasn't long before the whole thing grew too big for Luke to stay involved. As long as it was Donovan and a handful of trusted people, that was fine. But as the Division grew, it became more than Luke could stay involved with. He stayed close to Wild Bill, though, all the way up until his death."

"DEMON is the cryptid hunters, and DHSPD focuses on demons and magic, got it," Jo said. "But why are they coming for Harker?"

"He's unique," Pravesh replied. "There's never been another case of a vampire-human hybrid, and they want to see what makes him tick. And they want to know how to neutralize him."

"Haven't these people ever watched *Blade*?" I muttered. "Next thing you know, I'm gonna see 'Kill the Daywalker' spray-painted on the side of buildings."

"You joke, but that's their plan," Pravesh said. "They don't just want to study you and know how to put you down if they need to. They want to kill you and everyone else with a drop of cryptid blood or an iota of paranormal ability. They've gone one hundred percent radical, and Shaw and the rest of the new leadership are pushing a 'humans-only' doctrine from the top down."

"What about Bubba?" Flynn asked. "That redneck from Georgia. He works with them, doesn't he? I've always heard he was decent."

"He is, and he did," Pravesh said. "But he and his team disappeared into Faerie for a little over a year, and when he came back, he wasn't quite human. Or maybe he never was, but now they know about it. He was cut loose, his girlfriend was fired, and their team has scattered. All the other DEMON agents and contractors that we've encountered were terminated."

"Terminated?" Flynn asked.

"Not permanently, just fired," Pravesh said.

"Okay, then. DEMON has a new director, and she's a badass who wants to play vivisectionist with Harker. What do we do about it?" Flynn asked.

"Well, we could go knock on her door," I said. "And by knock, I mean kick it the fuck in, and by her door, I mean the black site I found just outside of Memphis."

"Good idea, but it's empty," Glory said, stepping into the room with the demon Faustus in tow. Glory looked like she'd just stepped out of the pages of *Rolling Stone*, with her artfully torn jeans, long blond curls, Victoria's Secret curves, and Chris Stapleton tour shirt. Faustus looked a little the worse for wear in a bespoke navy suit with no tie, but instead of his human face, he was sporting the jet-black skin of his true demonic self, complete with yellow eyes and short fangs curling over his bottom lip.

"Can we never do that again?" the demon asked as he followed my guardian angel into the room.

"What are you doing here?" I asked, then turned to look at Glory. "What is he doing here?"

"I brought him. We could use all the firepower we can get."

"Besides, I need to be out of Memphis for a little while," Faustus said, running a hand over his face and morphing into a muscular Asian man with a green mohawk. He caught my glare and shook his head. "Too much?" he asked, then shifted into a generic white guy in a Brooks Brothers suit, the kind of almost fit fortyish guy with gray temples and shoes too expensive for his credit line that would blend in perfectly with a bank town like Charlotte.

"Let me guess, you got caught cheating at craps, and Raxho decided you should go back to Hell and chat with Lucifer about your poor decisions," I said, looking at the demon.

"Something like that," he replied. He still seemed a little ruffled as he walked into the kitchen. Faustus opened a cupboard, pulled out my *Supernatural* coffee mug, and poured himself a cup. "Where's the Jameson's?"

"Under the counter," Cassie called. The demon nodded, poured a healthy slug of whisky into his coffee, and joined us at the table.

"What took you so long?" I asked Glory. "I thought you'd pop back here and be waiting for us on the roof."

"I would have, but it took me a while to find this idiot, then even longer to convince Raxho's thugs not to kill him." Raxho was the demon that ran the *Pearl of Dixie* floating casino outside Memphis. He hadn't struck me as someone who was particularly up for negotiations, but Glory can get downright persuasive when she wants to.

"That's a lot of hassle for one demon when we've got the whole Shadow Council we can call on," I said.

"Well, that's a little bit of a problem," Flynn said.

"What?" I asked.

"We don't have the whole Council. We've got, well, we've got us. In this room."

"What the fuck?" I asked, looking around the table. "Where's Adam?"

"He went underground at the first kidnappings. Luke was the only one who knew how to find him. I've left messages at his dead drops, but so far no response," Pravesh said.

"Watson?" I asked. "He's a bit of a prick, but he can shoot."

"He still can't get into the country," Flynn replied. "The same visa problems that kept him out of the Archangel hunt."

"I thought he was just bs'ing because he didn't want to help," I said.

"Well, if he is, then he's a consistent little shit," Jo said. "And Gabby's out. The idiot broke her leg chasing a werewolf in Chicago two weeks ago. She's on crutches for a month, more if she doesn't take care of herself. And Dennis is an angel now, so this is what you've got."

"It's okay, Mom," Ginny said, her voice very serious. "You can just say that Uncle Dennis died. You don't have to say he's an angel just because I'm here."

Jo's eyes whipped up to mine, and I shrugged. "Kids aren't my thing."

"Then don't treat her like a kid, Quincy," Cassie chided me. "Just treat her like that rarest of things—an adult you don't swear much around."

"Or a unicorn," Flynn said. "Since those two things appear with about the same frequency."

"Very funny," I said. I turned to Ginny. "Ginny, hon," I started, then took a deep breath. This was either going to go way over her head, totally freak the kid out, or, most likely of all, something I couldn't expect was going to happen. "We say Uncle Dennis became an angel because that's what happened. When I went away last year, it was to fight a really bad man in a really bad place. Uncle Dennis came with me to help, and when we won, he got to turn into an angel as a reward. He was tired of being cooped up in the computer, and when he got a chance to get wings, he took it. Now he's in Heaven," I paused a second, since I didn't know if that was true or not, but decided it was close enough for elementary school, "and that means he can't help us with this fight. Does that make sense?"

"Not really, Uncle Quincy," Ginny said. "But not a whole lot does. You guys are weird." She said this with the gravity of someone pronouncing a life sentence on an accused criminal and folded her arms over her little chest as she did.

"You're right, kiddo. We are very weird." I looked around the table. "Okay, this is the team we've got. Is there a plan?"

"Yeah, but I don't think you're going to like it," Flynn said, reaching for Pravesh's tablet.

Boy, was she ever right.

3

"Did I mention how much I hate this plan?" I grumbled as Becks put the Suburban in park.

"Only about a hundred times," she replied. "Now keep your head down. We don't know what kind of security they have."

"Does it matter?" I asked. "You're going to go in there, shit's going to hit the fan, and I'm going to blast through anything in my way to get you out. It doesn't matter if they have walls three feet thick, I'm just going to tear it all down if I have to."

"That's sweet. You're still in the doghouse, but that's sweet. Now sit here and listen in while Director Pravesh and I go pretend to be good little government lapdogs." Without waiting for any additional comment from me, Flynn opened the passenger door, slid out, and closed it again.

"This sucks," I grumbled from where I lay on the back seat. At least we were in a Suburban, which was almost long enough for me to stretch my legs out.

"Quit your bitching," Glory said from the cargo compartment. "You're not back here with Mr. Sulfur Breath."

"I brushed!" Faustus said. "And a hint of brimstone is purely an involuntary defensive reaction caused by close contact with divinity. I can't help it if our species are supposed to hate each other."

"Shut up, you two," I said. "This isn't easy when Flynn and I are tight, much less when she's pissed at me." I closed my eyes and sent my consciousness down the mental tether that linked me to Becks. I felt the wall come down, letting me all the way in, and I dove in head-first. I felt a jerk, like I was in a car that started abruptly, then I was looking through Flynn's eyes.

This feels weird, she said.

Yeah, I replied. *I'll try not to be too intrusive.*

Stay out of the mental equivalent of my underwear drawer, Harker. That stirred up all kinds of thoughts about Becks's underwear, which are really pleasant thoughts based on an even more pleasant reality, but not at all conducive to me paying attention to what's going on with her and Pravesh.

You're a perv, Becks thought at me.

I think I legitimately qualify as a dirty old man, I zapped back. *Heads up, first guard station.* I watched through Flynn's eyes like the most immersive first-person shooter game ever. She held out her badge to the guard, who inspected it and Pravesh's credentials, then picked up a phone.

What is he saying? I asked.

If I could hear it, you'd hear it, Flynn replied. I groaned a little, remembering how limited normal human senses are. I've always been able to see, smell, and hear better than most people, probably because of the unique heritage that makes me number one on DEMON's Most Wanted to Dissect list.

The guard came back to the door and opened it for the women, who walked in without a backward glance for the SUV. I felt Flynn's anxiety ratchet up a notch as the heavy outer door slammed shut, and she looked around. They were in a long hallway with a metal door behind them, sterile tile floors, cold fluorescent lighting, and off-white paint.

"Could they have made this place look more like a boring government facility if they tried?" Flynn asked.

"The picture of the current President isn't on the wall, and there's usually a silk Ficus tree in one corner and an American flag in the other. This place is boring even by government standards," Pravesh replied, starting off down the hall.

"Do you know where we're going?" Flynn asked.

"No, but it's not like there are many options." She was right. The hallway led forward to another door, this one with what looked like a pair of windows or shutters in it.

Do you need glasses? I asked. *Because your vision really sucks.*

I'm human, *Harker. I don't have super-senses, super-speed, super-strength, or any of that shit. All I have is a super-annoying fiancé.*

You're saying the engagement is still on? I sent a huge wave of relief down our link and felt Becks blush when she sensed it.

You aren't getting out of marrying me that easy, buster, she replied, and I could feel the little grin on her face. *Oh, and did I mention that I have a lot of cousins?*

Flynn and Pravesh walked down the hall to the second door, a generic hollow-core wooden number like you find in every office building ever built. Flynn put her hand on her service weapon as Pravesh reached for the knob. She opened the door, and they stepped into...another empty room. Not completely empty. It was furnished in early twenty-first century government office, this time complete with a photograph of the President and *two* fake Ficus trees, plus an American flag on a pole in one corner. But the reception desk was unmanned, and the computer was turned off. Another wooden door stood closed opposite the one they just stepped through, but there was no indication that anyone worked in the building.

Flynn walked around behind the desk and ran her finger across the monitor, coming away with a layer of dust. "This hasn't been used in a while."

"If ever," Pravesh said, looking around the room. "There's dust on the picture on the wall, too, and the fake trees."

"What the hell?" Flynn asked. "Why are there armed guards outside an empty building?"

"I don't know," Pravesh replied. "Let's see what's behind Door Number Two." She pointed at the door leading further into the office.

I don't like this, I said to Flynn.

I don't either, but we've got to look around, if nothing else. We're about thirty feet from the front door. How much farther back does the building go?

I can't tell. I can't see shit from where I am. It looked like a good-sized building from the Google Maps image. Maybe another sixty feet? Maybe a hundred?

Okay, Flynn replied. *We're going to keep poking around. There's got to be some reason there's security here. And that guard had to talk to someone when he checked our IDs.*

Be careful, I said.

She didn't reply, just drew her pistol and stepped to one side of the door. "You turn the knob, I'll sweep the room."

Pravesh nodded and drew her own weapon. "You go left." Then she turned the knob and threw the door open. I watched through Flynn's eyes as she stepped through the door, swinging left with her gun on a line with the center of her body, drawing a bead on…more nothing. She stepped clear of the entry to let Pravesh come through and turned to watch the other woman sweep her pistol to the right of the doorway, covering more empty hall.

They stood in a deserted hallway stretching out twenty feet to the right and left before it turned a corner farther back into the building. There was a door in front of them, which looked identical to the one they'd just stepped through, and the only thing different in this hallway from the first one they entered was the industrial grade carpet was tan instead of gray, and one of the fluorescent lights was flickering a little. The walls were the same mass-produced, bought-in-bulk eggshell, and the scent of disinfectant lingered in the air.

"Do you smell that?" Pravesh asked.

She doesn't smell shit, I thought.

Shut up. Just because no one in my family is a vampire.

That's low, I replied.

"No," Flynn said out loud. "I just smell some kind of industrial cleaner."

"Underneath that." Pravesh sniffed again. "Something...musky. I don't know what, but it's almost like there's been an animal in here recently."

"Well, if so, then it's the only thing that's been here lately," Flynn said. "Which way? Left, right, or forward?"

"I'm inclined to say forward, but we've found nothing behind the first couple of doors we opened, so why not try the hallway?" Pravesh said, starting off down the hallway to the right and waving Flynn forward.

Becks followed, her pistol pointed at the ground. She lined up her body directly behind Pravesh's left shoulder to keep as clear a field of fire as possible in the narrow hall. When they reached the corner, Flynn tapped the director on her shoulder. When Pravesh looked back, Becks pointed down. Pravesh nodded, then dropped to one knee and spun around the corner. Flynn followed, standing and sweeping her gun along the hall.

More nothing. This hall extended about fifty feet, with three doors on the left wall. The first two were closed, but the last one, this one metal instead of cheap wood, opened inward, and was slightly ajar. Pravesh and Flynn shared a look, then Pravesh nodded and started off down the hall, quickly but without a sound. She kept her pistol out in front of her, moving as she turned. When she reached the door, she pressed her back to the opposite wall and paused.

Flynn caught up to her and stood beside the door on the same wall, reaching out with her left hand to push it further open. As it swung wide, Pravesh stepped through, Flynn tight on her heels. A motion sensor kicked in, lighting up the dark room as they crossed the threshold, and the women froze at what they saw.

They were in some type of laboratory, and it had been absolutely *destroyed*. There were heavy metal tables overturned, smashed beakers and flasks all over the floor. Half a dozen computers lay in a heap in one corner, and a microscope jutted out of a piece of expensive-looking lab equipment.

"What the hell happened here?" Pravesh asked, looking at the devastation before them.

"I don't know, but it looks painful," Flynn replied. She pointed to a brown smear on the floor beside an overturned table. "That's dried blood, and there's spatter all over the wall over there." She indicated the far wall, where a spray of droplets had dried into a lurid Jackson Pollack display of violence.

"This kind of carnage, with that much blood…it took some time and made a lot of noise," Pravesh said.

"Yeah, but why didn't the guards say anything about it?"

"Maybe their whole thing is just keeping an eye on the gate and the parking lot? If they don't go inside, they might not even know anything is amiss in here. DEMON and the rest of the agencies that don't officially exist are pretty strict about compartmentalization. Those security guys were regular Army. I wouldn't be surprised if they had no idea what was going on in here," Pravesh explained.

"What *was* going on here?" Flynn asked. She stepped farther into the room, kicking aside broken glass as she went. The room was lined with stacks of empty wire cages, like the kind test animals are kept in, with a few glass aquariums stacked along the walls. "It looks like someplace that does animal testing, but that's not what DEMON is about, is it?"

"It's not supposed to be," Pravesh said. "Their charter is very similar to ours, officially. They are to study cryptids and paranormal creatures, develop methodology to protect humanity against them in case of attack, and monitor areas known to have heavy supernatural activity."

"Develop methods to protect humanity in case of an attack? You mean figure out how to kill them?" Flynn asked, her voice hard. "Is that part of your charter, too?"

"No," Pravesh said. "Our mandate is more specific. The Homeland Security Paranormal Division exists to monitor supernatural activity inside and outside the borders of the United States, and to defend the citizenry in case of an attack."

"Your job isn't to figure out how to kill cryptids?" Becks asked.

"We already know how to kill all the creatures we've identified. We exist to keep an eye on them, and to use that knowledge if the need arises." Pravesh's face was cold, her eyes lasered in on Flynn's. "I get that this is more personal to you than a lot of things about our organization because of your relationship with Mr. Card. But he is a creature of immense power and could unleash incredible damage if he went rogue. We exist to minimize the loss of life if that happens."

"By killing him." Flynn's voice was flat.

"If need be."

I'd like to see them try, I thought to Becks. *Don't sweat it, love. We knew this was why DHS had a Paranormal Division. They've just been more subtle about it until now. They never were the good guys, even when they weren't infiltrated by a half-demon psychopath.*

Still pisses me off, Becks thought back.

Yeah, I get that. But right now, you've got more important questions to answer.

Like what?

Like what the hell is scratching at the door to the room you're standing in?

At that, Flynn's head whipped around to the door at the end of the row of cages, about thirty feet from where she stood. She held a finger up to her lips and then noticed what I'd already heard, a furious scratching against the metal door that increased in pace every second.

"Director Pravesh, how good are you with that pistol?"

"I guess we're about to find out," Pravesh said, stepping to her right out of the line of the door and bringing her gun up. Flynn countered left and did the same, just as the center of the door shredded into shards of steel that flew into the lab.

I pulled myself back into my own head and sat up in the back of the Suburban. "Time to go, kiddies. They just called in the cavalry."

"What is it?" Glory asked, pushing open the back door and sliding out.

"There's a werewolf in a mad scientist's laboratory, and it's about to eat Flynn and Pravesh," I replied, jumping out of the SUV and sprinting toward the building.

"Well, that's not at all how I expected this trip to go," Faustus said from behind me.

"Obviously you haven't spent enough time around Harker," Glory replied. "Because that's pretty much *exactly* how I expected this trip to go."

4

I ignored the two soldiers charging out of the little booth with their sidearms out, counting on Faustus or Glory to handle my light work. I wasn't disappointed as I heard a *whoosh* behind me and a crash. Glory appeared next to me, and I looked over at her. "You handle the guards?"

"The demon threw them through a wall of the guard shack. I think they're alive, but possibly concussed."

"Better than I'd expect, given they just got their asses kicked by a demon. Can you teleport in there and find Becks?"

"No," she replied. "The whole place is warded six ways to Sunday. I can't even sense her. I'm surprised your link worked as well as it did."

"I might be hanging on a little tighter than normal, given recent events," I said as we reached the door. It was locked up tight, which I expected, but it also resisted my best efforts to yank it open, which I didn't. "What the fuck?" I asked, planting my feet and giving the handle a huge pull.

"Need a hand?" Faustus asked as he caught up to us.

"Nah," I said. "Plan B should be just fine." I let go of the door, took two steps to the right, and concentrated my will. A whirling sphere of red energy appeared above my upraised right palm, and I spun my hand, flinging the orb of power at the wall. The cinderblocks flew inward in a cloud of dust and drywall, and I stepped through the new door. "Even when people reinforce the door frame, they don't usually do much to the wall around the door. It's a flaw I've exploited more than once."

"I'll say this about your charge, Glory," Faustus said. "He does know how to make an entrance. Where are we going, Harker?" The demon drew a silver-toned pistol with a barrel almost a foot long from under his jacket, and I wondered for a moment exactly where he had it stowed, then decided I really didn't want to know.

"This way," I said, pulling open the hallway door and charging into the featureless building that I'd walked through Flynn's eyes just moments ago. It was just as boring the second time around, but this time it had a soundtrack of destruction coming from ahead of us. We'd just about reached the laboratory door when it flew open and Pravesh flew through it, crumpling against the far wall.

"Shit," I muttered. "Glory!"

"On it," the angel replied.

"Faustus, with me," I said, turning to the lab.

"Right behind you."

"This would be a great time to tell me you happen to have silver bullets for that hand cannon," I said.

"It would, wouldn't it?" he replied. "Unfortunately for us, we'll have to see what kind of damage a Smith & Wesson Five Hundred does to a lycanthrope."

"Are we compensating for something, demon?" I asked, looking at the oversized gun.

"No, but we certainly aren't going to show up outgunned," he shot back, elbowing me aside and stepping through the doorway.

I followed Faustus into the remains of the lab and walked into a scene right out of a horror movie. And I mean one of the good ones, where the monsters look real and you're pretty sure all the good guys are fucked, not one of the stupid ones where you know everyone has to survive until the sequel.

When I stopped looking through Flynn's eyes to run into the

building, there was one pissed-off werewolf in the room coming at her and Pravesh. By the time Faustus, Glory, and I made it to the laboratory, there were two werewolves and what I could only assume was a werebear, all converging on where Becks stood on top of a huge aluminum freezer.

I stepped into the room and yelled, "Hey, fuzzy!" All three lycanthropes turned to look at me, and I sent spheres of raw magical energy zooming right at their chests. My magical blasts hit the weres in the chest and hurled them back into the walls, and I looked up at Flynn.

"Becks, jump!" To her credit, she didn't hesitate, just flung herself off the top of the freezer at me. Glory streaked in, wings only half-extended in the cramped quarters of the lab, but still more than enough for her to fly across the room and catch my falling fiancée in mid-air. I turned my attention to the werebear, since he was the one getting up first.

"Faustus, you and Glory play dogcatcher. Becks, see if Pravesh needs an ambulance. I got Yogi." The bear must have been able to understand English in his fuzzy form because he let out a nasty roar when I compared him to the cartoon character. Oh, goody. I picked the one that was smarter than the average bear. Yogi stood up on his hind legs, his head almost touching the twelve-foot ceiling, and took a couple of wobbling steps toward me. Bears aren't all that good at the hind legs thing, and for lycanthropes, who don't spend all their time in bear form, it's even harder. Since I'm not a nice person, and I have an underdeveloped sense of fighting fair, I took advantage of the bear's shitty balance and fired another pair of purple energy balls right at its legs.

That was...less than successful. My idea had been to cut the bear off at its knees and end up with a bear lying on its stomach with its face well within kicking range, at which point I would commence to kicking said bear in said face. My result was that the bear fell down onto its front paws, let out a roar fit to send the MGM lion to the unemployment line, then charged at me on all fours without losing more than a second's momentum. I dove to my right, rolling on one

25

shoulder as I landed, and spun around as I came to a stop. I sprang up, only to see the bear had half-shifted back to human, and instead of a twelve-foot Grizzly Bear, I was now facing a nine-foot half-bear, half-man who was a *lot* better on his feet and still had arms the size of tree trunks and claws designed to rip me open from nuts to nose.

The werebear didn't punch me; he just shoved me in the middle of my chest, *really* enthusiastically. He slammed an open palm into my sternum, and I took flight like Superman. If Superman was loaded up on about two dozen tequila shots. Okay, probably closer to an even more inept Greatest American Hero, but I only had about half a second to contemplate my flight before I landed, wedged ass-deep into the drywall about four feet off the floor.

"Ow," I groaned, blinking to clear the sheetrock dust out of my eyes. All I saw was brown as a giant paw covered my face and the bear-man yanked me out of the wall and flung me the other way across the room. I was a little more prepared this time, and had farther to fly, so I was able to twist a bit before I slammed into the opposite side of the lab. Nothing broke my fall as I slid down to the floor in a heap, though, and I dropped like a very bloody stone to press my face against the cool, cool, tile floor.

"Harker, would you quit fucking around and blast that thing!" Flynn yelled. "We don't have all day!"

I couldn't think of any other pressing appointments I had for the afternoon, but since she sounded so damn impatient, I struggled to my feet, clawing up an overturned lab table and finally dragging myself mostly upright. My left leg didn't really work, and I was pretty sure I had three or four broken ribs, but as long as I didn't have to walk or breathe, I thought I'd be okay. Then I saw the bear coming my way. Yogi had shifted back to full Grizzly and was walking my way on all fours, just an easy lope as his basketball-sized shoulders rolled with each step. I swear I could see a grin across his furry muzzle as he stopped about eight feet away and reared up on his back legs, raising his paws to the ceiling and letting out another ear-shattering roar.

That quickly turned into a high-pitched screech of agony as I focused the remaining energy I had into a blade wrapped in purple fire and forged out of my own soul and sliced the bear from his nuts to his collarbone. My soulblade sizzled as it burned through fur and flesh, and I fell more than spun to the left as a torrent of viscera rained down from the werebear, who was already shifting back to human form as he dropped to the floor, dead.

"Now stand the fuck down!" I bellowed, putting just enough magic behind my words to make sure everyone heard me yell, but not so much that I passed out from the effort. It was a very fine line, made all the finer by the agony in my chest as my ribs started to realign and knit back together. I panted a couple of times like the world's oldest Lamaze coach, and hauled myself upright, using a flipped cabinet as a crutch. As I straightened up, I heard a litany of cracks and pops from my torso that sounded way too much like a bowl of breakfast cereal for my liking, and the world went white for half a second as I may have moved to a different plane of consciousness from the pain. Either that or I went to the place where curse words were invented, because new permutations of the word "fuck" flashed across my brain in time with my heartbeat.

The werewolves were frozen in place, one with its claws out ready to rip Faustus's face off, the other holding its paws up to fend off Glory's gleaming white sword. They were both in their intermediate forms—half-wolf, half-human, about seven feet tall and covered in muscle and bad intentions.

"Look fuckers," I said, my voice steadier now that my ribs were in more or less the right place. "Your heavy hitter is dead, and you're outnumbered. You can chill the fuck out and tell us what's going on, or we can paint the ceiling with your intestines. Your call."

"Can I cast a vote for the chilling out?" Faustus asked, stepping back from the wolf that was poised to give him an unanesthetized nose job. "Because this pistol is very impressive against humans but is less effective than a stern talking-to against lycanthropes."

"That's okay, Faustus," Flynn said from the doorway. "I've got your back, and I'm reloaded with silver nitrate-tipped hollow points."

Where the fuck did you get those? I asked her silently.

27

DHS has a stash of them. I figured we might run into some badass cryptids here, so I loaded up a couple of spare magazines.

You know what those are for, right?

Werewolves, right?

And vampires, I said. I felt the shock resonate across our bond. *Yeah, silver fucks vampires up, too. Those are vamp-killing rounds.*

Holy shit.

How about we not mention those to Uncle Luke? I suggested.

I'm good with that.

"You good with a cease-fire?" I asked the weres.

The wolves looked at each other, then at me and Glory, and nodded. Twenty seconds later, the half-wolves were gone, and two dark-haired muscular men stood before us. Completely naked.

"Clothes won't shift, huh?" I asked.

"Who cares?" the one nearest Faustus said. "Clothes are a pain in the ass."

*Well if you've got a body like that...*Becks thought.

Hey!

Sorry.

I turned my attention back to the large naked men standing in the middle of the devastation. "What the fuck happened here?" I asked.

"I think I can answer that," came a voice from the inner door of the lab.

"I was wondering if you were going to hide back there all day," I said to the figure looming in the shadows. "Were you waiting to see if your goons killed us all?"

"I was waiting to see if you were DEMON reinforcements here to retake their facility," the voice said. I watched as the shadowy form grew as it stepped into the lab. And grew. And grew.

"Well, that answers a question that's plagued humanity for a century or so," I said when I got a good look at the creature joining us in the room. "You're real, huh?"

"As real as vampires, werewolves, and demons," said the creature. "And wizards, I suppose."

"That's fair," I said. "What should I call you? Harry?"

"I wouldn't suggest it," he said with a scowl. "My name is T'morith. But you can call me Tim."

"That's a little anticlimactic, don't you think?" Faustus asked the nearest werewolf. "I mean, Tim?"

"I didn't name him, dude," the werewolf said, not amused.

"Okay, Tim," I said. "You wanna tell us why there's a bunch of lycanthropes and a Bigfoot in a government laboratory in the middle of Charlotte, NC?"

5
———————

A Sasquatch walked into a bar, and I wish anything I had to say after that was a joke. But it wasn't. And it wasn't a bar, but I did manage to find a dented flask of whisky in my coat that I drained as I perched on a lab stool and surveyed the room. The lab was trashed, and that was before I covered part of the floor in werebear guts. The whole place was littered with overturned and wrecked equipment, and Faustus had to scrounge the whole room to come up with someplace to sit. Glory just perched on top of one of the lab tables, her glowing soul blade laid across her knees as an incentive to good behavior.

Becks was gone, having helped Pravesh back to the SUV and on to the ER. The DHS director's eyes were having trouble focusing in the same direction, and she'd already puked once since she made her first abortive effort at standing up. I was pretty sure she was concussed, and I really didn't need another dead Homeland Security higher-up on my tab. I kept the connection to Flynn open so she could get the gist of our conversation with Harry and the Werewolfsons, but I directed most of my focus to the lycanthropes in the room.

"Okay, Tim," I said once he'd settled down onto the floor and the werewolves had gathered up a couple pair of tattered sweatpants. "You want to clue me in on what was going on here?"

The Sasquatch ran a hang through his shaggy hair in a remarkably human gesture, then let out a long sigh. "I was minding my own business in the mountains of eastern Tennessee when a team of DEMON agents took my entire clan prisoner. They hauled us here and tortured us, for lack of a better word. They pretended to experiment on us, but they weren't learning anything. They just wanted to see how much pain we could handle before we broke and lost all sense of self. They brutalized my brother, my mate, my...son..." A big tear rolled down the Sasquatch's cheek, and he dashed it away with an angry swipe of a tennis racket-sized hand. "They made a tactical error when they brought Reginald and I into their 'testing room' at the same time." He gestured over to the remains of the werebear, which had shifted into human parts as he died.

"Their security forces could handle one of us at a time, or even two wolves or smaller Sasquatch, but a bull male and a massive grizzly like Reginald?" A vicious smile split his lips, and pointed teeth gleamed through his fur-covered mouth. "They didn't stand a chance. We made them pay for every indignity, every moment of torture, every murder they committed, and we made them pay in their own blood."

"Well, I believe I can say with some sincere perspective that you enacted a truly medieval retribution upon them. And I should know, as I actually lived through the medieval era." Faustus leaned forward on his stool. "Tell me more about the disembowelments. I do love a good evisceration."

I reached over and slapped the demon on the back of the head lightly, just enough to get his attention. Also, just as much force as I could muster since my ribs still needed another couple hours to knit back together. "Focus, Faustus."

"Oh come on, Harker, let a demon be a demon for a change," he protested.

"No," Glory said, tapping her fingers on the hilt of her sword. Her tone brooked even less argument than the scowl on her face, and

Faustus huffed grumpily but leaned back and motioned for Tim to continue.

"When was this?" I asked. "And what happened to the other cryptids that were being held here?"

"This was about eight hours ago. Some of what they considered the highest value targets were taken out as soon as the jailbreak started, hauled away in special cages—"

"And coffins," one of the werewolves chimed in. "They had coffins for the vamps. Silver chains for special lycanthropes, cold iron for the fae, hoods for that medusa chick—"

"There was a medusa here?" Glory asked.

Simultaneously, I asked, "Medusas are real?"

Glory looked at me like I was a particularly slow-witted child. "Q, some dude fought a terrorist on a bridge with a friggin' narwhal horn. At this point why would you think that *anything* wasn't real?"

She had a point. I'd fought dragons, demons, lycanthropes, vampires, and was now sitting across from a Sasquatch talking about the humans as bad guys. I had Frankenstein's frigging monster on speed dial, for fuck's sake. I didn't need to suspend my disbelief; I needed to fire it.

"Okay, you've got a point. I'll just assume that anything I've ever read about in a fantasy novel is probably real. That'll make life easier," I said. "What about the lower-value hostages, or test subjects, or prisoners, or whatever you want to call them? Where are they?"

"Some are dead," Tim said. "A lot of them are dead, come to think of it. Most of us don't really like other supernatural beings, and there are a few that look at the rest of us as a food source."

"Some are just fucking psychopaths," the second werewolf said. "There was a redcap in here, and that little bastard was bad news. He shredded about half a dozen guards before he just waltzed out the front door, blood dripping down the back of his neck from his hat as he walked away."

"And that happened a good bit, too," Tim said with a nod. "Many of the cryptids just left, seeing a chance at freedom and running straight for it."

"Why did you stay?" Glory asked. Her voice was soft, like she was talking to a skittish animal, and by the way Tim's shoulders tensed when she posed the question, it was pretty well-founded caution. I was almost healed, but still pretty tired. I didn't want to throw down with a Sasquatch and two werewolves, and whatever he was about to tell us had Tim *really* pissed.

"They took my mate. They had been...experimenting on her. On her...reproductive system, trying to...*breed* her, like she was some kind of farm animal. I stayed to see if I could find any records of where they would take her, or if she was even still alive. I found her. Her body. Mangled almost beyond recognition and thrown into a heap with other 'biological waste.' I only recognized her because I know her scent as well as my own. After I found her, there was no one here to punish for their crimes, so I waited. I waited until I could..."

"Beat the ever-loving fuck out of the sons of bitches who came in to retake their lab until somebody told us what they did with our people," the bigger of the two wolves said. The smaller one, who looked like a younger brother, nodded and cracked his knuckles.

"Who did they take from you?" I asked.

They shared a glance, and I held up a hand. "Look, you didn't stick around here just to fuck shit up. If all you wanted was to raise hell, you'd be downtown ripping into douchebros at some nightclub. You stayed here for the same reason Tim did, the same reason I'm here. They've got somebody you love. I can't help you if you bullshit me. But if you're straight with me, and you'll play things my way, maybe we can work together to get our people back."

Faustus looked at me, then Glory, then the hairy trio. "You pick up more strays than a dogcatcher, Harker."

"Says the demon rolling with the Reaper," I said.

Big Wolf's head snapped up. "Reaper? I've heard of you."

"All good, I hope," I said with a sideways grin. It wasn't going to be good. Whenever anybody heard of me by that nickname, it was *never* good.

"It was, believe it or not. I've got some cousins in Ohio. They told me about you coming up there a few years ago and taking care of a little demon problem they were having. Said you were kind of a dick, but somebody they'd trust in a fight."

"That's a solid assessment," Glory said.

I whipped my head over to her and had to laugh as I saw her and Faustus both nodding. "Okay, fine. Yeah, I remember those guys. They gave me beer, and I helped them kill demons. You good to work with me? Get your sister back? Get justice for your mate?" I looked between the wolves and the Sasquatch.

"Who do they have of yours?" Tim asked.

I thought about it for a second before I answered. My relationship to Luke wasn't a secret per se, but we didn't broadcast it. We also didn't want everybody and their brother knowing he was in Charlotte, but it seemed like that ship had sailed. "My uncle."

"Your uncle? Who's that? And why would he be here?" Tim asked.

"He's kind of an adopted uncle," I said. "He was close to both my parents, and after they died, and he realized that I was…different, shall we say, he took me under his wing. No pun intended."

"You gonna tell us who he is, or we just gonna sit around and jerk off all night?" Smaller Wolf asked, with appropriate hand motions.

"He goes by Lucas Card, but most people know him as Vlad Dracul."

There was a moment of silence before Big Wolf let out a low whistle and said, "Fuuuuck, dude. Your uncle is Count Dracula?"

"Yep."

"And they took *him*?"

"Yep."

"That's ballsy."

"Stupid is the word I'd use," I said. "Because they were lucky when they got the drop on Luke, but that luck has run right the fuck out. Because now I'm coming for them, and nothing is going to keep me from getting Luke back."

"If he's alive," Tim said.

"He's alive." I may have said that with a little more edge than I initially intended, because the big Sasquatch's head snapped up.

"Quincy, he has a point," Faustus said, holding up his hands as I whirled on him. "Think about it. Luke is one of the most dangerous monsters in history. It would be sheer folly to keep him alive. If they have a list of specific supernatural beings too strong to attempt to capture, Luke would be near the top of it."

"He's alive," I repeated. My voice was low and steady, but I couldn't hold back the power glowing in my eyes. My guts and mind both whirled at the mere thought of a bunch of second-string government assclowns taking Luke out. He'd survived Van Helsing, two world wars, more monster fights than anyone could count. There was no way. "I'd feel it if he was dead."

"Are you sure, Quincy?" Faustus asked. "You have many abilities, but I've not known you to be terribly psychic."

I stood up and turned to the demon, my hands clenched at my sides. "Are you forgetting about the telepathic link I've got with Becks? I'm tied to Luke, too. Not the same way, but...I'd know." I let my words trail off, then looked at Tim. "I need you to take me through this place, and fast. If DEMON has a cleanup team coming, we need to gather any information we can before they get here." I didn't add that I needed to find some evidence of Luke's survival. Looking at the Sasquatch's face, I didn't need to.

6

Tim's words echoed in my head, warring with my own thoughts for dominance. A chorus of "they murdered him" danced with "he can't be dead" until a nasty number called "but what if he is?" cut in, and so on and so on until I couldn't take any more talking. I shook my head, trying in vain to clear my thoughts, and looked at the assembled cryptids and supernatural beings. This had to be the weirdest *Avengers* knock-off in history.

"Take me through the facility," I said to Tim. "Faustus, you and the doggos go through any intact computers and file cabinets you find. Grab anything that looks like it might be useful. We'll take it back and..." I stopped myself before I said, "We'll get Dennis to crack them open." Unless Dennis had turned into the Archangel of Hacking and Helping Out Asshole Demon Hunters, he wasn't going to be cracking anything open. No Dennis, no Luke, no Shadow Council, except for Jo...I was starting to feel almost as alone as when I was hiding out in Tennessee.

Cut that shit out, Becks's voice cut through the fog of my dark thoughts like a knife.

What? I asked, though "whined" was probably a better term.

You're wallowing. That's not what we do. We don't wallow. We kick ass, we take names, and we occasionally chew bubble gum. But we do not wallow. I didn't commandeer a magical helicopter and fly five hundred miles to drag you back here for a goddamned pity party, so pull your head out of your ass and get to work. Jesus Christ, Harker, did you leave your balls in Memphis?

I smiled in spite of myself. *I missed you, too. But as a motivational speaker, you're a little more* Full Metal Jacket *than* Rudy.

Rudy dies at the end, Becks replied. *Not exactly the climax I'm looking for out of you.*

Oh really?

That didn't come out right. Before that moment, I never knew it was possible to hear someone blush telepathically.

Let's get our boy back, and then we'll worry about making things come out right, I replied. *And thanks.*

I love you, you big idiot.

I love you too.

I know. Now get the fuck to work so you can start apologizing. I expect it will be a long process, involving much chocolate, a lot of expensive dinners, and possibly some very sparkly jewelry. I felt her close our connection down to its normal trickle, and I returned my focus to the room around me.

"Everything okay, Q?" Glory asked.

"It is now," I said. I stood up and turned to the Sasquatch. "Let's go, Tim. Glory, will you supervise Faustus and the pups?"

"Not a problem."

Faustus gave me a lopsided grin. "What's wrong, Quincy? Don't you trust us?"

"Since the werewolves were trying to rip my guts out ten minutes ago, and there are *entire operas* written as cautionary tales against trusting you, no. I don't trust you any further than I can throw Bigfoot here."

"We really don't like being called that," Tim said. "Feels...undignified, somehow."

I looked the giant, fur-covered cryptid up and down. "Fair enough," I said after a moment. "Sasquatch it is." No point in being any more of a dick than usual. If he didn't want to be called Bigfoot, then I wouldn't call him Bigfoot. "Let's go. As soon as I find some evidence that Luke is alive, we can work on finding him. Then we get to the fun part."

"The fun part?" Tim asked.

"Watching him murder every motherfucker involved in this shit-show," I said.

Tim led me through a heavy steel door in the back of the lab into a narrow hallway. There were no windows, and the lab's lights didn't reach that far, so I called up power and shaped it into a floating globe that hovered just above my head and cast a soft white light all around. "That's better," I said.

"Not bad," Tim replied, "but do you ever even think of reaching for a light switch?" The fluorescents overhead flickered on as he pressed a panel on the wall by the door.

"Nobody likes a smartass, Tim." I dispersed my glowing ball and followed the Sasquatch deeper into the complex. The hallway ran for about thirty feet before we came to an identical steel door. "Anything behind here?" I asked.

"Not that I know of," Tim replied. "As far as I know, me and the weres were the only folk left alive, except for the guards outside."

I thought about the swarm of supernatural creatures descending on my adopted hometown and shuddered. Charlotte was not ready for a cryptid invasion. Not that any place really would be. "How many creatures escaped?"

"I have no idea," Tim replied. "I don't know how many were held here. I saw twenty or more leaving through various doors or holes in walls and ceilings. I don't know which of them would want to stay near humans, and which ones, like myself, would prefer our solitude." He looked at me, and even through the mass of fur on his face, I could see the pain in his eyes. "We just wanted to be left alone. All we ever wanted to do was live in harmony with nature and raise our children in peace. Why couldn't we do that? My La'narta never hurt a human in her life. Neither did I, until today. But I swear to you, Reaper, if I get back to my home, my people will never be taken unawares again."

"Call me Quincy," I said. "Or Harker. The whole 'Reaper' thing is good PR for when I have to deal with the bad guys, but it's not something I like to answer to."

"I shall do that, Harker. And thank you. It is good to know that not all humans have become heartless bastards." He turned and yanked the steel door open, stepping into the next room. I decided to just ignore the fact that I'm not completely human. No point muddying the waters. If me treating him with the barest minimum of compassion and understanding meant he might not kill an innocent human, I was willing to deal with a little minor deception.

The next room was a giant…holding room was probably what the assclowns that ran this site called it, but prison or kennel was a more honest name. We stepped into a small open space in a maze of cells. There was a hall in front of us, and one branching off to either side. The path in front of us ran about a hundred and fifty feet straight ahead, with cells on either side. I stepped forward and ran my fingers across the door hanging from the hinges to my right. It was three-inch thick steel, and as I touched it, I could feel the magic crawling over the surface. The metal was bent and twisted, and only the top hinge was still attached. Black scorch marks marred the inner surface of the door, and deep claw marks ran the length and width of the metal.

"What the fuck were they holding in here?" I asked, sticking my head into the cell. It was your basic jail cell, with a metal bunk affixed to the wall, a toilet and sink with a water fountain, plus a pair of video cameras mounted in the corners of the ceiling. Every wall was black with soot, and the concrete floor had more of the deep gouges where whatever they were trying to contain had done its damnedest to dig its way out. Some of the scratches went several inches deep into the concrete, and I knew I *really* didn't want to run into whatever was locked up in this joint.

"That was Ernie. Ernie is a half-dragon, of the red variety. He didn't take well to confinement."

"No shit. Wait, *half*-dragon? You mean somebody banged a *dragon*?"

"Happens more often than you think. What? Don't you read,

Harker? There are whole genres devoted to cryptid porn, and shapeshifters are one of the most popular types. After all, they aren't always giant scaly beasts. And I've heard that some of their human forms are very appealing. If you're into hairless mates."

I thought back to the fight atop the Pyramid in Memphis. She was a fine-looking human, if terrifying, but maybe my fear of her roasting my nuts off tempered the attraction somewhat. "Yeah, I could see that. I've only met one dragon, but she was a hottie."

Tim raised an eyebrow but took the high road and ignored my pun. "Ernie was not happy at being contained, and he used every tool at his disposal to make sure his captors knew it. I would not have wanted to be wearing a DEMON uniform when he got free."

"Then what happened? You went apeshit in the lab and started a jailbreak? Just randomly pushed buttons until all the cage doors opened?" Something in this didn't make sense, and I wasn't sure if Tim was holding out on me, or if there was shit going on behind the scenes that he knew nothing about. My money was on the latter, though.

He thought for a few seconds, then shook his head. "No. I mean, yes, Reginald and I decided that enough was enough, and we attacked our captors in the laboratory. But neither of us knew how to operate the electronic locks. They were sealed with access codes, and we didn't have those codes. I expected to destroy a few guards and so-called scientists, then be shot. I had accepted my fate and was going to be with La'narta again."

"But then something happened," I said.

"Yes. The alarms were blaring, and I heard more guards coming toward the lab from the holding cells, but then I heard screaming. A lot of screaming. And no more guards came in. Reginald and I...I'm not proud of this, but we killed everyone we could find. Guards, scientists, assistants—anyone wearing a white coat or a DEMON identification badge was fair game. And if I'm being honest, I didn't really look to see if they were wearing a badge. I just killed anyone in arms' reach." He bowed his head. "I suppose I became the monster they expected me to be."

"We all have our times where we're monsters," I said. I thought back to what I'd been able to learn about the carnage I unleashed across Europe in the forties. That was the time that I earned the nickname "Reaper." "I've been there. I've got more blood on my hands than I can ever wash off. All we can do is try to help enough people to somehow balance the scales. Now what happened after you killed everyone in the lab?"

"I came back here," Tim said. "I came into the cell area, and I found Zane and Ari, the werewolves you met earlier, arguing about what to do. Ernie had already blasted a chunk of ceiling to rubble and was stretching his wings to fly out. There was a redcap washing his face with the blood of a guard, and several spell casters in a circle muttering to each other. In a matter of moments, everyone but myself, Reginald, and the werewolves were gone."

"Why did you stay?" I asked.

"Zane and Ari are young, and Reginald felt a responsibility to get their bloodlust under control before he took them out into the world. I had nowhere to go, and nothing to go home to, so I decided to stay and see if any reinforcements came. Then I could try to get some answers as to why they took us, and who was in charge. Then I could get justice for La'narta, once and for all."

"Even if it cost you your life? Because whoever started this isn't likely to be left unguarded."

"My life is the most worthless thing in the world to me right now," the Sasquatch replied. "The only thing that matters is making someone pay for this. Pay for the blood they've shed."

"Okay then," I said. "Ass-kicking it is. Let's see if we can find any clues as to who threw gasoline on the fire you started, and then see about going up the chain of command and killing every motherfucker who even thought this place was a good idea." I stuck out my hand, and Tim wrapped it in his huge, hairy paw.

"Ass-kicking it is," he said with a fang-baring grin that made me shiver a little.

7

The rest of the holding area looked a lot like the first bits— bent and battered doors hanging open, scarred walls from claws, some brown streaks on the walls where someone or something beat itself bloody trying to escape. We found the remains of two guards lying in a corner, their faces literally peeled off and their stomachs ripped open like they came with zippers. None of the internal organs were anywhere to be seen.

"That's fucked up," I said.

"That was the redcap," Tim replied.

"What did it use to cut them open like that?"

"Fingernails, I think. I'm not really sure. I didn't see it. Ari did, and he told us about it. He was shaking when he came into the lab, and it took him a little while to be able to speak. I think it rattled him."

"Really?" I raised an eyebrow. "What kind of person could be rattled by something as nonchalant as an evisceration? Pansy."

"I sometimes forget that not everyone kills and guts animals every day. And that's what these guards were to us—animals. They treated us like we were no better than playthings, simply existing for their amusement. I feel no remorse for their deaths. As you would say, in your own particular eloquence, fuck them."

He had me pegged. That is pretty much what I would think about the death of someone who treated me or any of my people that way. "Fair enough," I replied. "Still gross. I'm not surprised the pup was shaken." I started to walk to the door, planning on going farther into the building, when I heard a noise. I held up a hand to Tim, and he froze. I motioned in the direction the sound came from, around a corner and up an aisle of the pens we hadn't checked.

Tim fell in behind me as I crept toward the corner, my pistol drawn and held low in front of me. I turned the corner, bringing the Glock up to sweep the area in front of me for threats, but there was nothing there. The hallway was completely empty. I turned to Tim, one eyebrow up, but he just shrugged. Then something changed in the Sasquatch's face, like he realized something, and he held up one finger to his lips.

I had been just about to say something, but I let the words die on my tongue as Tim pointed over my shoulder. He leaned down until his fur tickled my ear and whispered, "I smell something. I don't recognize the scent. It's not human, but there's something there."

I saw nothing, but that isn't really all that unusual with magical beings. I slipped into my Sight, and the supernatural spectrum blazed to life. Traces of magic dotted the walls and floor, probably from the blood of cryptids and fae that died here. I looked farther down the aisle, and there she stood, pressed up against the wall, still as a statue.

She must have been one of the fae, but I didn't know what kind. Faeries were never something I studied much, because I didn't have to. They typically kept to themselves, so I seldom had cause to kill one. Sure, every once in a while a redcap would murder a family outside a small town, or a hobgoblin would wander into a city and leave a trail of bodies in its wake, but those were easily explained away as human serial killers. A few bullets tipped with cold iron instead of lead or copper, and *voila!* Problem solved.

This was no hobgoblin. This was a willowy female, taller than my own six feet and change, and almost perilously slender. I couldn't make out her features, wreathed as she was in magic, but I could see the tiny trembling in her arms and fingers, even from thirty feet away.

"You can drop the camouflage," I said. "I can see you. We won't hurt you." I tried to keep my voice as warm and non-threatening as possible, and hoped she didn't recognize me. That usually doesn't happen until I tell someone my name, but the results are unpredictable once I do.

The faerie stepped away from the wall and shimmered into view. It was wild, watching her just *appear* like that, like something from a science fiction movie. One moment she was invisible to the naked eye, blending in perfectly with the pitted and blood-spattered surface of the wall, then the next minute she was standing there, a tall, slender woman with stringy brown hair and almost preternaturally long arms and legs. She was gaunt, with a long oval face and pointed chin, sharp features, and long ears sticking out from behind her hair that tapered to a point.

She held out her hands in a placating gesture and said something in a lyrical language that I didn't understand at all. The words sounded more like the wind whispering through tree branches than syllables, or maybe water burbling over stones in a shallow brook.

"I'm sorry," I said. "I don't understand you. We're not here to hurt you. We just need to find someone. A friend of mine. He was held captive here."

She cocked her head to the side, and her mouth moved as if she was chewing on something, then she spoke again. "I just want to go home," she said, in perfect, if accented, English. She sounded...French, which made no sense. But since I was standing in a super-secret government facility talking to a faerie with a Sasquatch watching my back, I suspended my disbelief over her accent.

"How did you get here?" I asked. "Maybe we can help you get home if we know where they grabbed you."

"I don't remember. I was in the mortal world...I was given a task... it's all fuzzy. I don't recall much. Just two men, and a stick that lit up at one end, then iron, and pain. What did they want with me?" she asked, and a lone tear rolled down one cheek. I took a step forward but froze as the woman took two frantic steps away from me.

"It's okay," I said, keeping my voice low and soft, as if I was talking to a skittish animal. "I promise, I'm not here to hurt you. You can stay here, it's fine. Or you can come with us. But I have to try to find my friend."

Harker, what are you doing? Becks asked in my head.

She's terrified. I can't just leave her here scared out of her skin.

Yes, you really can, Flynn argued. *We've got a horde of random monsters roaming through the city, a rogue government agency bent on murdering every supernatural creature they can find, and Count Dracula is missing. All we need now is the Wolfman and the Mummy to show up with Adam in tow, and we can make our own Hammer movie!*

I didn't realize you liked old horror movies. And we already have two werewolves, so we're good there. Let me just make sure this chick isn't either going to get herself killed or suddenly murder a bunch of people, then we'll get back on task. Deal?

Deal. I could hear the reluctance ringing loud in her mental voice, but since she was still at the hospital with Pravesh, it wasn't like she could do much.

I turned my attention back to the faerie, but Tim interrupted me before I could speak. "What were you pondering? You were very...focused."

"Oh, yeah. Sorry about that. I have a...mental link with one of my partners, and she was asking me exactly what I thought I was doing."

"That is a fine question," the Sasquatch said. "There is no immediate threat from this creature, and we have much ground to cover. If she does not wish to accompany us, we should proceed with our plan."

"You're right," I said. I turned to the faerie. "Last chance, lady. Me and Big Fuzzy here are going to go deeper into the facility, looking for my friend and any clues on where the assholes that ran this place went. You can come with us, as long as you promise not to murder us when we aren't looking, or you can stay here. It's your call. But we gotta get a move on. There are sure to be reinforcements coming, and I don't want to be here when they arrive."

The faerie woman looked me up and down, then looked at Tim. "I...remember you. I heard your voice from inside my cage, I think."

"Yes," Tim said, pointing to a cage about three away from where we stood. "They kept me in there. I said many unflattering things about my captors and described in great detail the unpleasant things I planned to do to them when I escaped."

"If I come with you, will I get to help you do those unpleasant things to the ones who imprisoned me?" she asked, a wicked glint in her eyes.

"Absolutely," I said. "Now let's move out. We've got a lot of building left to search, and I don't want to leave the doggies and the demon alone with Glory too long."

I turned to head deeper into the building, Tim and the faerie on my heels. "Are you concerned that the demon will corrupt your guardian angel?" Tim asked.

"Not really," I replied. "But if they spend too much time together, I'm afraid she'll be a good influence on Faustus. Sometimes you need a bad guy on your side, and the last thing I need hanging around is a demon with a conscience."

8

The rest of the facility was empty except for the corpses. A lot of corpses. Enough corpses to make me realize that DEMON might have been pretty aptly named after all, since at least two-thirds of the dead bodies weren't human. There were vampires with silver stakes in their hearts, werewolves shifted back to human form and riddled with bullet holes, decapitated hobgoblins and faeries, a nixie that had been drawn and quartered, and several women that looked completely human, but their dead bodies still radiated magical power. Seems like the government's witch hunt had gotten literal.

"This is...disturbing," Tim said as we made our way back into the lab. Our search had been fruitless, so I hoped that Faustus and the puppies were able to dig up some information we could use.

"Yeah," I agreed. "That was a lot of dead people, and dead not-people. I've been around my fair share of mayhem, and that was a lot, even for me to take. How about you?" I addressed that last bit to the faerie woman, who still hadn't told us her name, or even what type of fae she was.

"It reminds me of some of the purges I witnessed at home," she said. Her voice was cold, and when I turned to look at her fully, it was obvious she wasn't paying attention to her surroundings anymore. Whatever she was seeing, we weren't it.

"Where's home?" I asked, trying to keep my tone casual. I was really racking up the supernatural sidekicks on this little adventure, and I wanted to know as much as I could about all of them.

"I am of the Summer Court," she said. "My name is Ilandrane, and I am one of Her Majesty Titania's ladies-in-waiting. My rightful place is at her side, ensuring that all her needs are met, not here, in this drab world, surrounded by these colorless walls, and wearing this... horridly dull excuse for a dress." This was more than she had said in the half hour we'd been exploring the building, and her whole demeanor had suddenly shifted, as if she only now remembered who she was.

"Well, Ilandrane, I'm Quincy Harker. Pleased to meet you." I held out a hand, but she just stared at it. "Usually we shake hands when we introduce ourselves. It's a quaint little custom, but I like it." I don't like snobs, and if this was the real Ilandrane, we might have an issue.

She looked at my hand like it was a dead fish, then reached out and gave it one limp shake. "I've never touched a human before. You're...warm."

"You still haven't touched a human," Tim said.

My head whipped around, and I reached out a tendril of power, just enough to have a spell ready in case the Sasquatch wanted to throw down now that we were close to his reinforcements. "What did you say?" I asked. My voice was hard as granite, and if he was any judge of human facial expressions, he could tell that his next words were going to be very important.

"I said that you're not human. Not completely human, anyway. I don't know exactly what you are, Harker, but you don't smell like any human I've ever encountered, and I've been around a while."

"How long is a while?" I asked.

"I don't remember the country before there were white men here, but I do remember the West when it was still wild, let's just leave it there." Seems Sasquatch lived at least as long as me. I filed that little tidbit away in case I needed it later.

I looked over at the faerie. "He's right," I said. "I'm pretty much unique, and not exactly human, although I can usually see human from here. But yes, we are warm-blooded. Faeries are too, right?"

"Yes. Most of us, at any rate."

She didn't seem very inclined to continue the conversation, but I wasn't inclined to just drop it. I did what I do—I pushed a little. "How did you get here? To our world, I mean. I assume the DEMON agents captured you and brought you to this facility, just like everyone else."

"Yes," she said, looking around. "They dragged me into this iron shell and imprisoned me within steel walls. It was horrible. I could feel the cold iron pressing in on me, sapping my strength, making it impossible for me to escape or touch my magic." She looked haunted, and my stomach clenched as I imagined the torment she endured here. Then her face relaxed, and her posture eased. "But that is over, and soon I shall be restored to my lady's side. I came here in search of a human. For breeding. Fae men of noble blood have historically weak constitutions; thus it is imperative every generation that some number of women of standing take human consorts. I was...selected to be one of them. I was sent from my lady's court to find a suitable mate and return with him to Faerie." She looked at me for the first time, really *looked* at me, and I suddenly had a deep and personal understanding of how a bull feels when he's being auctioned off at a stockyard. She scanned me head to toe with an appraising eye, then shook her head as if she remembered something. "But you aren't really human, are you?"

I sensed an out that would neither hurt her feelings or insult the magical creature standing in front of me and possibly piss off her boss, the queen of the goddamned faeries and probably incite an interdimensional political incident and bring a fuckton of faerie knights galloping down I-77 on their unicorn steeds, all looking to carve recompense out of my ass for whatever grievous insult I'd inflict upon this woman for not banging her.

Instead, I just shook my head, put on my best regretful grimace to hide the dancing going on inside my head, and said, "No. I'm sorry, but I'm not human. We don't even know if I *can* father children, but if I can, they wouldn't be what you're looking for."

She didn't look convinced. "Perhaps not, but perhaps you are, as you claim, close enough to human to be acceptable. I will continue looking for a suitable mate, but if I do not find anyone better, you may have to suffice."

I didn't have anything to say to that and wasn't completely sure whether I was relieved or insulted, so I just stuffed all that aside and turned my focus to Faustus and the doggos. In this situation, the demon and werewolves were *definitely* the safer conversation.

We'd reached the door to the lab, and I was surprised to find it closed. "Didn't we leave this open?" I asked Tim.

He nodded, then motioned for Ilandrane to move behind him. The faerie took several steps back into the hall, pressed her back against the wall, and did that *Terminator* camouflage thing again. I felt a tingle on the back of my neck as she touched magic, and my eyes widened a little. Then I cursed myself for being a dumbass. Of course she has magic, she's a frigging *faerie*. I chalked my ridiculous surprise up to the number of unfamiliar elements I was dealing with today, drew my pistol, and yanked open the door to the lab.

Only to get pelted in the shins by quarters thrown by a pair of werewolves and a demon. "Dammit, Harker!" Faustus yelled as I walked in. "I was winning!"

"What the literal fuck? We were sweeping the building for dangerous predators and you three were in here pitching pennies? What are you, nine years old? In 1962?" I scooped up the quarters and slid them into my pocket. If they couldn't keep a grip on their money, that wasn't my problem.

"You wanted us to search the lab for relevant documents and any portable electronic storage. We did that. It's over there." He pointed to one of the lab tables, which had been righted and was now holding a pair of bulging briefcases and three laptops. "All the computers are password protected, and the documents are either in code or heavily redacted, or they're just written in Nerd, which is not one of the seven languages I am fluent in."

"Only seven?" I asked.

"My Aramaic is rusty," he admitted. "Not much call for that anymore, and since I never intend to return home, I've let my Enochian studies slack off a bit, too."

"Seems fair," I said. "What's wrong with them?" I pointed to the werewolves, who were frantically sniffing the air and looking around the room, their eyes rolling around a little. I'd never known a lycanthrope who could lay their ears back in human form, but that's exactly what these guys were doing. They reminded me of terrified animals when there was a nearby predator they couldn't see. Or basically any dog when Luke was around.

"I don't know," Faustus replied, walking over to the taller of the weres. "What's going on, Zane? Do you smell something?"

"There's something dangerous here," Zane said, his head whipping from side to side.

"That wins the award for most obvious statement of the day," I said. "You've got a pair of werewolves, a Sasquatch, a demon, and a faerie. I think 'dangerous' is an understatement, pal."

"Not dangerous like you, or like us. Old danger. It's not something I recognize, but my instincts are going nuts. Like a goose walking over my grave, except the goose stopped there and is tap-dancing. What faerie?"

"He means me, dog," Ilandrane said, stepping through the doorway into the room. Zane and Ari both let out little whines deep in their throats, tiny, scared sounds that made them look small just from the utterance.

"Yeah…we gotta go," Ari said. "Thanks for not murdering us, and we hope you find your friend."

"Uncle," I corrected.

"Whatever," the terrified werewolf replied. "But we gotta be someplace else. Anywhere, really. And we gotta be there right fucking now.

Bye!" He grabbed Zane's elbow, and the pair almost bowled each other over in their haste to get out the door.

I looked at Tim. "What the fuck, dude? Did your boys get into the catnip?"

"I think you should ask her," the Sasquatch replied, nodding at Ilandrane.

"Good idea," I agreed. "Okay, Ilandrane. Why were those guys scared outta their minds of you? Do they know you? Is there something about you that I need to know?"

"All you need to know, Harker, is that I have decided after watching you more closely, that you are not acceptable breeding material, and as such, I shall be taking my leave of you. I have neither knowledge nor concern about the fears of a pair of curs such as the ones who were here. Thank you for ensuring my safety to this point, but now I bid you *adieu*."

With that, she swept past me and walked out the lab door. I watched her turn right toward the front of the building, then she was gone, leaving me standing there with my mouth hanging open. "Huh," I said. "Well, I guess I don't have to worry about marrying a faerie princess now."

"Good thing," Faustus said. "Because regardless of Detective Flynn's response to that, which I am certain would be…extreme, from what I have heard of marriages between the fae and humans, you likely would not enjoy the experience."

"Why is that?" I asked.

"They can be…extreme in their desires, shall we say."

"Shall we say something more specific, like anything that will let me know if I should be okay with her wandering around in my city?" I growled at the demon.

"I'm sure it will be fine. They usually only sample two or three potentials before settling on a mate," Faustus replied. "The body count shouldn't be *that* high."

"Goddammit," I muttered. "She's going to go out and bang a bunch of dudes and kill any of them that don't make the cut to be her husband?"

"Pretty much. But for the one that she does select as her mate, the rewards will be extraordinary. Extraordinarily painful, that is."

"We have to follow her. She definitely took an interest in either Ari or Zane," Tim said. "They are young and stupid, but mostly good-natured. They do not deserve to die like that."

"How do you know she was interested?" I asked. "Looked to me like she was kind of a bitch to them. Called them dogs, you know."

"I smelled her desire. Pheromones. She was much more interested in mating with one of them than she was with you. She emitted practically no scent when she spoke with you, but when she saw the wolves, it was almost enough to knock me down. I expect that is what they were responding to."

"I don't know whether to be insulted or relieved," I said. "Okay, let's get after her. We've got enough dead cryptids lying around without her going all praying mantis on those guys." I took one step toward the door when Becks's voice erupted in my head, almost driving me to my knees.

HARKER! Get your ass over here!

Where? I asked, blinking rapidly to clear the stars from my vision. It felt like a flash-bang went off in my head.

The hospital. I'm at Presbyterian with Pravesh. The emergency room. There's a vampire here, and I think he's been starved. He's blood-crazy, and I don't know how much longer we can keep him contained. Pravesh is barely able to stand, and the hospital security are not up to this.

Fuck. I'm on my way.

"We've got a situation at the hospital where Flynn and Pravesh are. A vampire situation. I have to go."

"We'll hunt down the faerie," Faustus said.

"I'll hunt the faerie. Alone." Tim's tone brooked no disagreement, and I bit back a chuckle as Faustus's eyes went wide.

"That's good," I said. "Faustus, you get all this shit back to my place and get Cassie and Jo to start going through it with you. Tim, you chase down the faerie. If you need me, I dunno, send up a flare or something." I rattled off my number, just in case he had a cell phone hidden somewhere on his person. I didn't want to think about where he would be carrying it, but then as soon as I thought that, I couldn't think about anything else.

I sprinted out the door and down the hall toward the hospital, hoping for a good, bloody vampire fight to clear my head. I had a shit-load of monsters loose in my city, and we were no closer to finding Luke than we were when our chopper landed. In short, this sucked.

9

It took me almost fifteen minutes to get from the converted warehouse north of town to the emergency room entrance at Presbyterian, with Flynn giving me updates the whole way. When I burst through the doors, a security guard with a big gut and a Taser walked up to me, his strut reeking of self-importance.

He held out a hand and said, "Hold it right there, buddy. You're going to have to go to CMC Main. The ER is shut down—"

"Fuck off. I'm here to fix your vampire problem," I said, pushing him aside. I might have put a little too much mustard on that push, as he went sprawling to the industrial tile flooring. "Sorry." I looked down at him. "Where is the cop and the fed? The ones with the real guns?" I eyeballed his Taser with all the disdain it deserved. I'm sure less lethal options are great in most scenarios, but this wasn't most scenarios. At least it wasn't for this guy. It was a pretty run of the mill morning for me.

"Back there, but you can't get through. The junkie—what the fuck is that guy on anyway?—he did something to the door. It won't open for anyone. I think your friends got everyone out, but I don't know what happened to them."

I did. Thanks to way more telepathy than I ever wanted, I knew exactly where Becks was. She was locked in one of the ER rooms with Pravesh, a mother with a sick little girl, and a guy who looked like he OD'd on something. They had the door secure, but it was just a matter of time before the vamp either broke through or found easier prey.

Becks, I'm here, I said. *Stay down. It's going to get loud and messy.*

I was counting on loud and messy when I called you in.

I walked to the door leading back to triage and the treatment rooms and jiggled the handle. Sure enough, it was locked, or stuck, or blocked. Whatever. The door wasn't moving. Not without some serious persuasion. Fortunately for me, I'm a pretty persuasive guy.

I took a step back from the door, then turned to the security guard. "You're gonna want to get behind cover. Something solid." He looked at me, realized there was not a single humorous bone in my body, and scampered around behind the nurses' desk.

I drew in power, holding both hands out to my sides, elbow high. I pointed my palms at the door, focused my will through my hands, and shouted "*DISCUTIO!*" Force flew from my hands, a pillar of pure energy streaming toward the doors with every ounce of anger I had stored in my body. And with the events of the last twenty-four hours, that was a lot of ounces. My rage slammed into the doors, and metal and wood didn't stand a chance. The doors disintegrated, and a shower of splinters, screws, and shards of metal flew through the mostly deserted emergency room. Mostly, except for one pissed off vampire who looked at me like I was an all-you-can-eat buffet, complete with chocolate fountain.

She was small, maybe five-six, with long straight red hair and the perpetually flushed complexion that shrieked her Irish heritage to the heavens. She was barefoot, and her hair was matted with blood, which covered the lower half of her face and her hands up past both wrists. Gaunt arms and legs stuck out from the rude armholes and bottom of the shapeless shift that barely covered her, similar to what Ilandrane had on. It must have been the uniform for female captives at Cryptid Gitmo. Blood covered the front of her chest, too, in colors ranging from the dark brown of stains that were many days old to the bright crimson that was obviously fresh from the tap.

That tap was a lanky black doctor that lay at her feet, his arms and legs stuck out at weird angles from his body and his neck twisted in a creepily unnatural fashion. His eyes stared out at me, but he'd seen his last patient chart. I may not have a medical degree, or any degree if we're being honest, but I've gained a lot of experience with corpses in my ridiculously long life. And this guy was all kinds of dead.

His killer, on the other hand, was exactly the wrong kind of dead. And by "wrong" I mean "moving around, supernaturally strong, hungry, and really pissed off." She grinned at me as I stepped through the wreckage of the door, her smile completely destroying any hope I had of looking like a badass when I entered through my own explosion.

"Are you here to take me back, human? I'm never going back. I'll rip you to shreds first. I'll snap your femurs like pretzels and suck every drop of marrow from your bones!" She ran at me, and she came *fast*. She might have been near-starved when she got here, but drinking the good doctor apparently gave her plenty of energy because she covered the fifty feet between us in the blink of an eye. Lucky for me, I know how most vampires fight.

There's a pattern to fighting a predator, especially one that's accustomed to being the top of the food chain. It's always going to expect to be invincible, and if you have just a little more ability than the monster expects you to have, you end up with quite an edge. If you've spent a good part of a century sparring with the most famous vampire in history, that doesn't hurt, either. So when she charged me, obviously expecting me to go down as easily as the dead doc in spite of me literally blowing the doors off the joint to get at her, I was ready.

I summoned a round shield of energy around my left arm and swung it up, letting her momentum slam her face into the unyielding manifestation of my will. And my attitude. Most days it's more attitude than will, and this one was no exception. When she stepped back, staggered, I lowered my shield and blasted her in the face with a bolt of raw mystical power designed especially to punch a hole straight through her skull.

Except her skull wasn't where I needed it to be, which meant I just blew up a rolling IV stand and melted a clock. I felt the air move behind me and dropped to my knees as she slashed through the space where my head had been just half a second before. I rolled forward and spun, drawing my pistol in what was nowhere near as smooth a motion as I wanted it to be, but I was facing in the right direction and armed, if I was stuck on my knees.

Or I was armed for about the blink of an eye, until the little blood-sucker slapped the gun right out of my hand. "No fair," she said. "I can smell the silver. We're doing this the old-fashioned way." Then she leapt at me again. In a movie, that would be the point where I lean backward in a badass dodge like something out of *The Matrix*. But since no one has ponied up to buy the film rights to my life yet, reality was much less awesome.

Reality was me flopping flat onto my back and wincing as I felt one of my knees bend in a really awkward fashion. Reality was the vampire chick landing on her hands, letting her momentum carry her into a handstand, then stop in mid-flip, spin around, and push off from the floor with both hands. That sent her into a high arc that drove her down onto my chest with both feet like a really bloodthirsty lawn dart.

She broke so many ribs landing on me, my chest sounded like bubble wrap. I couldn't scream because it takes air to scream. I could only shove her off me with my left hand while I called power around my right and made a dome over my entire body. I lay there panting under my shimmering forcefield as the vampire shrieked and clawed at it, trying vainly to catch even a little of my breath. I put one hand on each side of my ribcage and pushed inward, feeling a lot of dislo-cated bones *snap* back into their rightful place. I drew in a huge breath, and as soon as my lungs were full, I let out a scream fit to wake the dead.

My vision went white with pain, and I might have even blacked out for half a second, because the next thing I knew, there was a weight on my chest again, and when I opened my eyes, a smiling face with dripping fangs was just inches from my own.

"Hi there," the vampire said as a little drop of blood rolled off her chin and dripped into the hollow of my throat.

"Hi."

"You're fast."

"Not fast enough."

"Not even close."

"Then why am I still breathing?" Not the first time I've asked that question in my century-plus life, but one of the few times there was no existential whining associated with it.

"I wanted to make sure you could see."

"See what?"

"My face. Because it's the last thing—"

I cut her off. Not with a witty retort, my ribs still hurt too bad for that. I cut her off with a headbutt right to the nose. It doesn't matter how strong a creature is, if it's based off basic human anatomy, a shot to the bridge of the nose is going to hurt like a son of a bitch. She screamed and reared back, an involuntary reaction to getting your nose aggressively booped, and I took the opportunity to throw her off me. I rolled to my feet just in time to catch her wrist as she swiped at my throat, apparently abandoning the plan of ripping my throat out with her teeth and deciding to settle on slashing me to ribbons with her claw-like nails instead.

With her wrist clamped in my right hand, I spun around, using her momentum to speed her progress. I yanked her into the air and flung her across the ER, sending her into a wall where she slid to the floor beside an overturned rolling workstation that let out a series of angry beeps, then fell silent.

I didn't bother looking for her there; she wouldn't have stuck around. Instead, I took the few seconds of reprieve to push one last stubborn rib back into place, yell "Motherfucker!" at the top of my lungs, and manifest my soulblade.

"Come on, bloodsucker. Let's finish this up. I want to get home in time for *Jeopardy*."

"Home, you arrogant bastard? I haven't seen my home in *three years*.

Three years those pricks kept me locked up, feeding me just enough blood to keep me conscious but never enough to not feel starvation lingering in the back of my head. Three years of being chained to the wall and shot, stabbed, set on fire, beaten, doused with acid, and subjected to every kind of pain imaginable, just so they could examine how long it took me to heal. Three years of watching those humans, those *cattle*, poking and prodding at superior species like they had some kind of divine right of science. Like they were *anything* worth considering. Three years of wondering if today would be the day they finally cut off my head, or burned me to death, or jabbed me with a silver stake. Three years—"

"Three years of practicing this stupid fucking monologue?" I said, stepping around the nurses' station and coming face to face with her. "That's long enough for you to learn that brevity is the soul of wit. Now let's finish this, bitch."

10

"I'll show you a bitch," the vampire snarled, and then it was on. She sprang at me again, but this time I was able to sidestep her charge and bring the instrument tray I had in my hand up to collide with her face. She dropped with a *thud* but was back on her feet almost before I could blink.

But not before I could cast. I released the magic I'd called up with a shout. *"Mordaro!"* Blue energy washed over the furious bloodsucker, but she couldn't escape the spell. She threw a punch, but her eyes widened as she realized that she was now moving at normal speed. Normal *human* speed.

I grabbed her wrist and ducked, spinning around and pulling on her arm. She came off her feet like they were spring-loaded, and as I jerked her arm forward, she flew over my head into a nearby wall. She went down in a cloud of sheetrock dust and mangled aluminum studs, but she was right back up as soon as she could untangle herself.

"It's going to take a lot more than that, fuckwit," she growled. She moved forward, more stalking than charging now. She stopped just outside of arms' reach and moved to the left, her hands held low, palms up, ready to grab me and rip my throat out. She was fully vamped out, fangs extended, eyes completely black, and bloodlust written in every line of her face.

I've fought vampires before, and with a lot of them, if you can get them to slow down for a second and see that you're not easy prey, you can stop a fight before it ever really begins. This chick did not have that kind of sanity left. The only way this fight was stopping was with one of us dead. True dead.

Still, I had to give it a shot. "You don't have to die today. What they did to you was awful, but you can't take it out on innocent people."

"Innocent? These people aren't *innocent*. They're the ones who want to put me in a cage and see just what kind of monster I am. They're the ones who want to charge admission to gawk at the monster. They're the ones who would just as soon stake me through the heart as look at me!"

"But they didn't do any of those things. They just got sick, or injured, and came to the hospital for help. Instead of help, they found you. You want to show people you're not a monster? Stop acting like one."

"Go fuck yourself, you sanctimonious prick."

That was totally my line, but for the moment she wasn't breaking any more pieces of me. My "slow down" spell was only going to last about another minute, so I needed to figure this shit out, and fast. The vamp was still moving left, and I wasn't sure if she was trying to get to something or just maneuver me into someplace I didn't want to be. Then I saw it. She didn't care where I was. She was putting herself between me and Becks.

Fuck. I was out of position, and if she put everything she had into getting it open, there was no way that door would hold. *Becks, do you still have those vamp-killer rounds?*

Yeah, I've got one magazine loaded with them. But she moves too fast. I can't get a bead on her.

I think I've got that handled. She's slowed down with a spell right now. At least for another few seconds.

You want me to just open the door?

No. I want her to break it down. I just want you to be ready.

62

I felt her swap out magazines in her service weapon. *I'm as ready as I'm gonna get.*

Okay, let's see if she'll take the bait.

I let my eyes widen and took in a sharp breath, as if I'd just realized what she was doing. "No!" I shouted, charging straight at her.

"She matter to you, Hunter? Well too bad, because I'm going to have her for dinner!" The vampire took two long strides, put both hands on the door to Becks's room, then dug her fingernails into the wood, leaned back, and yanked the door off the hinges and backward through the jamb. The door used to open inward, but with that kind of strength, it pretty much opened however she wanted it to.

The vamp stepped through the splinter-strewn doorway, turned to the right, then Becks unleashed a little bit of noisy, lead-filled Hell right into the bloodsucker's chest. I heard five quick shots, then a pause, then five more. The vampire was staggered now, leaning with one hand on the doorframe, blood pouring from her chest. A couple of Becks's shots missed, punching holes in the drywall and making me very happy there was no one else in the ER bays, because they would be having a very bad day.

The vampire lurched back into the main body of the emergency room, looking around for any escape from the hail of pain she was in. There was no respite coming. Instead of safety, she found me, and while I've been called a lot of things, "safe" has never been one of them. I raised both fists to chest height, focused all my will, all the pain of broken and dislocated ribs, all my anger and fear at Becks being in danger, and I shouted, *"INCENDEMUS!"* at the top of my lungs.

Streaks of fire shot out of my hands, slamming into the vampire and knocking her back into the wall. I walked forward, channeling more fire as I went. My vision narrowed until my focus was absolute. There was only one thing in my mind—burning this undead asshole to ash. She messed with the woman I loved, and she was going to die for the last time.

I poured energy and flame into the vampire until there wasn't enough left of her to fill a shoebox. The walls were scorched down to the studs, and the tile where her corpse would be if there was enough of her to call a body was melted to slag. I saw soot-blackened concrete under the husk of her body. I let the fire go, and the energy and rage flowed out of me like a tap. I sagged against the door of the emergency bay and looked over to Becks.

"I think we got her."

"Ya think? Harker, one of these days you and I are going to have a conversation about overkill," Becks said.

"I've always said that if something is worth doing, it's worth overdoing." Then the pain and exertion caught up to me, and the last thing I remember was watching the lights rush away from me as I fell to the floor.

"You are an unbelievable dumbass." Those were the first words I heard upon waking.

"You're welcome," I said as Flynn's face slowly came into focus. She leaned over me, her dark eyes full of worry.

"I thought you were dead, you prick." She slapped me on the shoulder, and I winced. "Did that hurt? Good. No, I'm sorry. Shit, Harker, you just make me crazy. It's like you're the baddest dude in the room, but then you do shit that pushes even your limits of survival. It scares me, you know? It's like I can't tell if you do this stuff because you want to kick ass and save people, or if you want to figure out how to die."

I thought about that for a second, probably longer than I really should have. I didn't want to die. Hell, now that I was back with Becks, I even mostly wanted to live, which was a welcome change. But I couldn't argue with her. There was something in me, something dark and ugly, that pushed me to do more and more stupid shit just to see if this was the thing that finally killed me. I didn't need to stand over the dead vampire pouring magic into her ashes until I passed out. That was just me making a point. Making a point to a pile of ashes. If I had a therapist, she'd have a field day with that one.

"I just don't want anyone or anything to hurt you," I said. "I might have gone overboard a little this time, though."

"Might? You dick. I'm glad you're not dead, but I'd really like for you to stay that way."

"Me too," I said.

"Really?" I could see from the look in her eyes that she wanted the real answer, not whatever bullshit I came up with off the cuff.

"Yeah," I said. "I'm not gonna bullshit you. I'm pretty sure I *can't* bullshit you, especially not with you this close. I want to live. For the first time in a long time, I don't just want to keep surviving. I want to *live*. That's what you do to me, Becks. You make me want to live. I know I do stupid shit, and take crazy risks, and it doesn't always look like I do, but I do. I'm not gonna say there haven't been some dark times. Memphis got bad. Not just because you weren't there, but what that demon did, what he made people do…it was a bad scene, and it took me right up to the edge of a really dark place. But I'm not there anymore. I'm here. With you. And I'm gonna stay here. For a long, long time."

I watched her face as I talked. Watched it go from pissed off and scared to sad to hopeful to tearful and (I hope) happy. When I was done talking, she bent over the hospital bed and kissed me. This wasn't the kind of "I missed you and I love you but I'm gonna kick your ass later" kiss that we shared when I first got home. This was a "don't you ever leave me again" kiss, and I kissed her back with every ounce of permanence and dedication I could muster.

"I love you, you big dumb asshole," she muttered as she lay her head on my shoulder.

"I love you too, but do you think maybe you could take the restraints off? I don't mind you tying me up, but this doesn't really seem like the time or place. If we can postpone our little bondage experiment until later, I think it would be a good idea."

Becks straightened up and slapped me in the shoulder again, laughing. She placed both hands in the small of her back and straightened up, rolling her shoulders and stretching her spine. Then she undid the straps across my chest and legs, then unfastened my wrists and ankles.

"What's with the restraints?" I asked.

"It's the only way the staff would treat you," she replied. "They saw what you did, and after the vampire killed a security guard, doctor, and two nurses, they weren't going anywhere near you without some assurances."

"What did they give me? How long was I out?" I sat up and swung my legs over the side of the bed, looking around for my Doc Martens.

"They just gave you some IV painkillers and fluids. You were basically fine, just beat to shit. Careful of the...never mind."

I assume she was about to say "IV," but I snatched it out of the back of my hand before she could get the words out. "Do you know where my shoes are?" I asked.

"Over here." Becks bent down beside the lone chair in the room and picked up a white plastic bag with "Patient Belongings" on the side in big black letters. She dropped the bag on the bed beside me and picked up my Docs from the floor.

I dug my socks out of the bag and put them on, then my boots. I was just lacing up the left boot when the door to my ER bay slid open and Pravesh stepped around the curtain. She was leaning on one crutch and had a large bandage over her left eyebrow, but aside from that and some bruising, she looked fine.

"Good to see you, Pravesh. I was worried you were dead."

"I'm touched, Harker. Didn't expect you to care." But there was a smile on her face as she jabbed at me. Pravesh and I weren't tight. Never would be. I've got too many issues with authority for that, but we'd reached a pretty solid working relationship regardless. After all, when you plan an assault on Hell with somebody, you find ways to get along.

"Purely self-serving," I said. "I just don't want to break in another government lapdog." I stood up and grabbed my pistol and wallet out of the bag. I slipped the Glock in its holster into the back of my jeans, dropped the wallet in my front pocket, and turned to Becks. "Surprised I didn't wake up in one of those stupid gowns. Was I not out long enough for them to strip me down?"

"No," she said. "They didn't want to touch you that much. Harker, you set fire to someone with magic from your hands. You scared the *fuck* out of the people around here."

"Is that your way of saying I might be able to get a break on the bill?" I asked. She just rolled her eyes.

"If you're finished with your standup routine, can we get out of here?" Pravesh asked. "I have a feeling this won't be the last escaped cryptid we have to deal with, and I have a lot of data to analyze if we're going to have any chance of finding Luke before DEMON decides he isn't worth the effort to keep alive."

"Everyone else should be at the condo. I'll drive the Suburban. You two are too beat to drive," Flynn said, heading toward the door.

"What about my car?" I asked. "I…might have left it parked in the ER driveway."

"Yeah…about that…" Flynn said. "Your car got towed. Once the immediate threat was over, they reopened the hospital to ambulances, and it was in the way."

"What the fuck?" I asked. "I save the goddamn hospital and they tow my fucking car?"

"Don't screw with the parking lot security guards," Pravesh said. "They've got all the attitude of regular rent-a-cops, with none of the authority. The only power they have is the tow truck, and they aren't afraid to use it."

"Can I just go back to Hell?" I asked. "I mean, down there I knew who the assholes were. Everybody."

"Maybe, but let's make sure the monsters don't overrun the entire city first. Then you can resume interplanar travel," Flynn said.

11

B ack at the condo, we gathered everyone around the big dining room table for either a planning session for a supernatural invasion, or the weirdest Thanksgiving dinner in history. I sat at one end, with Becks on my right side and Jo on my left. Pravesh sat at the other end and stretched out her bum knee, with Glory on one side and Faustus on the other. Cassie bustled around in the kitchen making tea, but I knew full well she heard every word anyone said.

"Cass, you might as well come sit down. You know more about hunting bad guys than half the people at the table," I said.

She clucked her tongue at me and said, "Now Quincy, don't you be filling these children's heads up with all that foolishness. I'm just an old woman who don't know nothing about nothing."

"Yeah," I snorted. "You forget, old woman, I was around when you and Alex were out hunting together."

Jo's eyes widened and she turned around in her chair to gape at her mother. "Mama, is there something you want to tell me?"

Cassandra shot me a dirty look but came to sit by her daughter. "If I *wanted* to tell you, I wouldn't have waited until now. But I used to work with your daddy some. It wasn't a regular thing, and I never had it in my blood, like you and him, but I tussled with my fair share of vampires, werewolves, and ghouls in my day."

"Your mother was a badass," Glory said, leaning forward to look past Cassie at her daughter. "She would wait in alleys and parks, just sitting there as bait, until a monster tried to attack her. Then she would hold them off until your father came in with his hammer and killed them."

"It ain't as impressive as it sounds," Cassie said, looking down at the table. "And when it mattered, I wasn't enough to save Alex."

I saw the pain on her face as she thought about the night she watched her husband die at the hands of a werewolf. The same werewolf Jo killed almost twenty years ago when she took up her hammer. I wasn't there the night Alex Harrison died, but I'd heard the story from Luke once after way more wine than any reasonable person should consume in one sitting. Admittedly, I'm not what most people consider "reasonable."

It was 1987 in Phoenix, and Luke was helping Alex hunt a werewolf that had the local lycanthropes thinking about moving on to bigger and better things, like taking over the city and raising humans like cattle. It happens a couple times a century—you get a monster with a God complex trying to subjugate all of humanity. It never works out, but the body count can get pretty high until somebody, usually me or one of my friends, steps in and explains the error of their ways to the monster. Those explanations are usually very violent, and very bloody.

This wolf had killed a couple of cops, and the whole police force was going nuts looking for what psychopath sliced and diced their pals. Heavy police involvement usually makes it harder for my kind of work because what we do is pretty much murder a lot of the time. It's self-defense if you know all the details, but since lycanthropes revert to human form when they die, and there isn't a blood screen for werewolf, hunting shifters can be complicated.

The night it all went sideways, Luke wasn't with them. He was meeting with tribal leaders at the reservation just outside of town, trying to get them to help track the beast. In the meantime, Alex and

Cassie had lured the Alpha out into the open with Cassie acting as bait. She was a beautiful woman and had a scream that would make a B-movie horror starlet proud. In short, she made a great lure. The Alpha went for Cassie, she sprayed him in the face with an aerosolized silver nitrate she concocted, and Alex came rushing in with John Henry's hammer to finish the job.

The only problem was that the Alpha had been expecting them, had set the whole thing up when he saw that Luke was too far away to help, and sent a decoy in to come after Cassie. While Alex was pounding some hapless pack member into furry paste, the Alpha came up behind him and buried his claws in Alex's kidneys. He fought the best he could, but there was no way he was going to be able to go toe to toe with a fully grown werewolf with his insides all ripped out. Alex got in some good shots, but by the time Luke got to Alex's side, there was nothing he could do except wipe the blood off John Henry's hammer and take it home to wait until Jo was old enough to take it up.

Alex was another death in Luke's long history that he blamed himself for, no matter how many times Cassie told him it wasn't his fault. They'd been played. It happens in this game, but it never fails to make us angry when it happens, and I knew from the look on Luke's face every time he laid eyes on Cassie that guilt was one of the biggest things he felt. One of the biggest, but certainly not the only.

I blinked a couple times to bring myself back to the present. I *really* didn't want to know if Luke and Cassie had a different relationship than the typical Renfield, and it didn't matter. We needed to get him back, and now. "Okay, what do we know?" I asked, looking around the table. "We've got an abandoned DEMON facility on the north end of town, a similarly abandoned black site in Tennessee, a missing vampire, a fuckton of monsters released into the North Carolina ecosystem, and exactly fuckall for clues. Did that pretty much sum it up?"

"Yeah, pretty much," Glory said with a grimace. "I've got nothing, Harker. The folks upstairs are not talking about this, or if they are, they aren't sharing it with me. I think this falls into the 'mortals gotta deal with their own shit' category."

"Faustus, any news from downtown?" I asked the demon.

"I…don't really talk to anyone in Hell these days. I'm pretty much *persona non grata* down there, thanks to helping someone escape Lucifer's wrath. I think the bounty on my head may actually be larger than yours, if you can believe that."

"Okay, then. What's the plan?" I asked. "We've got to find Luke, and we've got to hunt down this Walston bitch and educate her on the consequences of fucking with our people."

"All the upper-level personnel at DEMON have gone completely dark," Pravesh said. "No one at DHS can find them, and no one at a lower clearance level than me ever knew they existed in the first place. I spoke to the Under Secretary, and he went all the way to the Secretary, but…"

"But what?" Flynn asked.

Pravesh's face flushed, and I could tell she was pissed. "The current administration has a bad habit of appointing people into Cabinet positions who are even less qualified than the typical Washington dipshit, so the Secretary is a useless twit who doesn't know enough to wipe his own ass without studying the effect it might have on his boss's approval ratings. I'm not sure he even knew DHS *has* a Paranormal Division until my boss spoke to him about this issue, and I'm one hundred percent sure he didn't know DEMON existed. All that to say that we're getting neither intel nor assistance from the top levels at DHS. The Under Secretary is good to authorize equipment, and I can allocate the few resources I have as I see fit, but otherwise, we're on our own."

"That's how we work best anyway," I said. "Jo, you and Pravesh start working on these computers to see if you can find anything on where they might be keeping Luke, or any cryptids they've abducted. Flynn, call in to your boss and let's see if we can track down some of the escaped monsters. Maybe one of them knows something."

"What are you going to do?" Glory asked.

I stood up and walked to the door. "I'm going to take a shower. I've been up for almost forty-eight hours, in which time I've fought a dragon, a bunch of demons, and a werebear. At this point I stink so bad I couldn't sneak up on a skunk in a sewer."

"That's what all y'all need to be doing," Cassie said, standing up. "I slept last night. Not well, but more than the rest of you. Faustus and Glory might not need sleep, but the rest of you do. Everybody go get some, even you two." She looked at Glory and the demon. "Then come back here and start on the stuff you just said."

I opened my mouth to argue, but Cassie held up a hand and nailed me with one of her "don't sass me" glares. I closed my mouth and nodded. "Yes, ma'am." I looked at the others. "She's right. As much as I hate to say it, we can't do anything for Luke if we're so exhausted we fuck up everything we try to do. Let's eat, shower, and sleep, then reconvene here first thing in the morning."

"It's early to be going to bed, old man. Your years finally catching up to you?" Flynn asked.

"A little. But I think it might take more than one shower to get all the soot, blood, and viscera washed off. Wanna come scrub the werebear guts off my back?" I asked, giving her an exaggerated leer.

"Well, when you make it sound that appealing, how could I say no?" She walked over to the door and stopped a few feet from me. "You know, you're right. You *do* stink. You should take that first shower alone. Then we'll discuss me washing your back for the next one."

She walked out, and I turned to the others. "Let's meet back here at sunup. If we can all get a good night's sleep, we'll be in much better shape to find Luke in the morning."

"Sounds good," Pravesh said. "We all deserve eight hours curled up around a pillow and a bottle of Scotch."

Yeah...we didn't get *close* to what we deserved.

1 2

There was a time in my life when a gorgeous blonde waking me up in the middle of the night meant I was getting lucky again. That time has passed, and when Glory threw open the door to my bedroom at two in the morning and flipped on the overhead light, I all but fell out of the bed in my surprise.

"What the fuck, Glory? Jesus!" I yelled, pulling the sheet up to cover my exposed privates. "Haven't we had the conversation about knocking? What if we were in the middle of something?"

"If you were in the middle of anything, it was carpentry, the way you were sawing logs," my guardian angel remarked as she walked over to my chest of drawers and started pulling out clothes. "Get dressed. We've got a problem."

"I've got ninety-nine problems and one of them is an angel with no sense of personal space," I growled as I stood up and grabbed the boxer briefs she'd tossed onto the bed. I looked over at Flynn, who was already up and walking naked to the bathroom. I paused to admire the view I'd been missing for half a year, only to catch a pair of black jeans upside my head as Glory continued to select my wardrobe.

I slipped on the jeans, then a white t-shirt with "The Mary Janes" scrawled across the front in pink letters. Becks came out of the bathroom as I sat down on the bed to pull on my socks and my boots. She walked over to the dresser, opened a drawer, and started to dress.

"You're lucky I don't have your shoes in my hand, Harker," Glory said. "Put your eyes back in your head."

"Nah," I said, my gaze firmly fixed on Flynn's shoulders, back, and everything else. "My eyes are good right where they are. I missed this sight."

"You're sweet," Becks said, turning around as she fastened her bra. I've never understood how women manage to basically dislocate their shoulders to fasten those things. They must have been invented by some nutjob king's torturer. "What's going on, Glory?" Becks asked.

"There's a new sculpture garden that appeared downtown tonight, right in the middle of the Epicentre," she replied, naming a shopping/eating/clubbing development in the center of Charlotte's Uptown district.

"That's nice," I said. "Public art is good for the masses. Tell me again why you woke me up?"

"You would think after all this time I'd be able to tell when you're being intentionally obtuse and when you're just an idiot," Glory replied, shaking her head at me.

"Let's chalk it up to me still being half-asleep and you talk to me like I'm an idiot. Not that I'll be able to tell any difference from how you usually talk to me."

"This sculpture garden looks suspiciously like a bunch of drunken karaoke fans in the middle of the Whisky River nightclub," Glory said.

"Aw, fuck."

"Yep."

"Medusa?" I asked, really hoping she'd say something about a spell, or a demon, or really anything that would be easier to deal with than a monster with a head full of snakes that turned people to stone with a gaze.

"Medusa," Glory confirmed.

"Wait, like Theseus and Medusa?" Flynn asked.

"Perseus," I corrected absently. "Do we know if she's still in the bar, or do we have to hunt her down?"

"Then who's Theseus?" Becks asked.

"Theseus killed the minotaur," Glory replied. "Everybody gets those two mixed up. Last I heard, she was still in the bar, but that was a few minutes ago, before I came to wake you. I sent Faustus down there to try and keep an eye on things."

"Isn't that a lot like sending a fox to watch your chickens?" I asked.

"As demons go, he's pretty trustworthy," Glory said. "Besides, he's fucking *terrified* of me. He's going to keep an eye on the medusa and let us know where she lands if she leaves the bar. The last word I got was that she was just sitting there drinking expensive bourbon."

"I've had worse nights," I said. "But without the karaoke. That shit's dreadful. You ready to roll?" I asked Becks.

"Let's do it." She was in jeans and a wine-colored sweater with her service weapon on her hip and a backup strapped to her right leg. We paused on the way out of the apartment to grab our jackets, and I picked up a Mossberg Cruiser shotgun with a pistol grip from the floor of the closet. I put it on a sling over my right arm and put my leather duster on over it. I felt like a *Tombstone* cosplayer, but I didn't feel like inciting a riot in my first two days back in town. Maybe for the weekend. I slipped my Glock in its holster at the small of my back and threaded my belt through the loop on a silvered Buck hunting knife. I slipped a pair of brass knuckles in each coat pocket and I was good to go.

I turned to the door and stopped as I saw both women staring at me. "What?"

"Are you expecting the Republican Guard, Q? It's one medusa," Glory said.

"The last time I went into a fight, I ended up dealing with demons in a Bass Pro Shops, a dragon in the parking lot, and an Archduke of Hell on the top of a pyramid. I have not had much in the way of reasonable fights lately. I will not be the one showing up with a knife to a gunfight."

"You remember that you're a wizard, right?" Becks asked.

"I don't know what medusas are vulnerable to. I've never fought one."

"Medusas?" Glory raised an eyebrow. "Pretty sure that's not right."

"Okay, medu*sae*, then. Whatever the fucking plural is. Let's go downtown, make this thing into a singular corpse, and then maybe I can get a little more sleep."

"Don't count on it," Becks said. "After you deal with the medusa, you need to find a way to restore all her victims to their normal forms."

"Do I have to?" I asked. "I mean, they were singing karaoke. They kinda deserved it."

W hisky River sits on the upper level of the Epicentre shopping/dining/entertainment complex, one of those things that would have been a mall if it were built twenty years earlier, but it wasn't, so it isn't. Glory and Flynn took the first set of stairs to the second level, which would let them skirt the upper walkways and keep an eye on the entrance to the bar while they approached. That left me to walk through the deserted plaza alone and take the stairs that came out right in front of Whisky River's doors.

I jogged to get there first, figuring that either I'd be immune to the creature's gaze, or I'd at least be able to protect myself magically more than Becks. I wasn't too worried about Glory, since angels don't have a whole lot of natural enemies on this plane, and I'm pretty sure some chick with a permanent bad hair day isn't on the list.

There were half a dozen statues littered around the promenade leading up to the stairs, all of them of men in their late twenties or early thirties, all of them wearing an infuriating smirk and the ubiquitous uniform of the Charlotte douchebag: khakis, an untucked dress shirt with the sleeves rolled up and the collar unbuttoned, and flip flops as their little spark of rebellion. They were all very original, just like every one of their buddies. Each statue had a look of surprise in his eyes to go with the smirk on his face, and I couldn't help but wonder if these assclowns getting turned to stone wasn't some kind of divine justice.

Faustus leaned on the banister at the top of the stairs, a cigarette dangling between his fingers and an amused expression on his face as I joined him on the mall's second level. "What's going on in there?" I asked.

"It seems she's stopped turning people to stone and is now making requests of the DJ and drinking," he said, taking a drag off his cigarette.

"I'm pretty sure you can't smoke here," I said.

"I'm a demon, Harker. Does that typically mean that I'm big on obedience? And let's face it, even for my kind, I'm a bit of an outlaw. Doing good and all that."

"More like refusing to go home when the boss calls," I replied.

"To-may-to, to-mah-to. Now what are you going to do about the snake? Go in there and charm her?"

I didn't even acknowledge the attempt at a pun. I try not to encourage him. "How many people has she changed? In addition to the ones out here, I mean."

"It looks like only three, maybe four. There's a clump of statuary at one end of the bar, and one lone dude decorating the hallway by the bathrooms."

"What do you want to bet every one of these guys either made some crude remark or tried to pick her up before she turned them?" I asked.

"That's almost a dozen guys," Faustus said. "You think they all managed to offend her in one night?"

I thought for a minute about the last few times I'd seen groups of young professionals get one more drink in them than they knew how to handle at Zeek's, the bar I worked at in Memphis. "I think I'm surprised there aren't more statues out here," I said. "Never underestimate people's ability to be assholes."

"I hang around you, Harker," the demon replied, finishing his cigarette and crushing it out with his shoe. "I am constantly reminded of the level of asshole to which a human can rise if given enough time and motivation."

"Stay here," I said. "Becks and Glory are right behind me. Have Becks line up a shot through the glass in case things go sideways."

"What about Glory?" he asked.

"We'll just let her do whatever she wants," I said. "It's not like we can stop her anyway."

"Good point," Faustus said to my back as I walked through the doors of Whisky River. The bar was brightly lit and decorated in roadhouse chic, with plenty of polished wood, tarnished brass, and neon beer signs. A middle-aged man with a scruffy salt-and-pepper beard sat on a stool behind a computer on stage, a flat-screen TV scrolling the words to that Garth Brooks classic "Friends in Low Places." A sign hanging on the front of the table he used as a mixing booth labeled him "DJ Tomato Slice," which seemed oddly fitting for a faux-redneck bar.

The medusa sat on a stool at the end of the bar as far away from the door and the cluster of stone douchebros as she could get and still have bar in front of her. She never looked back at DJ Tomato, just bobbed her heads along to the music. Her head was covered in tiny serpents that looked like black garter snakes, but which I knew were some of the most poisonous creatures to ever see daylight. She wasn't wearing a shapeless shift like the other escapees I'd seen. No, she wore a scoop-necked royal blue top with black leather pants and calf-high boots. She had cheekbones sharp enough to shave with, and her lips were the color of fire engines and sin.

She turned to face me as I approached, and I immediately cast my eyes to the ground.

"Don't worry," she said. "It only works if I want it to. If you're nice, you get to stay flesh."

I looked up at her. I felt my heart in my throat as we locked eyes, then I took a step forward. *Oh good,* I thought to Becks. *She wasn't lying. I didn't turn to stone.*

You mean you didn't know if she would turn you or not? Her emotions ranged from incredulity to exasperation, which was a familiar combination where I was concerned.

Well, I figured she had some level of control, or there would have been a lot more dead people. Not a lot of guys are going to avert their eyes from a gorgeous Greek woman in those pants.

Men are pigs.

Not gonna argue. In fact, I'm pretty sure that's what happened here. Notice how there aren't any statues of women?

Oh shit. You think she turned these guys because they were rude to her?

Yeah, probably.

You might not have been the best choice for negotiator, Becks said. *Just saying.*

Yeah, I had that thought, too. Oh well, I'm here now. Guess I'd better be on my best behavior.

Try to do better than that. Your best behavior often ends up with bloodshed and explosions.

She wasn't wrong. I turned my attention back to the medusa, who held up a hand as I drew breath to speak. "Sit down, Quincy Harker. Let's chat a little before we decide if we're going to do battle this night." She patted the wooden barstool next to her.

I sat down and took the bottle she slid my way. "Pappy Van Winkle," I remarked. "You have good taste."

"When you have lived as long as I have, you learn to appreciate the finer things."

I paused. "Are you trying to tell me you're not a medusa, but *the* medusa? I thought Perseus killed you."

"That's the story we put forth so no one would suspect that the lovely new bride Perseus brought home from his adventures was in reality the horrible monster that he set out to battle in the first place."

"Holy shit," I said, leaning over the bar and grabbing a highball glass. I poured it half full of bourbon and took a big drink, letting the rich amber liquid warm me all the way down. "You've been around a while."

"You could say that," she replied. "I have killed for much lesser offenses than these men offered me tonight. But they are not dead. Their condition can be reversed."

"Then get to reversing," I said. "Then we can finish this bottle, DJ

Tomato Sandwich can go home, and you can get the hell out of my city. We'll forget this ever happened."

"I don't think so," she said, smiling. She turned to look at me, and this time there was a golden ring around her iris that wasn't there before. "I think I'm going to make all of humanity pay for the indignities I suffered, for the pain that I endured as they ran their experiments on me. And I think I'll leave you here on this barstool as a monument to the hubris of the man they call Reaper, who thought he could challenge the medusa and live to tell the tale!" Her eyes flashed gold throughout, and I felt the paralysis take hold. The pain was immense as I felt my skin, my muscles, my blood begin to harden.

Just as her magic trapped me completely, I saw Becks and Glory burst through the door. "Get your eyes off him, you snake!" Becks shouted. "Nobody torments Quincy Harker but me!"

Yep, she still loves me, I thought, them my vision went white and I knew nothing but stone.

13

loating...
Weightless drifting...
Darkness warm and inviting...

"What the literal fuck?!?" I shouted as bright light stabbed my eyes, jarring me from the nicest dream. I was...I couldn't remember. But it was nice, wherever I was. Everything was peaceful, and nothing hurt, to paraphrase Vonnegut.

Here, not so much. Here I was awake, naked, and freezing my ass off. I stood on a marble floor that stretched out farther than the eye could see in all directions, with neither a wall nor a support in sight. It was an endless see of gray shot through with white and black veins that spiderwebbed through the stone and pulsed, as though the room was a living thing. I felt a vibration beneath my feet, a low steady hum that was beyond even my hearing, but I could feel it going up through the soles of my shoes all the way to my spine, making my bones thrum with it.

"*Vestimentum*," I said, reaching for power.

Nothing happened. Not just that no clothes materialized out of thin air, but *nothing* happened. There was no power coursing through me, no manipulation of the energy around me, nothing. I had no

81

clothes, and worse, no magic. I focused my will inward, reaching down into the heart of myself and was relieved to see I could still manifest my soulblade. It flickered a little, but the blade of pure will wreathed in purple energy was there.

"Trust you to immediately search for a weapon instead of an escape. You might be the most predictable human I've ever encountered, Quincy Harker. And I've dealt with a great many of your kind."

It was a testament to my iron will that I didn't piss myself at the sound of that voice. As it was, my mouth ran dry and chills crept over every inch of my exposed flesh, which was all of it. I turned around to see the most glorious of God's creations, Lucifer Morningstar, standing in front of me. The most beloved of the Host, the Lightbringer, the origin of betrayal himself…the fucking devil was grinning at me like I'd just given him the best Christmas present he could have ever asked for. Just what I want out of life—a happy Lucifer.

The last time I saw Lucifer, he wasn't at his best. As a matter of fact, the last time I saw the King of Hell, he was ten feet tall with obsidian skin and ragged, shattered slivers of wings hanging from his shoulders. The last time I saw Lucifer, he promised to destroy everything and everyone I ever loved before he finally took pity on me and dragged me down to Hell for my well-earned eternal torment.

He looked better now. I mean, judging from the eye-daggers he was flinging at me, he still wanted to floss his teeth with my Achilles tendons every morning, then grow them back overnight so he could do it again the next day, but he was back to roughly human form.

I've never seen Lucifer's true angelic form. No human has. There aren't any humans around from the time before Moses, at least that I know of. But from all I've ever heard, he was the most glorious creature God ever created, the most beautiful work of art the universe has ever seen. Too bad for him, he knew it. But even though he didn't have his angel mojo anymore, Lucifer was still a goddamned beautiful man, and he stood there in that faceless plane of marbled nothingness in a bespoke suit and handmade leather shoes, and he just oozed classy restaurants and dirty sex. His hair was dark and pulled back into a long ponytail at the nape of his neck. His skin was olive, and the dark hair and dark skin made his emerald eyes sparkle all the more in contrast. He smiled at me, and I'd swear I saw the tips of fangs along his lower jaw, but then his tongue slipped out over his lips, and I lost my breath. I understood exactly why he was The Tempter. Then I saw the hatred behind the lust, the hunger for my blood that lay under the aura of seduction he cast over me, and everything snapped back into sharp focus.

I opened my hand and let my soulblade vanish. I had no illusions about my ability to go toe to toe with the First of the Fallen. "Hello, Lucifer," I said. "Or do people really call you Lucy?"

"Do not confuse the very real danger you face with a television show, Quincy Harker. I have enough reason to want you dead. It is not in your best interest to give me more."

"How many do you need?" I asked. "I made you look like a douchebag in front of your entire realm. I'm pretty sure the last guy who pissed you off that bad was John the Baptist."

"No, I liked John," Lucifer said with a wave of his hand. A massive wooden throne with a thick red velvet cushion on the seat materialized, and Lucifer unbuttoned his suit jacket and sat down. "The Baptist, unlike his modern-day descendants, knew how to party. He was still hung up on Dad and his stupid rules and the Nazarene and his stupid forgiveness, but when I could get him away from all the praying and dunking, he was as willing as the next churchman to get drunk and laid. No, I think the last person who made me as angry as you was probably that little fuckwit Hitler."

I was honestly taken aback. "I expected him to be one of your favorites," I said. I was so stunned by Lucifer's words that I forgot who I was talking to and just blurted it out. "I mean, he was pretty much *the* greatest villain of the twentieth century."

"Sure, he was horrible and murdered eight million people. But if he wasn't such a little putz, he could have actually *won* the war. I gave him all the tools, but the idiot squandered them. By the time he finally hid in that fucking bunker, I was so tired of listening to him whine that I gave Eva half a dozen cyanide capsules and promised her that if she killed him, then herself, that I would make sure she didn't come to my realm and instead ascended to Heaven when she died."

"Did she? Go to Heaven, I mean?" If Eva Braun was in Heaven, I wanted to have a long chat with the fucking quality control guys up there.

"Of course not, you twit. For the one thing, she didn't follow orders. She didn't kill Adolf, just took a pill herself. She slipped poison into his food at dinner, but he didn't eat it, so she didn't hold up her end of the bargain. Besides, do you think *I* have any input into who Peter lets through his precious Gate? Fuck, Harker, how did you ever survive our last encounter if you're that stupid?"

"I got lucky, I suppose."

"Well, all that's over now, isn't it? You tangled with a medusa, and now you've turned to stone. That's not how I expected you to go out, but you never were one to follow the path anyone expected, were you?"

I stared at him. "I'm...dead?"

"As a doornail," the devil replied. "What do you think this is? A dream? A JJ Abrams movie?"

"I do have some trippy dreams," I said, turning in all directions trying to make out any features of where we were. The only thing I could see was Lucifer on his throne, that smug grin stretching unnaturally wide across his face.

"Welcome to...well, we've never really named it," Lucifer said, gesturing broadly around him. "For lack of a better term, we call it the Between. This is where we meet to discuss the disposition of particularly troublesome souls. Souls that I and my brothers in the Host both feel we have a valid claim on. Souls like you."

I had no idea what he was talking about, but if it meant he wasn't going to rip me limb from limb, I was okay with whatever he wanted to blather on about. I figured I should at least *try* to keep him talking, lest he get bored and go back to Plan A, the whole ripping me limb from limb thing. "Why can't I tap into my magic here?" I asked.

"Magic comes from life," he said, as if that explained everything. After a few seconds of me staring at him blankly, he figured out that it actually explained nothing, and let out a world-weary sigh. Nice to know my powers of exasperation extended to Archangels. "Did no one ever tell you how your magic works?"

"I took a few lessons when I could find someone through the years, but most of them were either charlatans, insane, or they had no real idea how their abilities worked. I've always just muddled through."

"Father, why hast thou forsaken me and saddled me with morons," Lucifer muttered. He looked back to me and adopted a tone that one would use with a particularly slow first-grader. "Magic is life. Life is magic."

"I thought friendship was magic," I interrupted.

"Do you want to know this or not?" he growled, and I saw a little fire flash behind the green of his eyes. "I'm only giving you this little bit of education because I'm bored, and I think there's a chance you may use it to your own detriment in the future, thus hastening you to my loathing embrace."

I made a "go ahead" gesture, but for all the nonchalance I feigned on the outside, Inside Harker was cutting backflips. I was getting a lesson in magic from Lucifer himself. If he didn't hate me to the white-hot degree that he did, this would be really cool.

"Everything that lives has a soul. Humans, dogs, cats, mice, crickets, eels, worms, trees, grass—everything. The souls of every living thing combine to fuel your magic. You're tapping into the life force of the whole world when you cast a spell. That's why you don't have any magic here. There's no life but your own. You can manifest your little sword because it comes from your own energy. But you can't do anything else. And you can't refill your stores of power, so if you keep your blade out too long, it will drain all of your personal energy and leave you nothing but a desiccated husk of a soul lying here on the ground. Go ahead, give it a shot. I'm sure you don't believe me, and I *really* want to see you give it a try."

"Nah, I'll trust you on this one." I recognized the truth in his words. I did feel a little weaker after manifesting the blade. And since he didn't seem inclined to destroy me in that moment, I figured I didn't need it. "Why could I use magic in Hell? There was nothing living down there but demons and Fallen."

"And souls," Lucifer said, still using the "boy you're a moron" tone of voice. "Hell is the greatest repository of human souls anywhere."

"Except for Heaven," I said.

He arched an immaculate eyebrow at me. "Do you really think there are more human souls in Heaven than Hell?"

He had a point. Most people generally suck, so it stood to reason that Lucifer's hotel would have fewer vacancies. "I just have to stand here with my dick in the breeze until your brothers show up, huh? Is that the plan, embarrass me to death? Not gonna work."

"Oh, I didn't know you wanted to be clothed." The devil waved a lazy hand through the air. Crimson light bathed me, and when I looked down, I was wearing the same clothes I'd had on back in the real world, where, apparently, I was now a statue.

"Thanks."

"Don't mention it. I want to torture you, Harker. I don't want to gawk at you. I'm far more interested in slicing open your abdominal muscles and tying them together behind your back than I am in looking at your tattoos."

"Let's hold off on the slicing for a little while longer, brother," came a genial voice from the left.

Lucifer and I both turned, and I took a step back in complete shock. Walking up to us, in jeans, Vans sneakers, and a t-shirt with Deadpool riding a unicorn, was Uriel. But the Archangel looked exactly like my friend Dennis Bolton, right down to his tight curly hair and the freckles on his nose.

"Hey there, Harker," Dennis/Uriel said with a smile. He turned to Lucifer, and his expression became decidedly *less* pleasant. "Lucifer."

"Uriel," Lucifer replied. "Nice shirt."

"Thanks. I like dressing like a human. Drives Michael absolutely batshit."

I gaped at the swearing angel. "Somehow I feel like I've corrupted an Archangel."

"Don't give yourself too much credit, Harker. Uriel has long been the closest of us to you hairless apes. You just gave him another thorn to twist in our brother's side." Lucifer turned back to Uriel. "Shall we get on with it, then?"

"Get on with what, exactly?" I asked. "What the fuck are we doing here?"

"We're negotiating, Harker," Lucifer said with a smile. "Both I and the Host feel that we have a claim on your soul. Now we're going to sit down and figure out who gets you. You really don't want it to be me."

Well, fuck.

14

"Do I get a vote in this?" I asked, looking from Lucifer to Uriel. Lucifer was right, I *really* didn't want him to end up with my soul as his punching bag for all eternity, but I also really needed to get back to Becks and the rest of my friends before monsters tore my city apart at the seams and the shady government douchebags that kidnapped Luke killed him. For good.

"Not really, no," Lucifer said, with that same shit-eating grin on his face. "You see, everything in your life has pointed you straight to Hell. You've committed murder more times than either of us can remember, you blaspheme literally daily, you cheat at cards, you spent a legitimate four decades as a reckless womanizer, and that's before we get into the amount of non-fatal destruction you've left in your wake. Let's face it, Harker, you're a lot like a natural disaster, only less discriminating in what you destroy."

Well, when he put it like that, I had to agree with him. I had unleashed more than a lifetime's worth of havoc, but in my defense, I'd lived more than a lifetime. "Why are you here, Uriel?" I asked. "You just come by to see an old pal before Lucifer rips my soul out through my nose and fillets it?"

"No," the Archangel replied, and this time he'd dropped the Dennis voice and moved into the deeper, more resonant tones of the ethereal creature he really was. "You have sinned, that is inarguable. As a matter of fact, you are one of the most accomplished sinners I have seen in centuries, especially for someone who honestly thinks he is doing the right thing. It's astounding how much devastation you can cause while trying to help."

"It's a gift," I said, bristling a little at the angel's "compliment."

He held up a hand, a placid expression on his round face. "But you have also done a great deal of good. You have served as a protector to the weak, and the defender of this world from many threats, and you have performed great service to the greater good. Not the least of which was keeping our brother from once again storming the Gates of Heaven and destroying much of what our Father has wrought."

"All, brother. I would have destroyed it all, if not for this meddling mortal. That's why he's *mine*. I get his black little soul as payment for him interfering in my plans." Lucifer's grin faded and I was reminded exactly how scary the First of the Fallen could be when he wasn't playing piano and drinking expensive Scotch.

"And that is why he is *not* yours," Uriel replied, his placid expression never wavering. It was a little creepy, if I'm being honest. Lucifer, for all he hated humans and had literally threatened to destroy everyone and everything I cared about, was open about what he wanted. Angels, in my experience, were all about the mystery. I don't like mystery. I like my bad guys to be bad and wear black hats. I like my good guys to wear white hats. That way it's easy to figure out who to shoot. All this moral gray area was confusing and just made me want to burn it all down.

"Okay, guys. Whose am I?" I asked. "And if you could decide who's got me so I can know who I need to beg for my return to the land of the living, that would be really helpful. I've got shit to do back in my body and don't have all eternity to sit around jerking it with you two dorks."

In hindsight, maybe insulting the two cosmically powerful beings currently discussing the disposition of my immortal soul wasn't my best idea, but nobody's ever accused me of being prudent. Both of them looked at me like I was some kind of never-before-seen brand of idiot, then turned back to their argument.

"Oh, fuck no," I growled, then took two steps forward. This put me right between the pair of them, and I reached out and grabbed them by their collars. I had a fistful of expensive Italian wool in one hand, and a wad of celestial angel dust pretending to be a Deadpool t-shirt in the other, and I yanked both their heads in until we were all three almost bumping foreheads.

"Look, motherfuckers," I said. I didn't stop at the time to think about the folly of my actions, which was good, since pissing oneself in front of the Devil isn't a great look, no matter how understandable a reaction it may be. "I'm not some pansy-ass Job wannabe just hanging out to be a bargaining chip in your game of who's got the bigger celestial dick. I've got a bunch of monsters to capture or kill, a rogue government agency to shut down with extreme goddamn prejudice, a relationship to repair with my fiancée, and a vampire to rescue. So if you two would kindly quit scratching your metaphorical balls and send me the fuck back home, I'd really appreciate it. Otherwise, whichever one of you pricks decides to keep me is going to have the biggest motherfucking problem child you ever dreamed of. Because I will either install a goddamn stripper pole right inside the holy gates, or I'll take over the top eight Circles of Hell and open it up to horror movie fans as a new Rob Zombie-themed amusement park and charge admission! Now send. Me. The. Fuck. Home."

I released their collars and stepped back, gesturing for them to resume their negotiations. Lucifer spun toward me, but Uriel put a hand on his shoulder. The Devil stopped and slowly rotated around to look at his brother. "The only reason that hand isn't shoved so far up your ass it tickles your diaphragm right now is that you are the least dickish of my brothers, by a very slim margin. But if you don't remove it right now, I make no promises that my restraint continues for another five seconds."

Uriel and Lucifer glared at each other for a full *fifteen* seconds before Uriel broke into peals of laughter that echoed off the marble floors. "Lucifer, you have developed a poetic sense of profanity in the millennia since I last sat with you watching the mountains form. Let's step back a moment and assess the situation. We both have a valid claim on the mortal—you for his soul, and the Host out of an unpaid debt. You can't just give him to Heaven after all the havoc he's wreaked, and we can't just let him go to Hell after all he did to restore us to ourselves. And he did keep you from murdering me forever, after all."

Lucifer looked a little abashed. "Sorry about that, by the way. Ambition clouding judgement and all that. If I'd really been thinking about it, I would have gone for Michael. Nobody likes him enough to mount a rescue attempt."

Having spent a little time around Michael in his Archangel form, I had to give the Devil his due on that one. If I had to choose between Lucifer restarting his War on Heaven or listening to Michael's judgmental ass for another hour, it would be a close fucking vote.

"Be that as it may, Harker did rescue me. He did save us from another War. And he did restore the Host to our rightful place in Heaven. We owe him. I'm paying that debt. He goes back." Uriel's voice was firm, his jaw set. He was a determined Archangel wrapped in a short white kid's body. It was a weird picture, but it worked somehow.

"And if I say no?" Lucifer asked, his voice taking on a sibilant tone that reminded me who the original serpent in the Garden was.

"Then we fight."

"I've never had a problem besting you, brother."

"But you've never been able to best all of us, *brother*." Uriel gestured to the blankness above us, and I looked up to see thousands of angels, the entire Heavenly Host, floating above us. They were all clad in gleaming white armor trimmed in silver and gold. They held swords, spears, halberds, and crossbows, all limned with ghostly flame. Thousands of angels, ready for battle, hovered above the three of us.

Lucifer flushed, and with a wave of his hand, cast a dark shimmer across the opposite side of the sky. It turned a burnt crimson, and horde upon horde of demon appeared, some flying on their own, others astride nightmarish winged mounts that looked more bat or desiccated buzzard than horse. "It seems we have a standoff, *brother*," the King of Hell said with a curl of his lip. "We could clash, right here in the space between, where neither of our armies has an advantage, and settle the eons-old question once and for all."

"We could," Uriel said, his voice as placid as a mirrored lake. "But while I see all of your Dukes and Archdukes, all your Princes and Lieutenants, you'll notice that my force is missing something."

I looked up, and after a moment's searching, I realized what he meant. There were no Archangels among the assembled armies. Michael was nowhere to be seen, waving his flaming sword like a banner. Azrael wasn't beating his black-tinged wings with bloodlust written in every wrinkle of his countenance. The forces of Heaven were arrayed against Lucifer, but the Archangels had devoted only a portion of the power at their disposal to this skirmish. They still had their heavy hitters in reserve.

"That's right, Quincy," Uriel said. "We didn't bring the big guns."

By the look on Lucifer's face, he came to the same conclusion I had: he was fucked. With a scowl at me and another skyward glance to the arrayed angel army, he took two steps back from us. He gave a deep bow and swept his arm through the air. At his motion, the demons vanished, and the sky returned to its "normal" featureless white. "I concede the day, brother. Quincy Harker lives to annoy for a little while longer. But eventually, *human*, you will do something that not even my tenderhearted brothers will be able to rescue you from. When you do, I'll be waiting. Toodles." Then he gave me a little wave, and in a puff of no shit sulfur-smelling smoke, the Devil vanished.

I felt a huge wave of tension flow out of me along with the breath I let out. "Thanks, Uriel. Now about that whole not being dead thing?"

The Archangel gestured to the assembled army of celestial beings, and they winked out of view. I wasn't sure if they poofed back to Heaven, or if they just turned invisible, but I made a mental note not to scratch my ass until I was sure. It's one thing to be crude in front of one angel; it's another thing entirely to be crude in front of *all* the angels.

Uriel looked at me, and the Dennis face melted into the angular, almost painfully beautiful visage that I more closely associated with an Archangel. He grew to his full height of nearly seven feet, and huge white wings flickered into view on his back. It seemed that the time to cosplay human had passed. "That was the only one of those I had, Quincy. I was betting literally everything on my brother loving power more than he hates you, and I won. This time. But there can't be another. That was the promise I made to the others of the Host—I would face down Lucifer and his armies for you. Once. But I cannot, will not, do that again. The next time you find yourself on Hell's doorstep, try not to ring the Devil's doorbell."

"Sounds like you're saying I had one Get Out of Dead Free card, and I just used it?" I asked.

"Precisely. Now go home, Quincy. And try not to die again."

I opened my mouth to assure Uriel that I had no intention of dying again anytime soon, but before I could draw a breath, everything went black and I felt every nerve in my body scream as I was pulled apart and sent back to Earth.

15

I woke up paralyzed. More specifically, I woke up in excruciating pain wrapped in what felt like a literal ton of concrete. I couldn't open my eyes, I couldn't open my mouth, and it took me all of about half a second to realize that I couldn't breathe. I was wrapped head to toe in something rigid enough to hold me completely motionless, and if I didn't get free in the next thirty seconds, I was pretty sure I was going to die.

And I'd just been told in no uncertain terms what would happen to me the next time I died.

Motherfuckers, I thought. *Couldn't even unfreeze a guy when you bring him back from the dead?* Panic rising in my throat and what little air I had in my lungs burning like I was huffing bleach, I concentrated on getting free rather than letting the whirligig of my thoughts take over. *Focus, Harker. Focus.* I reached out with my mind and found power all around me, *life* all around me, filling me almost by osmosis. I drew it inward, sucking energy in from all around me, shoved it into a little ball of power inside me, then did it again. And again. And again. When I was unsure which was more likely to kill me, asphyxiation or the overload of power I was holding, I cut loose.

Normally when I cast a spell, I use my hands as a focus, to aim the power at a specific point. Sometimes, like when I'm creating a shield, I wrap a part of my body in power. This time I just shoved it out of me in all directions, with as much force as I could muster, like a rock-wrapped, man-shaped grenade, sending shards of power radiating outward in all directions.

There was an eyeblink of resistance when the power couldn't penetrate the stone, but I poured more magic into it, sucked in more power from my surroundings, and used my body as nothing more than a conduit for it, like if you tied a balloon over the end of a fire-hose and turned the water on full blast. Except the balloon was solid stone and I happened to be wearing it over every inch of my body. I felt myself expanding, felt the strain between the power coursing through me and the stone refusing to yield, and I was getting ground to bits between. I wasn't going to make it. I couldn't draw enough power. I didn't have enough will.

Fuck. This is it. Goodbye, Rebecca. I love you.

Not today, motherfucker. Flynn's voice in my head was as much a snarl as a call, and I felt her latch onto my soul with everything she had. Usually when I feel Becks in my soul, it's like a candle in the dark, or a lighthouse guiding me home. She's a strong, steadying beam of hope and goodness that draws me out of the darkness and shows me how to get back to her. Not this time. This time she wasn't the guide who led me out of the darkness, this time she was the hand snatching my wrist as I plummeted over the falls, the lifeline that snaked out of the dark and yanked me up from the depths, this time she wasn't calling me home, she was goddamn *pulling* me.

I felt myself pulling back from the darkness, inching away from nothingness, and I found strength I didn't even dream I had. I drew in more power from around me and found myself able to pull in energy through Flynn as well, and as it blazed through me like a supernova, in the barest instant before I was nothing but a smear on the inside of the medusa's statue, the rock encasing me exploded into pebbles and I fell to the ground gasping for air.

I rolled over onto my back, sucking in oxygen in huge, whooping breaths and trying to remember where I was and how to stand up.

The ceiling of the bar flickered down on me in its red and blue neon-plastered glory, and the lazy swoop of the fan went *whoosh-whoosh-whoosh* as I relearned how to focus my eyes.

"...ow..." I croaked out a little gasp, all I could manage for witty repartee.

"Harker!" Flynn yelled, and I heard the *clump-clump* of her boots as she ran across the hardwood floor to kneel by my side. "Are you okay?" Her brown hair made a waterfall around us as she bent down to kiss me, then drew back. "Dude. You are *seriously* dirty."

"Yeah..." I managed to gasp. "Being turned to stone will do that to you. Medusa?" I asked, trying and failing miserably to stand.

"She got away. Glory's tracking her by the blood trail."

"Blood trail?"

"I shot her. But she's stronger than she looks. Took three in the chest and still ran off faster than I could follow."

"Glory'll get her." My throat seized up on the thick layer of dust I'd inhaled, and I couldn't speak, so I switched over to our private channel. *You saved me*, I said.

That's the deal. We save each other. It's kind of our thing.

I love you.

I know.

Pretty sure the guy said that in the movie.

If we're going to conform to normal gender roles, I'm going to give you shit about robbing the cradle.

Fuck it, I'll be your Leia.

You couldn't hold Leia's jock. That bitch was a general.

You're not wrong. Help me up.

Flynn scooted around behind my head and leaned down, putting both hands under my arms. "If you ever scare me like that again, I will fucking kill you."

"Don't worry," I said, my throat feeling like sandpaper. "Pretty sure that was my one pass. Anything like that happens again, I'll wake up turning on a spit in Lucifer's living room."

"Then let's try not to let that happen. Can you stand?" I nodded, and between the two of us, we managed to get me upright and over to a barstool. Flynn walked around and opened the cooler, passing me a Stella Artois. I popped the top off with my thumb, surprised at how much it hurt. I looked at the bloody slash and saw to my displeasure that it wasn't healing nearly as fast as it should.

"That sucks," I said. She gave me a questioning look, and I said, "Looks like my healing has slowed down. Hope it isn't permanent."

"Well, you did just come back from the dead. I guess that takes a little getting used to."

I drained the beer but waved her off when Becks tried to pass me another one. "Water," I said. "Need to cut the dust from my throat. Literally." She filled a pint glass, and I drained it down, then sucked down another one before I started to feel even remotely hydrated. I could breathe without breaking into a coughing fit, and I could speak without sounding like I gargled razor blades, but I was still weak as a kitten and had no idea if I was going to be fit to go another round with the medusa if Glory did find her.

It didn't matter, though. She was hunting the monster that I let get away, and I wasn't going to sit here and count my bruises while she ran headlong into trouble. I put a hand on the bar and the other on the stool beside me and slid down until my feet touched the floor. I wobbled for a few seconds, but the longer I stood there, the stronger I felt. I reached out to the magic and felt energy all around me. I opened myself to it, using that power to hold me up and let me fake being all right. "Let's go," I said, managing to get the words out with just a minor cough. I wiped the stone dust off the bar and looked at Flynn. "We need to get to Glory. You're driving."

Faustus stepped out of the shadows outside the door and gave me a nod. "You're alive. Good. How's Lucifer? Still hate you?"

"Still wants to eat your spleen every morning for breakfast like Prometheus, last I heard. How did you know that's where I'd go?" I glared at the demon.

"I didn't, but when you turned to stone, your lady friend there lost her absolute shit, telling us all that you were dead. I might not be as completely aware of your final destination as I am my own, but it was a pretty good guess that if you *were* dead, Lucifer's would be the first smiling face your soul saw in the Between. How'd you get out of it? Call in a favor with the Archangels?"

"Were you eavesdropping?" I asked. "Because that's pretty much exactly how it went down."

"Well, yeah," the demon said with a smug grin. "Of course it is. Lucifer wants to torture you until his torturing muscles get tired, which by the way is never, but you happened to save all of Heaven from another great war, so they figure they owe you one. If you weren't a complete moron, it wouldn't take much to set them against each other to send you back. But be careful, that kind of thing only works once, if ever, and it probably made Lucifer hate you even more. And I didn't think that was possible."

"Yeah, he said I pissed him off more than anyone since Hitler. And that was before I slipped through his fingers again." I leaned heavily on the banister as we went down the curved steps outside the bar, concentrating very hard on not taking a header all the way down to the promenade level.

"You should probably try not to get dead again for a while," Faustus said.

"I'll do my best," I agreed. "Becks, go ahead and get the car started. Faustus will help me the rest of the way."

"Why me?" she asked, obviously reluctant to leave my side.

"Because you're the human, so the cop that's putting a boot on the Suburban might listen to you instead of immediately shooting the black-skinned demon with yellow eyes and fangs." I pointed to the squad car pulled up behind our SUV.

"Goddammit," Flynn said, breaking into a jog. "Hey! Back off, patrolman!"

I managed to get an arm over Faustus's shoulders before I face-planted on the concrete, and he looked up at me with some concern. "Not to be a downer," the demon asked, "but how are you going to be any fucking use fighting this medusa? You can hardly stand, and I'm pretty sure your last conversation with her dispelled any thoughts you might have about being immune to her gaze."

"If I'm being honest with you, Fausty," I said. "And since I wouldn't get anything out of lying, I am being one hundred percent honest, I have no fucking idea."

"I think you'd better figure it out, and fast."

"Why?"

"Because unless he's decided on moonlighting as a living statue, that cop Flynn was running after just turned to stone. I think your snake-haired friend has come back."

Well, goddammit. This night sucks.

16

The medusa was walking the wrong way up College Street when I got to the curb, and Flynn had moved out into the middle of the street and stood there with her pistol drawn. I opened my mouth to yell something, but Faustus put an elbow in my gut that doubled me over. When I was back to my full strength, I was going to kick his ass for that.

"What the fuck?" I wheezed.

"Keep your mouth shut, Harker. If she hasn't petrified Flynn already, there's a chance she won't. Up until now everyone she's turned to stone has been male. Maybe her powers don't work on women?"

"More likely she just really doesn't like men," I said.

"Do you blame her? Most men are pigs."

I had to agree with the demon. Especially given all the years the medusa had lived through, women had been pretty horribly mistreated for most of them. Maybe Becks would have a better chance of not dying than me.

Try to talk her down, I said to Flynn over our mental link.

Down to what? She escaped from a secret government facility and turned a couple dozen people to stone. What could we possibly offer her?

When she and I were talking, before I pissed her off and she killed me, she said something about being able to reverse the process. Maybe we can work with that.

I'll try. But if this goes sideways—

It won't.

I know. But if it does...I love you too, asshole. Becks shut down our connection to the barest trickle, just enough to let me eavesdrop on her conversation with the creature while staying safely behind cover.

The medusa walked along the center of the street, either assuming that it would be pretty deserted at that hour or counting on anyone driving to avoid hitting her. She'd definitely been locked up for a while, and had never driven in Charlotte before her captivity, or she wouldn't make that second assumption. They invented NASCAR around here, and half the people drive like they're the second coming of Richard Petty.

"Stop right there," Flynn called out as she stepped into the street. She raised her Smith & Wesson and set her stance. I'd seen Becks on the range. The medusa was about twenty yards away, and I knew Flynn could put sixteen rounds in the creature's center mass before she got another three steps. What I didn't know was the range on a medusa's gaze, and that was what I was more worried about.

"I don't want to hurt you, sister," the medusa said, stopping in the middle of the street. "But I will not be caged again. You seem to work for someone with authority, so you should tell them that. If you try to lock me away, I will destroy everyone I see, including you."

"I don't want to hurt you, either. Why don't we talk about it and see if we can come up with a better solution?" Flynn holstered her sidearm and stood up straight. "Nobody else needs to die tonight."

"We may not agree on that point, but I can certainly say that no one else needs to die immediately. And if I'm being honest, I've only killed one person tonight. Most of these trolls are still alive, or can be if I decide as much."

"Then who did you kill?' Flynn asked. "And why did you kill them, if you left all these others alive?"

"His name was Quincy Harker, and he was much too dangerous to

101

simply suspend, like I have done with these others. He was a wizard and could have possibly captured me if I let him live. Too bad, he was kind of cute." Her snakes twitched a little at that, and I was simultaneously creeped out and flattered.

"Well, you didn't do a very good job at killing him," Flynn said, waving to me. "Come on out, Harker."

Staring daggers at Becks, I stepped out from behind the planter where Faustus and I were taking cover. "Hi there," I said with a wave.

The medusa turned to me, and now her snakes were a writhing mass of scaled fury whipping to and fro around her head. "How can this be? I have never had anyone survive my envenomed gaze in all the centuries I have hunted. Your soul should be plummeting into the deepest depths of Hell, where you will be tortured for time immemorial."

"Why does everyone think I'm destined to go to Hell?" I asked.

"Not everyone thinks that, Harker," Faustus said. "Just everyone who's ever met you."

"Thanks," I said, sarcasm dripping off my tongue. Focusing on the medusa, I said, "I did all that dying stuff. I got over it. Now I'm back. Like Flynn said, it's time to turn these people back into…people, then we can get together and find you a safe place to live without interference from humans."

The medusa turned to me, a smile brightening her face. "You'd do that? For me? Even after I killed you? I'm…I'm truly touched, Quincy Harker. Perhaps you aren't the monster everyone says you are. Perhaps you're really a good person. Perhaps you…think I'm a child, to be taken in by your lies and empty promises? You're just like every other human male since my Perseus died—worthless!"

Her eyes flashed gold again, but this time I ducked back behind the planter before her magic could petrify me. "Time for Plan B!" I yelled to Flynn.

"What's Plan B?" Faustus asked as he dropped to his ass on the concrete and pressed his back up against the planter next to me.

"Shoot anything that moves," I said, drawing in power and using it to stand. I limped across the promenade to take cover behind another planter, firing off near-blind shots at the medusa as I hobbled along. I heard the flat crack of Becks's pistol and the ricochet of bullets off asphalt as she unloaded on the monster. I hefted my shotgun then let it fall. I was too far away for buckshot, and as weak and off-balance as I was, I was just as likely to fall on my ass from the recoil as to do any real damage. I was still a good fifty yards from the medusa, and that's farther than I can count on my shotgun to do much without firing slugs.

"I don't want to kill you, sister, but I will," I heard the medusa yell, presumably to Flynn.

"Don't worry," said a new and very welcome voice. "You aren't killing anyone. You have five seconds to release everyone from your spell before I cut your head off and burn every one of your snakes to ash." I heaved myself upright, leaning on the planter, and saw Glory standing on the roof of our Suburban, flaming sword in hand and wings spread to their full width.

She was an impressive sight when she wasn't trying, but when Glory really concentrated on looking like an angelic badass, she put anything Boris Vallejo painted to shame. She didn't need a chain mail bikini, she was hotter than Hell in a full suit of plate mail, complete with gleaming white tabard emblazoned with a crimson cross. Her armor shone like the sun in the middle of the night, not just reflecting streetlights but glowing from within as well, bathing the entire promenade and street with near-blinding brilliance.

"You think to stop me, angel?" The medusa glared up at her, snakes whipping around her scalp and hissing loud enough to be heard fifty yards away.

"No," Glory said, her voice firm. "I don't *think* to stop you. I *am* stopping you. Now stand the fuck down before I get truly biblical on your scaly ass." As incongruous as the profanity was with the wings, I had to admit she was getting really good at it.

"You are a terrible influence on her," Faustus said.

"We all have our roles in God's plan," I said as piously as I could manage. Which wasn't very pious, but I was talking to a demon, which set a pretty low bar for piety.

The medusa glared at the angel, and I could almost *feel* the power in her gaze. Glory didn't bat an eye, didn't even flinch. She just floated down off the roof of the SUV and walked over to stand in front of the furious snake-headed woman. "You ready to talk, or are you just ready to die?"

"I'm not going back to that laboratory."

"Nobody is asking you to. You can go anywhere you want, as long as you return these statues to flesh and keep your temper in check."

"Why should I have to behave? I did nothing to attract attention from these...men. I merely walked to the tavern, looking for a drink. They accosted me, insulted me, propositioned me, and in one case, *assaulted* me. Me, the legendary medusa, and an overweight blowhard in a cheap suit had the gall to put his hands on me! Why should I turn any of them back to flesh? Give me one good reason why I shouldn't turn them all to stone all the way down to their heart, like I did your friend."

"Do you want me to try to reason with you, or do you just want me to say 'because I'll kick your ass' and move on?" Glory asked.

"I want a reason! I want to know why you are defending these scum."

I glanced over at Faustus. "She does have a point," I said, my voice low.

"Hasn't anyone ever told you it's bad form to agree with the monsters that want to kill you, Harker?" the demon asked.

"I'm working on my empathy."

"Work on it when there's no chance of any of us becoming lawn ornaments."

Is she still distracted? Becks's voice came in my head.

I looked to the left of Glory's confrontation with the medusa and saw Flynn creeping from car to car along the sidewalk, trying to maneuver herself into a clean shot. *Yeah, Glory has her talking and her back is to you.*

Let me know if she sees me.

Pretty sure you'll know.

"Don't try to sneak up on someone with a hundred eyes all around her head, sister," the creature called to Flynn.

She sees you, I said.

Why do I even try with you? Flynn stood up and pointed her pistol at the snake-haired woman. "Give it up, Medusa. You don't get to hurt anyone else tonight," Flynn called.

"What about the wrongs and slights that were done to me? Who will make them pay for their mistreatment of me?" The monster never took her eyes off Glory and her flaming sword, but we all knew she was talking to Becks.

"You think that's mistreatment? Try being the only female detective in a precinct. You end up changing clothes in a broom closet because there's no better locker room. You never leave your coffee on your desk unattended because you really don't want to know what they'll put in it. You just assume that every guy in the building is eye-fucking you, co-worker and perp alike. But you put up with it because the other options are to lay down and die, or to walk away and quit. Either way, the bastards win. And I'm *not* going to let them grind me down. Now why don't you turn these lovely sculptures back into douchebags, and we can all go get a drink somewhere?"

"I am not going for a nightcap with the medusa," Faustus said under his breath where only I could hear him. Or at least he really hoped only I could hear him.

"Don't worry, you weren't invited," I said. I heard nothing for a long moment, long enough that I stuck my head out from behind the planter. I saw Glory and Flynn each standing within five feet of each other, on either side of the medusa. Flynn had her gun holstered and her hands out to her sides, palms out. Glory still held her flaming sword, but it was pointed to the ground, not threatening.

"I'm not interested in some bond of sisterhood," the medusa said. "I just want to be left alone. I want to be able to go somewhere, have a drink, and not be harassed. Is that too much to ask?"

"No, it's not," Glory said. "It doesn't happen often, but it should. But maybe we back off on the petrification for those offenses, okay?"

"If I say no?"

"Then I shove a flaming sword through your heart and hope these folks turn back to flesh when you die."

"If I restore these humans and leave, you won't follow me?"

"Not even a step," Flynn said.

"You won't help DEMON apprehend me and perform experiments on me again?"

"We're pretty interested in shutting DEMON down right now," Flynn replied.

The medusa lowered her eyes, took a deep breath, and looked to Flynn. Her snakes were lying flat against her skull now, indistinguishable from hair unless you got really close. "Fine," she said, and raised a hand into the air. It glowed with the same golden light that had turned me to stone, then I felt a wave of power sweep across the entire area. I staggered back as the energy coursed through me, and when I looked around, the cop wasn't a statue anymore, just a man looking at his gun in confusion.

All around the Epicentre, stone men were turning to flesh and staggering, some dropping to their knees on the sidewalk. As I watched, several of them vomited, one fainted dead away, and the rest looked for a place to sit down and examine themselves for signs of stone, I guess. By the time I looked back to the medusa, she was gone.

Where did she go? I asked Flynn.

Does it matter? She's gone, and as long as she doesn't go on a sculpture garden rampage again, she can stay that way.

Yeah, I guess. Still want to punch her.

Why?

She killed me, remember?

You got over it. So get over it. If you don't stay dead, it doesn't even really count as dying.

You're awfully sanguine for someone who isn't doing the dying.

Yeah, but I'm the one who's driving you home, now quit your bitching and limp your half-dead ass over here and let's go get some sleep. That sounded like a fantastic idea, so I got Faustus to help me to the car, and we went home in hopes of finally sleeping until my eyes weren't full of sandpaper.

Of course, shit never turns out like we hope.

17

Getting out of the Suburban in my exhausted and injured state was pretty easy—I just opened the door and fell out onto Faustus and Glory. I even made it to the elevator without issue. The trouble started when the elevator opened at my floor, and I realized that's exactly where I was—the floor. I looked up at the angel, the demon, and my fiancée, and said, "A little help here?"

Together we managed to get me into the apartment, through the living room, and onto the bed. Flynn knelt down to take my boots off, and Glory and Faustus headed off to do whatever immortals that don't need rest do when they're saddled with humans and whatever I am.

"Are you really that beat, Harker?" Flynn asked, looking up at me. "Or are you just playing for sympathy?"

"I'm pretty fucked up," I said. "I think I'm still healing faster than a normal human, but I'm weaker than I can ever remember being, and all my senses are dulled. It sounds like there's cotton in my ears, nothing smells right, and everything more than thirty feet away is a little fuzzy."

"That sounds uncomfortably like being human." Flynn tossed my Doc Martens into a corner, yanked off my socks, then got up and sat on the bed beside me. She unbuckled and unzipped my pants, then looked down at me. "Don't get any ideas. I just thought you'd be more comfortable without your pants on."

"I almost always am," I said. "And as much as I love you, your virtue is safe from me until a time when I can, oh I don't know, move." I lifted my ass to let her pull the jeans down my legs, then sat up and yanked off my shirt. I sat there on the edge of the bed in just my boxer briefs and leaned forward, resting my elbows on my thighs. "I'm pretty fucked up, Becks."

"What else is new?" she asked, standing up and stripping down to her underwear. She walked over to the dresser and pulled out a Reckless Kelly tour t-shirt that was more holes than shirt, threw that on, and came back to sit next to me. "Seriously, though. What is it? Are you worried that something happened to you when you...?"

"Died," I said. "The word you're looking for is 'died.' And something *did* happen to me. I'm weaker, I'm slower, my senses are dulled, and I haven't touched magic since I came back. I had enough power stored up in myself to break free of the last of the stone, but I haven't drawn any more in since then. I don't even know if I can."

She stilled beside me, her eyes widening at that last bit. "Have you tried to call up the magic?"

"No. I'm afraid of what might happen. If...magic has been such a big part of my identity, of *me*, for so long that I don't know what it will do to me if it's gone."

"But it's not." I looked at her, and there wasn't even the slightest hint of uncertainty in her face. "Just reach out and do something with it."

"How are you so sure?"

"Trust me. You are every bit the Quincy f'n Harker you have always been. I promise. Now reach out with your magic and call up one of those glowy purple balls you like to play with."

I didn't look at my hand. I didn't take my eyes off her eyes, big dark pools brimming with faith in me. I locked onto those eyes like I was scrabbling at that door in the end of *Titanic* and that bitch Rose wouldn't let me climb out of the water. After what felt like a year but was probably ten seconds, I felt something inside of me *click* into place, and the power was just...*there.*

It was like nothing had ever happened. I reached out to the magic and called up an orb of purple energy. I channeled more power into it, and it turned red, then blue, then I split it into three balls and started to juggle them. I tossed them all up into the air and let them cascade down upon the room, showering me and Flynn with cool, tingly, magical fireworks. I laughed and flopped flat onto my back with my arms spread wide. Becks laid down in the crook of my right arm and snuggled up against me, her dark curls spraying out across my arm like a blanket.

"Wow," I said. "That even fixed my senses. I can see, hear, smell... everything feels back to normal. I think I'm even healing faster. How did you know?" Unless she'd been doing some serious studying since I'd left, everything Rebecca Gail Flynn knew about magic, she'd learned at my side. And I didn't know what was wrong with me. But she knew how to fix it.

"There was nothing wrong with your magic," she said, leaning forward to kiss me on the cheek, the ear, the side of the neck. "There never was. You just convinced yourself that you *should* be all fucked up after dying, so you were. You just needed a kick in the ass to realize it."

"Yeah, all that makes sense in theory, but how did you *know*?"

She sighed and leaned up on one elbow. I followed the neckline of the t-shirt as it fell, threatening (or promising, depending on your perspective) a peek at the breasts contained therein. "Okay, one—pay attention, pig." She tugged her shirt back into place, and I reluctantly focused on her eyes. Not that I don't love Becks's eyes, but...

"I knew you still had your magic because you talked to me mind-to-mind, dumbass. That's not something normal people can just *do*. If you could still do that, it stood to reason that you could still do everything else. You just needed to realize it. And you needed me to show you. So I did."

"Have I told you how much I love you?" I asked.

"Yes, but not nearly often enough."

"I love you," I said, reaching up and pulling her down on top of me. She pressed her lips to mine and the real healing began.

———

I slept. I slept and I dreamt.

I woke up in Hell, but it wasn't Lucifer staring at me, his mouth twisted with glee at the idea of pulling my intestines out with red-hot pokers, then hanging me with them, only to cut me down, shove my guts back inside my throat, and do it all again. No, what awaited me in my dream Hell was worse than what I had waiting for me in the real thing.

I opened my eyes to a crimson sky, an ochre landscape, and a symphony of screams that could have been the soundtrack to a Hieronymus Bosch painting. Standing over me, wearing a disapproving glower perfected over more than a century of watching me make stupid decisions, was Luke. It wasn't the twenty-first century Luke I last saw half a year ago. It wasn't even the Luke I traveled Europe beside through the first half of the last century. Nor was it the caped figure with cartoonish hair and razor cheekbones that Lugosi so famously portrayed.

No, this Luke was the warrior of Wallachia, Vlad the Impaler, the man whose enemies cowered in fear at the mention of his name. This was Vlad the Dragon, the legendary Romanian noble who had his captives displayed on spikes outside his castle to frighten his enemies. He glared down at me wordless, a slight sneer peeling up the left corner of his mouth under the drooping mustache.

"What a waste," he said, spitting the words as though I was something disgusting he scraped off his boot. "I wasted a century on you, and you can't even keep a band of *humans* from invading my home and murdering me. That fat shite Van Helsing could have done a better job. Maybe I should have bitten his parents."

"Why are you here?" I asked, swallowing in a vain effort to clear my parched throat. Every breath was like gargling with broken glass as the searing heat broiled me from the inside out. "What do you want?"

"What do I want? What do *I*, want?" His dark eyes glittered with rage and spittle flecked his chin as he shouted. "I want to be alive, you imbecile! I want to not be splayed out in pieces across a cold metal table as pimply-faced PhD candidates extract tissue samples from every inch of me. I want to have never seen your worthless face! I want to have ripped your father's throat out and sent him down to my wives as food instead of as a plaything. I want you to feel an inkling of the agony I've suffered because of your failure, you insipid, whining pustule!"

I struggled to stand, only realizing as the ground scorched the soles of my feet that I was naked. Naked and flayed nearly to the bone in some places. Skin hung from my shoulders in long, ragged strips that sent fresh lightning bolts of agony coursing through my body if I moved. I looked down at my hands and saw that a couple of fingers on each hand were broken and sticking out in bizarre directions. As I gaped at my injuries, a drop of blood ran down my forehead to my nose, then splashed between my toes. Everything hurt, and every breath was agony. I looked up to Luke, but he was gone. I turned around in a circle, almost falling to my knees in pain as the shredded flaps of skin brushed against each other, but there was nothing around me but dirt. Dirt, and rocks, and searing wind, and…marble floors, and candelabras, and soft piano music playing.

I was in a ballroom, a vast expanse of black and white checker-board floor and Corinthian columns, the football field-sized dance floor jammed with men and women dressed in their mid-century finest. There were tailcoats and ballgowns, corseted waists and bared shoulders, slicked hair and long gloves. And every couple, all around me as far as I could see, was me and Anna.

I saw her everywhere I turned, but every time I reached out to cut in, her partner spun her away and left me clutching nothing but air. I heard myself laughing at me as the me that still held Anna danced away light as a feather, leaving me standing there in a black and white tuxedo, starched to the gills, with blood running freely down my arms and splattering to the floor. My shirt was soaked crimson, but no matter how much I bled, there seemed to be an inexhaustible supply of pain for me to spew all over the ground. I took three staggering steps after another Anna when suddenly the couples on the dance floor all stopped and turned to the piano, applause starting off polite and building to a roaring ovation.

I blinked and I was surrounded by red velvet and gilded chairs, but no one in the auditorium was sitting. Every soul stood roaring their approval, and I followed their gaze to the stage, applauding as hard as I could despite my palms being completely raw and splashing blood into the air every time I clapped. A slight figure stood on the stage, a boy of no more than twelve, his dark hair mussed and a little too long because I kept putting off taking him to the barber. I knew him before he turned, knew before I saw that while his back may have been clad in a tailcoat, his front revealed the infamous striped uniform of the camps with the lopsided yellow fabric star gleaming like gold from his breast. Edgar Treves, Anna's brother, the one I couldn't save from Auschwitz, the child who died because I wasn't strong enough, fast enough, everything enough to keep him safe. Edgar looked up from the stage to the box where I stood frozen and smiled at me.

I slept. I dreamt. I dreamt, and I woke up screaming, with tears pouring from my face and flames at my fingers.

18

"You look like shit," Glory said as I trudged into the war room and made a beeline for the coffeemaker. I yanked down the first mug I saw and poured it full of steaming black rocket fuel and tipped the entire cup down my throat without coming up for air once. I set the mug down on the counter, paused for a couple seconds, then refilled it and scuffed over to the head of the conference table, my Batman slippers making little *shup-shup* noises across the beige carpet. I sat down, stared deep into the ebon heart of my coffee for another few seconds, then took another long sip.

I couldn't *quite* feel the caffeine coursing through my veins and waking up the exhausted synapses and brain cells, but I was starting to feel a little closer to human. A couple minutes later, Flynn came out of the bedroom, looking far more put together than me in a pair of dress pants, chunky heels, emerald t-shirt, and blazer. She walked across to the kitchen with her arms over her head, pulling her long curls into a loose ponytail as she went. She looked in the open cabinet and froze, then turned around to look at me.

"That's my coffee cup."

I looked down. Sure enough, I was drinking out of a chipped blue Charlotte-Mecklenburg Police Department mug that looked to be twenty years old if it was a day. "Sorry," I said. "I'll make sure to wash it when I'm done."

Becks gave me a look that let me know that she was fully aware of exactly how much bullshit was glazing every word of that sentence, but she said nothing. "It's fine," she said. "I'll just use…another one."

Something in her tone told me it was very much not fine, but she didn't want to talk about it. Fortunately, we had other options. *What's up?* I asked.

It's nothing. It's stupid.

I'm pretty sure it's not stupid. I'm sorry I used your mug. I wasn't paying attention.

No, I get it. You never did get back to sleep, did you?

Memories of sitting bolt upright in bed at four a.m. ran across both our memories. *No. Never quite got relaxed enough. Feel like hammered shit this…morning? Afternoon? Fuck, I can't tell anymore.*

I get it. It's cool.

What's the deal with this old mug, anyway? You must have had it… Then I got it. *It's your dad's, isn't it?*

She didn't have to answer. We were mind-to-mind, so as the images flashed across her memory, I saw them too. Pictures of her dad sitting at the kitchen table with his newspaper folded over in front of him with only the sports page showing, that same coffee cup sitting on the paper leaving a brownish circle on top of the Braves box scores. Her dad setting that mug aside to give her a hug as she ran off to catch the school bus. Her sipping coffee from the same mug the morning she headed off to her Police Academy graduation. That coffee cup had been with her for more of her life's seminal moments than I had.

Wow. I'm sorry. I'll make sure to wash it. For real.

Please let Cassie wash it. If you try, there's no way it doesn't end up shattered. I could feel the smile behind the words and stood up as she walked toward me.

I put my arms around her. "I love you. Go make the city safe."

"I'll see what cryptids popped up overnight and call in with a list of what to chase and where. Then you can stay here looking for clues to get Luke back." She saw the shadow across my face and grabbed my chin. "He's alive, Quincy. You know he is. You had a dream, not a prophecy."

"Yeah," I said, but the word felt even emptier than usual.

"Trust me," Flynn said. Then she leaned in to give me another peck on the lips, and I threw my arms around her again. I stood there for a long moment, just feeling the safety of being in the arms of a woman who loves me, then I let her go.

"I'll talk to you in a bit," she said. "Now go find Luke."

I snapped off a really terrible salute, more Benny Hill than General Patton, and she chuckled at me. "Aye aye, cap'n." Becks turned and headed to work, and I was unapologetic in checking out her ass as she did. As the saying goes, I hate to see her go, but I love to watch her leave.

"You're incorrigible," Cassie said from the kitchen. I looked up, not having even heard her come into the room.

"You're not wrong," I replied. "I also don't give a shit."

"Pretty sure that's what incorrigible means, Harker," Jo said, coming in through the front door. "He staring at Flynn's ass again?"

"You know it," her mother said. "Cream and sugar?"

"Just cream, thanks." Jo came over to the table and sat down.

"What have you got?" I asked.

"A shitload of escaped monsters running around town causing all kinds of havoc, better than fifteen murders and 'animal maulings' right in the middle of the city, and a federal agency that's gone from being a secret to being a frigging ghost almost overnight." She pulled out a MacBook and fired it up, tapping the trackpad with one hand and drinking coffee with the other. I tried to work a computer before coffee once. I burned my finger clicking in my mug and tried to drink my mouse. I am not the best at multitasking before I've had caffeine.

"Give me the rundown on the worst of the cryptid attacks," I said. "Do any of them look like they're setting up lairs for the long run, or are they all just trying to get the hell out of town?"

"Most of them look like they're running away, but there are three that might be a long-term problem, just based on location."

"Run through them with me. Then once Flynn gets to work, we can get her to give us anything the CMPD has on those particular ones."

Cassie came and sat down at the table. "What about finding Luke? I understand we need to get these monsters off the streets and keep them from killing anybody else, but every minute he's in those people's hands, the more danger he's in."

I looked in her eyes, reached out and took her hands, and said, "Cassie, we have to accept that Luke's probably dead. Real dead. He would have been way too dangerous for them to keep alive once their base here was compromised, so it's more likely that they killed him to make him easier to transport and now they're somewhere in a remote lab doing nasty things to his body."

Her eyes widened, and she snatched her hands back from under mine. "What the hell is wrong with you, boy? This isn't some garden variety Edward Cullen wannabe moping around high schools trying to get laid. This is *Luke*. Count Dracula, remember. He is the monster other monsters' mommies used to tell stories about to get them to behave. This is the O. G. Bloodsucker, with a demon riding shotgun in his soul for centuries. You think a bunch of government pussies can kill *Luke*? If you believe that, you're dumber than you look, and let me tell you, with your mouth hanging open like that, you look pretty dumb."

"I...I don't think I've ever heard you use that word before," I said, my eyes still trying to bulge out of their sockets.

"I don't use it very often. I don't like it much. But sometimes I need to get your goddamn attention, and when your head is wedged so far up your ass you can't see daylight unless I cut open your bellybutton, bad language ensures that you fucking listen for a change."

I glanced over at Jo, who was hiding a grin behind her coffee cup, but there was no help coming from that quarter. "Um, okay, Cassie," I mumbled. "What do you think we should do to find Luke?"

"Sweetie, I don't have no idea. But I know he ain't dead. I'd feel it if he was. You would too. You know how that goes, because you and Detective Flynn got the same kind of thing going."

I opened my mouth to argue with her that the bond Becks and I shared was very different, then I let it snap shut. "You're not exaggerating, are you? You're *bonded* to Luke. Like Becks and I are. Like my mother was."

There was a *thunk* as Jo's mug hit the table, and she snatched up her computer before the dregs of the coffee soaked the keyboard. "What the fuck? Mama, is this for real?"

"More like Mina than like you and Rebecca," Cassie said. She turned to Jo. "When your daddy and me fought that big werewolf, the one that you killed when you took up the hammer?"

"Yeah," Jo said.

"Luke was there, too. The Alpha had him a whole pack, and every one of them was bloodthirsty bastards. Luke took out a dozen wolves on his own, covering our backs while me and Alex went after the Alpha. It should have been safer, what with there only being the one of him and two of us. It wasn't. He was bigger, and meaner, and faster than any wolf we'd ever seen, and he was smart, too. He didn't lose himself in the wolf when he shifted, like most of them do. No, he held on to every one of his faculties, which is not as common as you would think. When Alex went after him with the hammer, he just leapt past him onto me and ripped me open like I had a zipper running from my belly button to my throat."

"Holy shit," Jo said.

"Yeah, it was a bad night. It didn't get any better when your daddy tangled with him, but he held his own for a few minutes, anyhow. Luke saw how bad I was hurt, and we both knew I wasn't going to make it to a hospital. He told me his blood had healing properties, but there were strings attached. I asked him if I was going to have to drink blood, and he laughed, said yes, but just this once, and we would be linked forever from that moment on. Your daddy screamed for Luke to quit jabbering and do something, so he opened up his wrist. I pressed my mouth to it, and I drank."

"And you healed," I said. "And you had a vampire in your head from that moment."

"No, it wasn't as much as all that. It was more vague. Like I could feel him, and I could always find him, but we can't talk in one another's heads like you and Rebecca do. It ain't like that at all. But he's alive. I know, because I can still feel him in the back of my head. He ain't close, and he's hurt, but he ain't dead. I swear this much to you, Quincy."

There were a lot of things I wanted to ask her, and not a single one I wanted to ask with her daughter sitting right there staring at her. I just nodded, reached out, and patted her hand. "Okay, then. Let's find him."

Then the phone rang and everything we'd planned went straight to shit.

1 9

I picked up my phone from the table and swiped a finger across it to answer, then pressed the circle on the screen to turn on the speaker. "What's up, Becks? I've got Jo and Cassie with me."

"We've got a problem."

"You wanna be a little more specific? Last time I checked we had a bunch, and that's even before we get my therapist to give us her list."

"There's a goblin slicing its way through Concord Mills. And it's out of my jurisdiction. CMPD can't do a damn thing about it."

"Fuck me," I said. "I'll get Pravesh, and we'll haul ass up there. She should be able to get the locals to unbunch their panties about letting us take care of the wee beastie. But Flynn?"

"Yeah?"

"Please tell me it isn't in the Bass Pro Shops. If I never see another one of those places again, it'll be too soon."

I heard her laughing as she hung up on me, and I looked up at Jo. "You stick around here and stay on the hunt for Luke. I want one of us on that at all times, and it'll be good to keep somebody in town for whenever the next monster attack happens in the city. I'll take care of this shit." I stood and walked to the closet, prepared to arm myself but stopping when I remembered I never restocked the closet after last night.

"Shit," I muttered, then went to my room and collected my pistol, a couple of silvered knives, and a short sword that I'd carved some protection runes into. "Hey, Glory?" I called to thin air, hoping she was paying attention.

"What is it this time, Harker? I was practicing my harp." Glory appeared behind me in thigh-high boots, tight black leather pants, and a Led Zeppelin 1977 tour shirt with her blond curls cascading down her shoulders.

"You totally don't play a harp."

"If I do, you'll never know about it. Where you're gonna end up, the band sounds a little different."

"Where I'm going to end up, the house band will *rock*," I fired back. "We've got a goblin problem."

She looked around the living room, then said, "I don't see any goblins. Are they really small? Like bedbugs?"

"They're at Concord Mills."

"What is it with you and Bass Pro Shops?"

"They're not at the...never mind. Will you get Pravesh and meet me in the parking garage? We're going to need her credentials."

"What am I, your fetching angel? Call her ass."

"Fine," I said, pulling out my phone. "Will you at least get Faustus? I don't have his number."

"I'll get Pravesh," Glory said, turning and walking to the door like her ass was on fire. "I *really* don't want to walk in on him doing...well, anything. With anyone. Ever."

I wondered for a second what kind of shit Faustus was into, then I realized that was nothing I wanted to know about the demon living down the hall, and just went and pounded on his door.

After a few seconds of beating, with no answer, I put my face to the door and yelled, "Faustus! If you aren't out here in three seconds, I'm going to blow this door to splinters and bill you for the repairs!"

I counted to two, sheathed my fists in pure kinetic energy, and was just about to blow the door to toothpicks when it opened up and a skinny woman in her late twenties with a nose like a hatchet and a face like a horse came out in a lacy thong with a leopard print spandex tube dress clutched to her chest. "Fausty says he'll be out in just a second. He had to go wee-wee."

She clumped past me in five-inch Lucite platform shoes with gold-fish swimming in the heels and made a beeline for the elevator. I watched her press the button to call the car, then calmly pull the dress over her head and down almost far enough to cover the bottom of her butt cheeks. She looked down at a cell phone that I seriously didn't want to think about where she was carrying, and without a backward glance, got onto the elevator.

I turned back to the door and was reaching out to knock again when it opened up and Faustus stepped out. He was wearing his human face, and most of a set of human clothes. He pulled on a tight black t-shirt with a lighter black logo on the chest and tucked his shirt into the buckle of his spiked black leather belt. He wore dark jeans and red Chuck Taylor high tops, and he grinned up at me as he walked past. "I see you met...Ivory. That's her name, Ivory. Or maybe Emerald. Or is it Ruby? Whatever. You met my latest gem. Charming girl. Quite the hand with a cat o' nine tails, which is fast becoming a lost art. Not so good with the candle wax, but she's young. And she can tie knots like a sailor, I promise you. Where are we going?"

I stared at him, this millennia-old demon who still managed to find as much pleasure in debauchery as he had when the world was new, and just shook my head. "The mall. Goblins."

"The big mall? With the Bass Pro Shops?"

"I wish everybody would just shut the fuck up about Bass Pro Shops!" I nearly shouted. "Come on." I turned and stomped off, getting to the elevator just as Glory and Pravesh walked up. Keya was walking better, but she still had a pronounced limp and was walking with a cane. I could see the outline of a brace around one knee under her black pants, and her pistol made a blocky bulge under her blazer.

"Good morning, Glory," Faustus said, and there was an odd tone in his voice. I gave him a hard look and almost fell over laughing when I realized what was going on. He was looking at Glory like I often looked at Flynn. The demon had the hots for my guardian angel. I opened my mouth to drop a huge load of snark on his head, but one look from Glory cut that shit off at the pass.

"Hello, Faustus. Let's go. Harker, you drive. Pravesh's leg is still giving her problems."

"I can drive," the Homeland Security director protested.

"My job is to guard this moron," Glory replied, pointing at me. "Which is hard enough with just bad guys trying to kill him. You adding to his danger level with half-assed reaction times and a bum leg only makes my life more difficult. It's difficult enough on the best days, and I'd appreciate if we don't make it worse, just for a couple hours. 'Kay?"

Pravesh nodded, then reached into her pocket and passed me the Suburban keys. "I guess my car is still impounded?" I asked.

"Yeah, and we wouldn't all fit in your little Honda anyway. Why don't you get a decent ride, Harker?" Glory asked as we got onto the elevator.

"My car is very reliable. Besides, Luke has all the awesome cars. I don't want to steal his thunder."

"Not to mention that as long as every one of his cars is better than yours, anytime the two of you go anywhere, he demands you take his car anyway," Faustus added.

"He ain't wrong," I said. I watched the elevator doors slide shut and wondered exactly what kind of shitshow we were heading into.

The answer was "spectacular." A spectacular shitshow was exactly what we rolled up into when we turned into the parking lot of Concord Mills Mall. A huge, sprawling thing with an interior walking circumference of over a mile, Concord Mills was the largest shopping center in the Charlotte area by a long shot. We needed to track down a goblin in an outlet mall haystack.

Police cars blocked every entrance, sending their blue and white lights strobing across all sides of the mall and every car trying to get out of the jammed parking lot. A broad-shouldered black woman came over to the SUV, her hand up and a "don't fuck with me, I ain't in the mood" look on her face.

"Mall's closed. Turn it around." She was making the "turn around" motions with her hands before I even got the window rolled all the way down.

I held my credentials out the window and flipped them open, just like I learned watching the feds on television. "Homeland Security. We got a call about a terror threat in the mall."

"It's no kind of terrorist, just some psycho kid with a butcher knife gone bugshit in the food court and started murdering everybody. Who called you? Nobody told me anything about it." She was positioned just to the left of the driver's side front wheel, where it would be hard for me to move forward without running her over. I noticed her right hand drop to the butt of her pistol while her left reached for her radio. The look on her face told me this was about to go sideways, and I started to call up power when I heard the door behind me open.

"Officer?" I heard Faustus before I saw him, then he stepped forward into my line of sight. "Officer, I need to tell you the truth. We are with Homeland Security, but no one called us in officially. We have a contact inside your organization, and whenever something out of the ordinary happens, we get the call. That isn't a kid with a knife in there; it's a goblin of some sort. We're the best people you have to deal with threats of a supernatural nature, mostly because we *are* threats of a supernatural nature."

With that, Faustus reached up to the top of his head with both hands and grabbed a fistful of wavy brown hair. He got a good grip and pulled his hands apart, ripping the false face he wore right down the middle and showing his true visage to the cop. I watched from behind as his gleaming obsidian skull came into view and knew by the cop's expression that she was getting the whole enchilada: jet black skin, sharp little fangs where humans have incisors, and yellow eyes glowing at her from inside his ebon face.

Her eyes got big, then huge, then closed abruptly as she fainted dead away in the middle of a traffic jam. Faustus caught her before she hit the ground, then looked around like he wanted us to help him. "Don't just stand there," he called. "Give me a hand!"

I looked at Pravesh, then into the rearview mirror at Glory, and we all simultaneously started to clap. Our numbers were few, but our snark was mighty, and we applauded like the curtain had just dropped at The Met. I even let out a "Bravo!" for good measure.

The demon didn't even deign to look at us. He just dragged the cop over to a grassy median, propped her up under a bush, and got back in the back seat. "That didn't go quite as expected, but it did get the desired result," he said as I put the SUV in gear and pulled into the parking lot.

"And we found out where the cryptid is," I said. "I can park near the food court and that'll narrow our hunting ground a little. I hope."

"Sounds like a plan," Glory said. "Keya, you've got to stay with the Suburban. You can't walk enough to go after even a small goblin, and this one doesn't sound like the innocuous type."

"Are there innocuous goblins?" I asked, my education on the species being limited to dungeon crawl video games.

"Not really, no," Pravesh said. "I'll stay here and keep the car running in case you need a quick retreat."

"Oh, come on," I protested. "It's one goblin. We'll be out in five minutes. I mean, seriously, how bad can it be?"

Someday I will learn not to ask stupid questions.

20

I walked into the mall with a demon on one side, an angel on the
other, and "Stuck in the Middle with You" running through my
head. The place was pretty sparse, and the people we did see
were either shoppers streaming toward the exits or employees pulling
down security doors and hauling ass out the back. That was good,
since whatever we were chasing was likely to be hazardous to their
health.

As we made the turn to head to the food court, I watched a woman
carrying a toddler trip over a bench and go sprawling. Glory flashed
over to her side, catching her before she slammed the kid into the
floor. She glanced back at me. "I'll help these people get out safely."

"Good call," I said. "You do the guardian thing; we'll hunt the
monster. It's only one goblin. How bad can it be? Ow!" I turned and
glared at Faustus, who had just punched me in the arm.

"Don't jinx it, damn you," he snarled at me.

I was too far away to communicate mind-to-mind clearly with
Becks, so I settled on calling Pravesh on my cell. "Anything new?"

"Not in the thirty seconds since you left me, Harker," came the
clipped reply. "Have you seen it yet?"

"I don't even know what 'it' is supposed to look like yet, much less if I've...oh. Never mind. We found it. Gotta go." I didn't wait to hear Pravesh yell at me; I just hung up the phone and slid it into my pocket. There was pretty much no question about what we were after because I was staring into the food court and it looked more like an abattoir than a place to get a smoothie. Unless you were in the market for a strawberries and spleen breakfast shake.

"Well, I guess we know what we're hunting," Faustus said.

"Oh yeah," I agreed.

"Did I mention that I have an urgent dentist's appointment? In Kansas?" He turned and took one step back the way we came, but I reached out and snagged the back of his collar, halting his escape. "Come on, Harker! That was *not* part of the deal. I'll face a lot of things, but a redcap? Nah, I gotta draw the line somewhere. This is that somewhere."

"A redcap, huh? That fits," I said, looking at the creature standing atop a table and jumping rope with an intestine that had until recently been happily intestining away inside a blond college-age girl who worked the ice cream counter. I knew where the guts came from because one end was still attached to the girl.

The other end was clasped in the spindly fingers of a gray-skinned creature with black hair hanging lank over its misshapen skull and bulging black eyes. The only solid indicator that this creature was fae were the pointed ears, but when it turned to me and grinned with three rows of pointed teeth, I knew that it definitely wasn't local. The monster wore one of those shapeless hospital gowns like all the other escaped cryptids I'd encountered, but it had stolen a UNC Tar Heels hat from somewhere and smeared blood all over it, dyeing it bright and brutal red.

There was plenty of red to go around because I spotted a dozen corpses in just my first glance around the food court. There were dead employees, dead customers, one security guard with his face peeled off, and a couple of people covered in so much blood and gore that I couldn't tell if they were civilian or mall worker. Frankly, I was just assuming they were all human, because it was really hard to tell because of all the blood. The place looked like a red paint factory exploded, but the coppery scent that seeped into my very skin told the true story. There were literally gallons of blood splattered across the Concord Mills food court. I was *never* eating at that Sbarro's again.

"Yeah..." I said, focusing power into my palms. "I'm gonna need you to put down the viscera and step away from the dead people. I think we're going to have to take you in." I didn't know what we were going to take it into, but since that's what all the cops on TV say, I said it.

The redcap dropped the intestines to the floor with a *splat* and a small spray of blood, then it hopped down off the table and moved toward us, stopping to kick the corpse of a pair of geriatric mall walkers in jogging suits and headbands, then splashing for a second in a puddle of blood like a psychotic toddler in the front yard after a rainstorm.

"Take me in?" the redcap asked, kicking at a lump of flesh lying on the tile. The lump, probably something that had once been important before it was removed from its original owner, rolled a few feet and stopped. "I don't think you're taking me anywhere, human. I think I'm taking you. Taking you apart!"

It sprang at me, and it came fast, drawing a pair of long curved knives from nowhere I could see and sprinting forward faster than any human ever could. But not nearly fast enough to get to me. I shifted energy into a shield around my left arm and pulled that in front of myself as I flung a sphere of crackling energy at the oncoming redcap. It sprang high into the air, easily avoiding my attack, and came down a mere ten feet in front of me.

Which also put it a mere ten feet from the barrel of my Glock, which promptly disgorged ten rounds of nine-millimeter hollow-point ammunition into the creature's chest. I watched all ten rounds strike the redcap between its belly button and its throat, then fall harmlessly to the ground, all the kinetic energy spent without putting a single scratch on the creature.

"Huh. All that shit about nothing but cold iron hurting you fuckers is true, huh?" I asked, slipping my pistol back into the holster. The redcap hadn't moved since I shot it, just stood there with its head cocked to one side, studying me.

"What *are* you?" it asked, its brow coming together in a "V."

"I'm Quincy Harker, bitch," I said, and I swung both hands in front of my chest, palms out, and channeled pure magical force into the redcap's face. A stream of blinding white light cut through the air, and the fae dodged frantically to the side.

The gangly redcap kept half a second ahead of the twin beams of energy blasting from my hands, which brought it right into the reach of Faustus and the sawed-off shotgun he pulled from under his jacket. I stopped blasting as the creature froze, staring at the demon, then grinned and said, "Brother, we have both been villainized by humans for centuries. Let's set aside any petty differences and tear this arrogant wizard to bits, shall we?"

Faustus glanced over at me, and I worried for a second that he was thinking about it. Then he smiled at the redcap. "Let's not," he said, and pulled the trigger, sending a blast of buckshot right into the fae monster's chest.

The redcap slammed back onto the floor with a *thud*, smoke billowing up from its chest. Faustus turned to me with a broad grin splitting his face and said, "See, Harker? It's not so hard. You just put the barrel of the gun right up to the monster, and you pull the trigger. No special equipment or magic needed."

I stared at Faustus, stunned. "How did you know to bring cold iron shells?"

"What do you mean?"

"I shot the fuck out of that thing and it never even flinched because fae aren't vulnerable to lead or copper. How did you think to pack iron shot? Where did you even *find* iron shot?"

"I didn't. I just grabbed the shotgun out of your—*urk!*" The demon's explanation was cut off as a pair of curved blades appeared out of his midsection, their tips crossing just about where I expected Faustus's belly button to be. The redcap rose from its knees, lifting Faustus as it went, until the skewered demon was held high above the monster's head, raining blood down upon the tile like a broken sprinkler. With a grimace, the creature rotated its blades inside Faustus's belly, then pulled its arms down, shredding the demon and sending a cascade of intestines and a kidney tumbling to the food court floor with a meaty, wet *plop*.

The redcap stood in front of me, gore painting its face like a scene from a *Carrie* remake, and I watched in revulsion as a long, pointed tongue snaked out to lick its lips in a gruesome parody of a smile. "Yummy. Demon viscera. Been a while since I tasted one of Lucifer's lapdogs. Wanna show me what angel tastes like, cherub?" the fae asked Glory, who flew in from helping civilians escape. She hung in the air, a stunned look on her face as Faustus bled out all over the floor.

"Get Faustus out of here," I said. Get him healed if you can, get him, I dunno, absolved if you can't. If he goes to Hell, he's fucked."

"Pretty sure that's why it's Hell, wizard," the redcap said, its words slurred as it kept trying to lick all the blood from its face like a kid chasing the last morsel of ice cream on its chin. "Now do you want to join your damned friend, or do you just want to get out of my way while I track down the last fat humans hiding in the far corners of this buffet?"

"Gonna have to go for 'C, none of the above' on that one, pal," I said, reforming the shield around my left forearm and calling up my soulblade. It flickered a little as it manifested, hopefully not showing the redcap how tired I was from drawing power almost constantly for the past seventy-two hours or more.

"Having some performance issues, wizard?" the monster asked, baring two rows of its teeth in its grin. So much for it not noticing the distinct lack of mojo in my magical sword. "That's okay, I hear it happens to all men sometimes. Like death. Death happens to all men, too." Then it crouched, dropping almost all the way to all fours, and sprang at me like the world's most murderous bullfrog.

I spun right, lashing out with my soulblade and carving a long slice in the creature's flank. Out of the corner of my eye, I saw Glory hoist the shredded Faustus into her arms and leap into the air, her wings appearing in a flash of white light. Then she was gone, streaking through the air to wherever the fuck she thought we could find a demon healer that would cross Lucifer enough to help Faustus. Maybe somebody owed him a favor, or Glory, because trading on my name was going to get her both jack and shit.

A crackle of energy and pressure as the redcap's knife scraped across my shield was my only warning that the creature had spun around, and I ducked under a slash that would have sliced through my carotid like tissue. I felt a few clipped hairs sprinkle down onto my ears and thrust forward with my blade, feeling it meet resistance as I stabbed the redcap in the midsection.

It let out a screech of pain and rage, and its slashing switched to hammer blows on my shield, trying more to break the arm behind it than get through the disk of magical energy. I poured more will into the shield, seeing my sword flicker again as my reserves depleted rapidly.

"How long can you keep this up, wizard? I feel your shield weakening. Your sword can barely cut my flesh now. You're getting weak. You're going to die, human, and I will paint my face with your blood and wear your entrails for a necklace as I kill every creature within a hundred leagues of this place. You mortal fools will know not to cage a lord of the fae!"

I gave a shove with my shield to create space, and when the redcap slipped on a puddle of blood, I planted a foot in the center of its chest. The creature went sprawling, and I dropped my sword and shield, allowing them to vanish into the aether as the redcap sprang back up, its blades low and ready to slice me from nuts to nose.

But I had other ideas. Flinging power out at the faerie, I shouted, *"TORPEO!"* at the top of my lungs, imbuing the word with every bit of power I could spare. The redcap froze, my paralysis spell not enough to hold it for long, but I only needed a second. I manifested my soulblade again and stepped forward, spinning in a circle to build up momentum. I struck the redcap in the side of the neck with my magical blade of pure energy, and it cut through flesh, muscle, sinew, and bone just like it was wet spaghetti. The monster stared at me for a long second, eyes frozen wide, before its head toppled back off its shoulders and landed with a wet *thump* on the food court floor.

The extraplanar creatures remains immediately began to sizzle and smoke, and within ten seconds, there was nothing left of the redcap but a puddle of disgusting black goop on the floor and a scene in the mall that looked like it was something out of a *Saw* movie. I let out a long sigh and walked over behind the counter at the Great Steak & Fry Company stand, yanked a plastic cup out of the dispenser, and poured myself a beer. After that fight, I fucking deserved it.

But I didn't get to finish it because just as I got my heart rate back to normal, my phone rang. I didn't recognize the number, but I answered anyway. Too many people in too many places trying to find Luke for me to screen my calls.

"Harker, it's me," came the familiar voice.

"Glory? Where are you?"

"I'm at Mort's with Faustus. You'd better get over here. We've got a problem." The line went dead, and I stared at the screen. *Because of course we have a problem.*

Once upon a time, Mort's had been a relatively safe, if sketchy-looking, bar on the south side of Charlotte, wedged back at the end of a long driveway stretching between an adult video shop and a strip club, right across the street from a pawn shop and a gun store. All it needed was a liquor store, and that block would have hit the cycle of sinful business establishments. Now, the exterior of Mort's looked the same—cracked parking lot with weeds growing in the corners, low-slung white cinderblock building with four rectangular windows along the front, all blacked out by careful application of aerosolized cooking grease and cigarette smoke. The same dingy, hand-scrawled "OPEN" sign was in the window nearest the door. And the same tattered and faded burgundy awning provided absolutely zero protection from the elements for the customers.

The difference began when I walked through the front door and didn't need to go through my typical routine of assaulting and insulting Doug the Door Demon. There used to be a vestibule where Doug could examine everyone trying to come in through the main entrance and evaluate them for trustworthiness and ability to pay the cover charge. Which was a load of shit. It was just a small foyer that gave Mort a chance to trap anyone who wanted to start some shit and deal with them before they got near his glassware.

But now Doug was gone, relegated to some minor functionary's role back in Hell, and the inner door stood wide open. I stepped through, the first time I'd been back to Mort's since Orobas, the Archduke of Hell, murdered Mort's half-demon daughter Christy. That was partially my fault, but Mort forgave me almost as soon as I helped him take his revenge on Orobas. Last time I saw Mort, he was on the outs with both the legions of Hell for torturing Orobas and with the Lords of Chaos for not taking Oro's place among their number when he killed the demon. Oh, and Mort had reinstated the Sanctuary inside his bar. Just not for me.

I was on high alert when I walked into the bar, and it looked even worse than the last time I was there. But in a totally different way. Then it looked run-down and scuzzy, like you could catch the plague just by running your hand across the bar. Now it looked like you could broker a real estate deal in the front room and probably get a blowjob in the back. It had that kind of slick Hollywood filthiness that hipsters love in their slumming. The floors and walls were clean but painted with a wash of gray to make it look dingy, even though you could almost smell the paint, it was so fresh. The pitted and cigarette-burned linoleum flooring was gone, replaced by a dark hardwood or laminate floor that perfectly set off the aluminum legs of the chairs that surrounded the custom tables carved out of bourbon barrels and fashioned from huge wire spools. It all had the sterile feel of very safe grunge, and I hated everything about it, from the energy-efficient LED lights in the ceiling to the craft beer taps lining the bar.

There were still plenty of demons in the joint, and they weren't all wearing their human suits, but there were plenty of humans, too, and where it used to be a respectable group of thugs and murderers mingling with their supernatural counterparts, now it was something even worse—bankers.

I walked up to the bar and glared at a skinny dickhead in a Brooks Brothers suit, pink shirt, and purple tie loosened just enough to say

"I'm chill" but not loose enough to say "I'm really a human being, not a soulless corporate drone masquerading as one."

The bartender walked over, a fake smile plastered to her face. She was pretty, and as far as I could tell without invoking my Sight, human. She was a black woman in her mid-twenties, with dark skin and an afro as wide as her shoulders. She wore a Mort's t-shirt with a pentacle on it, and jeans. "What'll it be, stranger? Haven't seen you in here before."

"It's been a while," I said. "I need to see Mort. Tell the flesh-borrowing shitball that Quincy Harker is here. Or you can just take me back to where the angel and the demon are."

She smiled at me, but it was a tight, mirthless thing that didn't touch her eyes. "Now I know you're new. There isn't really a Mort. It's just a name the owner thought sounded good when he opened up. But his name is Stephen, and he's a very lovely man, so I don't appreciate you calling him names. And I don't know what you're talking about with an angel and a demon, so unless you're going to order a drink, I think you should probably leave."

I watched her hand drift forward under the bar and I gave my head a shake. "Don't try it. You can't reach that shotgun before I can punch your dental work out the back of your head. Now call your fucking boss and tell him Quincy Harker says to get the fuck out here right goddamn now before I begin to cause a scene." Through all of this I'd kept my voice low and my face smiling, but now I let it slip and called power up into my eyes, making them blaze purple.

She blazed right back at me, her own eyes emitting a yellow glow that extended out to peel away the sections of illusion closest to her face, and I saw the fangs and hungry smile that screamed "succubus" in every language I'd ever heard.

"Well, well, well...the Reaper himself, right here in Mort's. We had a pool, the employees, on how long after we remodeled that the place would end up trashed. Looks like Aaron the dishwasher is going to win. He had seven weeks."

"We don't have to fight," I said. "I just need to get to the back room with my friends, then I'll be out of your hair."

134

"Nah," she said, more of that yellow glow surrounding her and dissolving every bit of the human façade she'd been wearing. Now she looked like a succubus—reddish skin, narrow features, cheekbones you could carve wood with, and absolutely zero interest in wearing clothes if there's a chance their nudity could distract an enemy or prey. And her nudity was plenty distracting, let me tell you. I didn't even know it was *possible* to pierce some of the places she had jewelry attached. "I think I'll just do what the sign says."

She pointed to a familiar sign, one that I'd seen hundreds of times in Mort's. It read, "Sanctuary—All are safe within these walls. Anyone violating the Sanctuary of this space will be summarily destroyed. Do not fuck with anyone. Period." That Mort, such a poet. Underneath the last sentence, someone, presumably Mort, had taken a Sharpie and scrawled, "Except Quincy Harker. If that fucker shows up, kill his ass on sight."

"Well, fuck," I said, turning to see every non-human in the bar, and two very brave or stupid humans, moving toward me in an ever-shrinking semi-circle. I counted two run-of-the-mill Pit Demons, the succubus bartender who'd now abandoned her post and was moving in on my left to get a better swing at me with the baseball bat she'd brought out from behind the bar with her, one huge hairy dude that I assumed was some flavor of lycanthrope, and a pale emaciated little bastard with thin stringy hair hanging down over his greasy forehead who was obviously a vampire that followed the *Nosferatu* fashion style as opposed to the more popular "I'm immortal and rich as fuck" style that Luke preferred. There was a pair of humans in the back, one with a long filleting knife in his hand and the other a big guy in a tight t-shirt with brass knuckles on each fist. This was going to hurt.

I reached out to draw in power and my eyes went wide as I felt myself blocked, cut off from more than a trickle of my magic. A glance at the ceiling told me that when Mort redecorated, he worked nullification runes into the crown moulding, and I could tell the tables were bolted to the floor in a similar style as at Zeek's bar in Memphis, intentionally arranged to disrupt the flow of energy in the room.

"There's a very thin layer of salt poured on top of the slab, too," said the bartender with a vicious grin. "Just enough to scatter most magic. Doesn't fuck with those of us who start the day with some inherent abilities, like strength, speed, and the ability to rip a human being limb from limb, though."

"Probably doesn't do fuck all against a bullet, either," I said, drawing my Glock and putting a round through the center of her forehead. She dropped like a sack of potatoes with a fatal head wound, and I spun to face the rest of the advancing pack of monsters. I drew the silvered blade from my left hip and pointed it straight at the were-whatever. "This one's got your name on it, fuzzy."

He took a step back, but snarled at me. "You can't kill us all, Harker."

"One—you wanna fucking bet? And two—even if I can't, which one of you pricks wants to be the next one I *do* kill. You?" I pointed my gun at the nearest demon's face. "I'm sure Big Daddy Luce will just wrap you up in a hug and give you a participation trophy if you show up back at home with a story of having the Reaper six feet in front of you and fucking it up so badly your meat suit doesn't work at all anymore. That'll go over real well."

I turned to the vampire. "What about you, Toothy? I learned to fight from Count Fucking Dracula himself. What makes you think you are big enough for you to step in the ring with me? They brass? Do they clang together when you try to walk sideways? Or did you just get all swept up in the fun and want to play with the cool kids for a change? Go take a goddamn shower, you rancid scrotum wart. And how about you, you trying to win a prize for your fucking *American Psycho* cosplay? Or do you think you're Christian fucking Grey and I'm your Anastasia? Either way, move another fucking inch and we'll see who's walking on goddamn sunshine."

I looked around at the now-cowed monsters, knife in one hand and still-smoking pistol in the other. Nobody moved. "Well, come on! Come at me, you chickenshit bastards! Let's do this, you gutless bags of demon splooge!" I felt my face getting red and could almost see the vein bulging in my own forehead as I sprayed spittle all over the nearest creatures. They stepped back. One step, then another, then another, until, en masse, they all turned and walked back to their tables to nurse their drinks and pretend they hadn't just gotten scolded into paralysis by a *human*. I mean, as far as *they* knew, I was human.

"Hey kid," I said to the barback, who was cowering on his knees behind a keg of Stella Artois. "You just got promoted to bartender. Now buzz me back through to Mort's office and clean up the dead demon in the floor." I walked to the door at the end of the bar and stood there tapping my foot for a moment until I heard the magnetic lock *click* open.

"What the fuck took you so long?" Glory snapped as I walked in. All thoughts of triumph at backing down a bar full of monsters vanished when I got a good look at Faustus.

"Jesus Christ," I muttered, then moved forward. "Time for that later. This looks bad. What can I do to help?"

22

F austus was stretched out on Mort's pool table, and every inch of the felt was stained red demon blood. Glory was on the table beside him, up on her knees with both hands pressed to the demon's midsection. She was covered in crimson up to her elbows with splatters all the way up to her face, and the ends of her curls were red where they had dipped into the bloody mess that was Faustus's chest and stomach area.

"Get over here and channel for Miranda," Glory said, jerking her head at the other woman in the room. Miranda was a young woman with a long blue and green mohawk lying flat against one side of her skull, with pagan symbols tattooed into the sides of her head. She wore a nose ring, a lip ring, and a bunch of studs, hoops, and bars glinted from her ears. Her clothes were completely incongruous with the rest of her look, as she wore nicely pleated gray slacks, clunky black shoes, and a dark blue camisole top. A jacket to match the pants lay on a chair beside her, making it look like a punk rock star had come from her day job as an investment banker to come heal the demon in the back of the monster bar.

My uncle is Count Dracula, and this shit was weird even for me. I walked over and nodded to the woman. "Miranda? I'm Harker. What do you need me to do?"

"Call your Sight so you can see what the fuck is going on, for the first thing," she said. She wasn't angry, just abrupt.

I did as she said, and once I shifted over to the magical spectrum, I saw that Faustus was in way more trouble than was immediately apparent. His metaphysical form had been shredded by the redcap's claws even more than his body, and essence was pouring out of him at an alarming rate. Demonic essence isn't pretty. It was like a creeping mass of black tar oozing out of his chest and puddling up until it spilled over the edge of the pool table and dripped down onto the floor, where it vanished, presumably back to Hell. Other Faustus was getting less and less substantial with every moment, becoming almost translucent as more of him bled away. Miranda glowed with a cool green light, and I watched as her hands moved over the demon's body, cauterizing wounds and stopping the flow of Faustus's soul. But that kind of work takes a toll, and I could see her getting weaker as she poured more and more of herself into her job.

I stepped forward, spinning out a tendril of myself to connect with the young witch. I saw and felt the questing stream of magical energy weave through the air until it touched her back, then we both stiffened as the link was formed, immediate and *tight*. It was different than the bond I shared with Flynn, where we passed information, affection, pieces of ourselves back and forth along the link. No, this was a siphon, pure and simple. This connection existed for one reason—to send energy from me to the witch, and there was no option for it to go in the other direction. I was the donor in this energy transfusion, and there was nothing I could do about it short of severing the connection and letting Faustus die.

I thought about it. I'd be lying if I said I didn't, because there was an instant there when I wondered if I should really help keep a demon alive. It did run contrary to pretty much everything I stood for, and it wasn't like I didn't have other shit to do. I had a bar full of monsters that wanted to rip me limb from limb and were likely going to object to me leaving without donating a pound of flesh. I had a city full of escaped cryptids to track down. I had a rogue government agency with way more information on me and my friends than I was the slightest bit comfortable with. I had a missing uncle/mentor/father figure that I needed to rescue. And I had a demon lying in front of me on a pool table bleeding in the physical and spiritual realms with only me to help save him.

A demon. And not just a demon, a *legendary* demon, who had corrupted more humans throughout history than any other low-ranked Hellspawn in history. A demon bad enough to have plays, books, and operas written about him. A demon that might be working alongside me today, but was just as likely to sell me out to the highest bidder if it became convenient.

Except he hadn't. He had every opportunity to give us to Lucifer when we were in Hell, and if there's ever been a bounty worth claiming, I was it. But Faustus didn't just not hurt us, he *saved* us. Then he pitched in again when it was dragon-fighting time in Tennessee, when he could have just as easily bailed.

Yeah, he was a demon, but God help us all, he was a friend, too. And I don't have enough of those to let them die in front of me when I can do anything to stop it, so I stiffened my spine, locked my knees, and reached down and out around me with my magic, looking for any source I could draw from to feed more juice into the witch's healing spells. There was no salt under the floor back here, letting me tap the magic without a problem, and when I did, I felt the link widen as I became little more than a conduit for Miranda to draw in more power to fuel her magic. I was the routing station, but as fast as power flowed into me, she pulled it right out, leaving my nerves raw and scorched.

For long seconds it seemed like nothing was happening. Nothing good, at any rate. Life force still flowed out of Faustus and along the floor before dissipating into nothingness. He still lay coma-still on the table, his obsidian skin unusually ashy and chalky. Glory kept her hands deep in the demon's guts, pinching off something vital, I guessed, because any time she shifted her weight, a narrow stream of blood would spurt up from his midsection.

I felt my hold on the magic, and consciousness, slipping as I channeled more power in moments than I'd allowed to pass through me in some entire years. My vision got all starry around the edges, and I felt beads of sweat pop out on my brow. I locked eyes with the witch, who shook her head at me. Her unspoken message was clear—if we stopped now, Faustus was dead, and severing the bond in mid-transfer was just as likely to send power coursing into both of us, killing us stone dead from the backlash.

"Not today," I said through gritted teeth. I moved my right foot forward, slow and sluggish like I was dragging it through mud against the tide. When I put it down, I used all my strength to haul my left foot up to meet it. Again, I strained to move through the currents of magic swarming around the table, and despite the power fighting us every step of the way, I did it once more. And again. And again, until I was leaning on the edge of the pool table with my elbows.

I bent down to Faustus's head, marveling at how pale someone with midnight-black skin could get, and I hissed through gritted teeth. "Not today, you motherfucker. Someday Lucifer is going to get his hands on both of us, and that's going to suck cosmic donkey dick. But today is not that day. I've got shit to do, and you've got mortals to swindle and a guardian angel to annoy. So wherever you are in there, Faustus, you listen to me. You need to sack up and fight this shit, or I'm going to Hell with you and if you think Lucifer will fuck you up, just imagine what seeing me without coffee will do to you."

Motivational speech over, I let my head sag until it almost touched the table. The crown of my head brushed against Faustus's cheek, and as I thought about the amount of blood in my hair *again*, I felt the power streak from me directly into the demon. There was still a steady flow going from me to Miranda and being spun into healing energy, but this was another conduit of pure magical energy streaming from me to Faustus, like I was the squirrel touching both power lines at once.

It felt about that good, too. My nerves felt like they were being scraped with sandpaper before, but now the sandpaper was coated with glass and lemon juice. I opened my mouth to scream, but only magic flowed out. I was leaking magic from the corners of my eyes, it was dribbling out of my ears, and twin streams of it poured from my nostrils. I was being simultaneously scoured from the inside and ripped apart by fingers of pure lightning and flame. Just when I thought my eyeballs were going to explode from the energy coursing through me, the power receded.

Not much. Not enough to make it stop hurting, but enough that my vision was more than just rainbow swirls of energy dancing in front of my eyes. Enough that I could straighten up, severing the physical connection to Faustus, but not cutting off the flow of energy between us. I blinked rapidly, trying to focus on the images in front of me rather than the ones printed on the backs of my eyeballs from the inside. As my vision cleared, I felt a persistent slackening of the magical transfer, as though someone slowly turning off a faucet.

After long seconds of agonizingly slow reduction on the channeling, I was able to once again make out details of the scene on the table in front of me. Glory still knelt astride Faustus's chest, but she sat upright now, with her hands on her thighs instead of buried up to the wrists in demon guts. Miranda leaned beside me on the table, her hair hanging in front of her face in damp, lank strands, breath coming in great gulping gasps.

"That...sucked," said the exhausted witch. A man I hadn't even noticed until now rushed over to pull a chair up behind Miranda and guide her down into it.

"Rest. That was a lot more than we thought it would be. If I had known it was going to be that difficult, I would have told the angel to piss off when she called."

I recognized the tone and the words, if the vocal chords were new. "Mort?" I asked.

"Who else would it be?" The passenger demon looked like nothing if not a stereotypical college professor in khakis, a tweed jacket with leather patches on the elbows, a French blue dress shirt with the top button undone and no tie, and loafers, complete with pennies shining from the slit in the tongue. The body he was wearing was youngish, mid-thirties maybe, and handsome in a bookish, nearsighted way, as if he peered at the world through thick glasses. He didn't wear spectacles, but he had that pinched look to his brow that made it look like he should.

"Oh, I don't know, Mort. Maybe I thought the person in that body was the person who, wild guess, belonged in it?"

"That's terribly small-minded of you," Mort said, walking to the small bar in the private room. "Drink?"

I raised an eyebrow. "Does this mean you don't want to kill me?"

"I never wanted to kill you, Harker. Oh, don't get me wrong, I might have wanted you dead, but I don't like to get my hands dirty. I wouldn't do the deed myself. And I'm ambivalent as to whether or not I still want you dead, but your willingness to help one of my oldest business associates certainly speaks well to our ability to remain in the same building without bloodshed."

"Then you might need to redo the sign over your bar," I said. "It kinda encourages people to try to kill me."

"I'm simply trying to skip the intermediate steps. Whenever you come in here, there's bloodshed. This way we get it out of the way before drinks are poured. Easier on the glassware that way."

"That's a very orderly approach for someone who's supposed to be a Chaos Lord now," I pointed out.

"Oh that? I was fired. I'm back to being a demon, a passenger in willing souls, and the purveyor of the finest moonshine in North Carolina. Now, would you like a drink, or are you going to grill me on my employment status? Besides, I think you may need information that I have access to."

He said my magic words: booze and information. Well, mostly booze. I bellied up to the bar to drink the demon's liquor and see what news he had for me.

23

I sat down at the table with Mort and looked around for someone either willing or reasonably capable of pouring me a drink. I was, in a word, shit out of luck. Glory was off the table and making a beeline for the restroom, presumably to wash off the worst of what looked like a solid gallon of demon blood that she was wearing. Miranda, the witch, was legit passed out facedown on a table about six feet from where Faustus lay, still out cold but no longer in apparent danger of bleeding out. I sighed and looked over at my demonic host. "You want a drink, Mort?"

"Always, Harker."

"What can I get you?"

"Macallan 30 Sherry Oak. Bring the bottle. And you should get something for yourself. I think you're going to need it."

"I figured I'd just have what you're having," I said, standing up. That took a lot more effort than normal, and parts of me hurt that I usually wasn't aware of, like my entire nervous system. I was pretty sure my eyeballs would pop if I sneezed wrong, so I moved across the bar like I was walking on thin ice.

"Don't kid yourself, Harker. I've seen you drink. There is nothing about you that is worthy of a thirty-year-old single malt. You may help yourself to anything on the bottom shelf or in the beer cooler, however."

"You're all heart, Mort." I grabbed the Macallan off the top shelf, a bottle of Gentleman Jack for myself, put a couple of ice cubes in two glasses, and made my way back to the table.

Mort looked at the glass I set in front of him with the kind of disdain usually reserved for people that shit on your rug. "What is in that glass?"

I looked but didn't see anything out of the ordinary. "Nothing. Just a couple ice cubes. Is there something I'm missing?"

"Yes, Harker, and that something is taste. One does not dilute proper Scotch with water, frozen or otherwise." He plucked the ice cubes out of his glass and dropped them into mine.

"Thanks," I said. "I've never noticed ol' Jack minding if there was a little ice in the mix." I pushed the bottle over to him, and he poured himself a healthy drink. Then he sniffed the whiskey, eyes closed, looking like a sommelier, only more innately evil. This is why I don't go out. Too many pretentious fucks out there laying their judgement down in the way of my drinking. Ain't nobody got time for that.

By the time Mort had taken one sip of his Macallan, I was on the second glass of Jack and well on the way to muting the howling coming from every fiber of my magic-scorched being. "What's the news, Mort? You got intel on Luke? DEMON?"

"Are you calling me 'demon' or are you asking about the nefarious organization that has been hunting and exterminating members of the local supernatural population? They are truly poorly named, given the potential for confusion their very name engenders."

I shook my head a little, took another drink, and stared at Mort. "What do you know about the shitshow that my city has become, Mort? I know DEMON, the agency, is behind it, I know they've taken Luke, and I know their local base of operations is shut down. What I don't know is who is calling the shots over there, how to get to them, where they took Luke, or if he's even still alive. I'd really like to know all of those things before I leave here tonight."

Mort looked at me over the rim of his glass. "Well, Quincy, as they say, if wishes were horses, beggars would ride. We can't always get what we want, and all that. I don't know who is leading the charge to eradicate all paranormal life in the area, and I don't know where they took your uncle. I do know that Vlad Tepes still lives, at least as of the evacuation of their facility here. Several of my customers were part of those who managed to escape, and I have heard from more than one source that your uncle was hale, hearty, and in good health, if furious, when they got free."

"You know that he was alive when the shit went down. But nothing more than that. Thanks, Mort. Next time I need some absolutely fucking useless information, I know where to find you." I stood up, then put a hand on the table as the room spun around.

"Sit down, Harker," Mort said. "You can't even walk to your car, the shape you're in. You may as well listen to what I have to say while you recuperate. Neither of those things should take very long."

I glanced around at my companions, but neither of them looked like they could make it to the car under their own power either, so I sat back down. "Go ahead, Mort. Talk. And where did you get this body? Usually you go for something, I don't know…interesting. I don't think there's a more milquetoast option in the city than this."

"You might think that, but the coeds certainly don't. Professor Green is going to have some serious 'splainin' to do when I give him his body back, but it's been a fun couple of weeks, I promise you that."

"You're a little disgusting," I said. "And what the fuck can you do to get fired from Chaos? Did you organize your sock drawer or something?" When last I saw Mort, he'd been taking over as one of the minions of Chaos in exchange for them letting him dismember and eventually kill the demon Orobas, who had killed Mort's daughter Christy, in no small part to get to me. To say my relationship with the hitchhiker demon was complicated was to vastly understate the degrees to which we both respected and hated each other.

"I don't want to get into it. It wasn't pleasant, and I had to give up a lot of equity in Hell to find them a replacement they would accept. Let's just say that I owe Lucifer a *lot* more souls now and leave it at that." His hands shook just the tiniest bit as he poured more Scotch into his glass, and I knew I wasn't getting anything else useful out of him on that front.

"Okay, I'll let it go. What have you for me on this DEMON shit?"

"It's more than just them hunting monsters in Charlotte. They've gone nuts everywhere. It seems to be localized to the US, though. Their operatives in other countries are as confused as you are. And it's not a Church thing, totally a State thing."

"What do you mean?" I asked.

"You know how DEMON has a lot of ties to the Catholic Church and their various occult divisions?"

I just looked at him.

"Seriously?"

"Look, Mort, I work for Homeland Security. They've never been on my radar. I know that redneck guy of theirs killed a bunch of vampires here a few years ago, but that's the only time they've been in my backyard that I know of, so I haven't paid a lot of attention. Besides, the whole wearing a lot of flannel and traipsing around in the woods hunting Bigfoot isn't really my thing. I'm more the hunt down evil necromancers and burn them from the inside out type."

"That makes sense, I guess. Well, they do work with the Church a lot. So much so that they're pretty much the new Templars. Some of them are for real the new Templars, complete with magical weapons. But none of this has anything to do with the Catholics."

"And you know this how?" I asked.

Mort just stared at me like I was three of the stupidest things he'd ever seen. "Do you really think there is any place in the world with more undercover demons than the Catholic Church? We've got people in there at every level, all the way to the top."

I narrowed my eyes and Mort shook his head. "Okay, not *the* top. That guy's legit holy, and most of the ones that work in the Vatican are on your side. But we've either got our guys wearing human suits or we've got humans that we've co-opted at every level of the Church below that."

"You make it sound like you're intelligence agents," I cracked.

"Who do you think founded the KGB, jackass?"

"Get to the point, Mort." My glass was mysteriously empty again, so I poured more Jack into it. Obviously there was a flaw in the tumbler somewhere.

"The point is this shit goes all the way to the top of DEMON, which goes all the way up in your government. And what I'm hearing is that everything they're doing here is a smokescreen, that there was really only one target they were looking for." He pointed one manicured finger at my nose. "You, Reaper. This whole thing has been a cover to get their grubby hands on you."

"Yeah, I got that already," I said. "There's never been anything like me, so they want to cut me in half and see if each half will grow into a full Harker."

"Lucifer fucking forbid that," Mort said with a shudder. "One of you is bad enough. You don't seem nearly as worried about that news as you should be."

"A shadowy government agency is hunting me. Big fucking deal. I fought Nazis, Mort. I went to Hell. Less than a week ago, I fought a dragon. It's going to take more than some pencil pushers in off-the-rack suits to make me break into a cold sweat."

Mort leaned back in his chair and laughed at me, shaking his head incredulously. "Jesus Christ, when I'm away from you for a little while I manage to somehow forget the incredible hubris that fills your every fucking cell. Yeah, you're a one of a kind creature, like a goddamn unicorn. Big fucking deal. There are *actual* unicorns out there. You being a unique kind of monster isn't enough to spend literally millions of dollars to hunt down hundreds or even thousands of magical beings just to hide the fact that they're really after you. That is someone with a *serious* hard-on for you, and not in a good way. Who hates you that much, Harker?"

I thought for a second. "Shit, Mort, when you put it that way, I have no fucking idea. I mean, there are probably dozens of people who don't like me, and most of those wouldn't have shed a tear if I never came back from Hell, but other than Lucifer, and maybe Asmodeus, I can't think of anybody with the kind of stroke to do what you're describing that hates me that much. And this has been in the works too long for it to be either of them. Lucifer only considered me a minor annoyance until about six months ago, and Asmodeus has hated me for a long time, but it only kicked into hyperdrive in the past few days, which lets him off the hook, too."

I took a second and ran over the "Wants to Murder Me" list I keep in my head a couple more times. "Nope, I got nothing."

"Then you better get to thinking because whoever is after you has a fuckton of resources and a shitload of cash," Mort said, standing up and taking the Macallan back over to the bar.

I felt that tickle I sometimes get on the back of my neck when life is about to go from shitty to spectacularly shitty. "How do you know how much cash they've dedicated to hunting me?"

"Because I know how much it cost for me to promise to turn you over to them if you ever showed up here. And it was a big number. Really big. I'm thinking of moving the bar closer to Uptown kinda big."

"You sold me out," I said. I wasn't even surprised. You lie down with demons, you get up with...well, the metaphor falls apart, but that's not the point. "How long until they get here?"

"Oh, they aren't coming until I call them. And I'm not going to call them until Harrison gets a few minutes to play with you." Mort pressed a button under the bar, and I heard the magnetic *click* of the door into the back room opening again.

I looked to the door and saw a huge half-dragon standing there, a baseball bat in each hand. They looked like toothpicks in the giant's grip, and he was broad enough to have to turn sideways to get through the door. Once he made it fully into the room, he took a few swings with his bats to get the height of the ceiling measured, then started toward me with a grin.

"Mort, why does the half-dragon want to beat me into paste? Is this more of the big bucket of money you were talking about?"

"Oh no, Harker. This is personal. Remember Stewart, my bartender?"

"Not really." I stood up and shoved furniture aside to try and give myself as much dodging, weaving, and diving room as possible.

Glory came out of the bathroom, looked at the mob forming up with blood in their eyes, and let out a sigh that only a truly long-suffering guardian angel can muster. "Dammit, Harker, what now?"

"He worked here after...Christy," Mort said, jogging my memory.

"Oh yeah." I remembered him. I remembered killing him by freezing him from the inside out. "He was kind of a dick."

"He was my baby brother," the draco said with a scowl.

"Well, goddammit," I said. "Come on then, let's see if I can wipe out your whole fucking generation." I reached for magic and hoped I'd recovered enough from healing Faustus to do more than stand there and bleed.

24

The draco didn't waste any time on small talk—he just barreled through the back room straight at me. I grabbed a chair and flung it at him as I sprinted across the room, but he flicked it aside with one bat, not even missing a step. I scurried backward and sideways, trying to keep Glory, Miranda, and Faustus out of the line of fire. I didn't give a shit about Mort. I wasn't sure the little bastard *could* be killed, and if he got roasted like a fucking almond, it served him right for not giving me a heads up.

I drew my pistol and squeezed off five quick shots. Three missed, but two slammed into the musclebound half-dragon's chest. Didn't do nearly enough damage. I saw him stagger back a couple of steps, but the bullets couldn't penetrate the thick scaly hide of the draco. I really missed fighting things I could shoot.

I burst through the door into the main body of the bar, trying to keep the draco's attention on me and get him away from the recuperating demon and the exhausted angel in the back room. Not getting Miranda killed was a bonus, but not my main concern, if we're being honest. Getting out of Mort's back room gave me more room to maneuver, but it opened me up to attack from more angles, since pretty much everyone in the building wanted to murder me. Looking around the room, I started to rethink wanting more bad guys I could shoot. This bar was full of them, and it didn't feel the least bit like an improvement.

"Stay back, he's mine!" the half-dragon bellowed as he came through the door.

"Fuck you, scaly," said the guy I'd clocked as a lycanthrope earlier. Sure enough, his features blurred as he started to grow and sprout hair all over his face and body. He managed to kick his shoes off before shifting into a seven-foot-tall half-wolf. He opened and closed his mouth a couple more times, but all that came out was an odd string of growls and yips.

I ejected the magazine from my Glock and slammed a fresh one home. I fired one more bullet at the half-dragon, this one glancing off his forehead to absolutely no effect. Note to self: don't bother shooting monsters in the head if they're both heavily armored and stupid as hell. No point wasting ammo. The last regular hollow point cleared, I turned the gun on the werewolf, who was stalking toward me with drool running down his chin.

"Come on, man," I said. "That's just fucking nasty." I raised the pistol, and I could swear the son of a bitch smiled at me. He stopped smiling when I put three silver bullets in the center of his chest. I looked around the room. "Anybody else allergic to silver? Oh wait, vampires are vulnerable to it, aren't they?" I leveled the pistol at the Nosferatu-looking bastard from earlier, but he blurred into motion and bolted out the front door.

I didn't have time to revel in my victory, though, because about four hundred pounds of muscle and scales slammed into me at a dead run. I felt something in my side crack, probably a couple of some-things, and my eyes crossed from the impact. My pistol flew across the room in the opposite direction from where I was headed, and I just managed to get my arms up over my face before the draco slammed us into the far wall. Drywall shattered, and I felt a couple other cracks through my ribcage as I hit the outer cinderblock wall.

The draco backed up, and I dropped to the floor. I looked up at the half-dragon, who grinned down at me, his snout filled with needle-sharp teeth. "You're going to pay for what you did to my brother, Harker. He was just a baby, and you killed him. For that, you suffer."

I opened my mouth, but nothing came out but a wheeze. It hurt to draw breath and I couldn't really make sound yet.

"What's that?" the draco asked, bending at the waist to bring his face down closer to me. "You want me to kill you fast? I don't think so. I think I'm going to take my time with you. I think I'm going to break one of your bones for every night my mother cried herself to sleep over her dead son. I think I'm going to peel your skin off real slowly, make you feel every second of it, and if you pass out, I'll wake you up with a little squirt of lemon juice in your wounds. How does that sound?"

I hissed out air again, trying to speak. The draco leaned in more, and as I tried to get enough air into my battered lungs to make words, he grinned and opened his mouth to speak again.

That's when I struck. I called up my soulblade and thrust my hand straight up, driving the magical sword into the half-dragon's open mouth and straight through to the back of its skull. I felt an oddly physical *crunch* as the energy blade pierced bone and brain. The draco's eyes went from smirking to wide to agonized in half a second, then the life fled from them as I twisted the blade and pureed his giant lizard brain. I managed to roll aside as he collapsed where I had lain mere seconds before.

I scrabbled out of the wreckage of the wall and the half-dragon, reaching out to a nearby chair to haul myself to my feet. A quick glance around the room told me I wasn't out of the woods yet, since there were nearly a dozen or more demons, cryptids, and random human assholes closing in on me with various weapons, claws, fangs, and spells at the ready.

"Okay, motherfuckers," I said, managing to make words despite the pain in my lungs. "Who's next?" I raised my soulblade in front of my face in a guard position, but that was the moment all my exertion came to a head and I reached the bottom of my well of energy. I'd used a *lot* of power channeling for Faustus, and I had to dig deep to manifest the blade long enough to kill the draco. My magic finally decided enough was fucking enough and left me hanging. The blade of brilliant white energy flickered a couple of times and went out, leaving me holding nothing but air and my proverbial dick against a bunch of monsters that wanted me dead.

What wall are you against? I felt Becks ask in my head just before I dove into what I figured would be my last bar brawl ever.

The one beside the front door. Why?

Duck.

I ducked. It was more like a somewhat controlled collapse, but we're going to call it a duck. As I hit the floor, the wall to my left exploded inward, sending a huge shower of sheetrock, cinderblock, and shitty beer signs across the entire bar.

"Back the fuck up, assholes," Jo said, stepping through the giant hole with her great-grandfather's hammer glowing in her hands.

The monsters stood there for a second, stunned, before a skinny Pit Demon charged at the pair of badass women standing in the slowly settling dust. Jo didn't bat an eye. She just stepped forward, let the hammer slip through her right hand as she swung, and smashed the silver head of the hammer into the demon's temple. The monster didn't exactly stop in its tracks; more like its head stopped moving but its legs didn't, so it kinda flopped on its back on the floor twitching for a few seconds before it went still.

Jo took one step forward and swung the hammer around to drop the head right on the dead demon's face, just in case there was any question about it ever getting back up. "Next?" she called, looking over the room.

The monsters stood frozen for a second, held in a collective hush like the breath before a scream. Then all Hell broke loose as half the beasties charged Becks and Jo, and half came rushing at me. The ones heading at me looked to all be supernatural, of course, because why would the guy who just got put through a wall by a dragon bodybuilder with a grudge luck out enough to just have to deal with humans?

My soulblade was useless, my Glock was forty feet away and probably under a table, my backup piece didn't have enough ammo to be useful, and I wasn't sure I could call enough magic to light a cigarette. Oh well, not the first time I've been biblically fucked in a fight. I drew the runed short sword with my right hand and a long silver dagger with my left and squared up to deal with the five nasties trying to surround me.

I had a pair of Pit Demons, a human with some kind of magical gauntlets on his fists, another werewolf in its half-human form, and a tall being that I assumed was some kind of faerie based on their ears, but I couldn't really pick out species or gender, or really anything but intent, because they definitely had some wicked plans for me with the curved short swords they were twirling around. I flung the dagger at the human, burying six inches of silver-plated steel in his gut and taking him out of the fight.

I yanked another dagger free as I ducked under one of the faerie's whirling swords. I lashed out with my short sword, trying to cut them off at the ankles, but I sliced nothing but air as they hopped over my blade, then my vision starred as I caught a foot in the side of the head. I rolled with the kick and let the momentum carry me to my left, out of the path of the kicks and stomps the demons aimed at me. I rolled to my feet, coming up inches in front of the demon with an upward slash of my knife that caught the pit-dweller right around where its navel should be and sliced it open all the way to its chin. I yanked the knife free and slammed the demon in the face with the hilt of my sword, sending it sprawling backward. It landed on its back and split open like an over-ripe tomato, spilling entrails and demon nastiness all over the floor.

I didn't have time to admire my handiwork, though, because the werewolf was on me, leaping onto me from the right and bearing me to the ground, its teeth snapping at my ear. I twisted, writhed, and contorted until I got a hand up in front of the wolf's eyes, and shouted "*LUMOS*" right in its face. My palm didn't explode with a stream of blinding light, but it did pop off with about the same power as a flash-bulb, which from an inch away was enough to get the wolf to rear back and shake its head. I took the half-second of opening and jammed my knife into its fuzzy neck, twisting as I pulled the silvered blade out. The wolf's eyes went wide as its blood painted my face and chest, and it slumped on top of me, dead.

I wriggled out from under the wolf just as the other Pit Demon reached down and hauled me to my feet. I looked at its grinning face and just shook my head. "Did you not watch what happened to your buddy?"

It didn't speak, just drew back both clawed hands, then froze in shock as both of my blades pierced its guts. I stabbed it in the abdomen with sword and dagger, right below the ribcage, then pulled my blades apart, effectively slicing the demon in half. It fell to the floor in a puddle of intestines, and I turned to look at the faerie.

"We gonna do this? I've got no gripe with the fae in general, so if you want to walk away, here's your chance."

The faerie smiled at me, a cruel grin licking the corners of its mouth. "You give me an opportunity to retreat when it is you that is clearly beaten. Why would I not remove your head from your shoulders and parade it through the streets of this city as proof of my prowess?"

"Because if you don't fuck off right now, my fiancée is going to blow your goddamn head off." To their credit, they didn't do the whole "do you expect me to fall for that?" shtick. They just turned around, looked at Flynn standing about eight feet away with a Mossberg 12-gauge pressed to her shoulder and a grim look on her face.

"I'm not going to argue that he doesn't deserve shooting, but if anybody murders Quincy Harker, it's going to be me," said the love of my life without even a hint of joke in her voice.

The faerie held their hands up, sliding the swords into scabbards so carefully built into the shoulders of their coat that I couldn't even see the blades when sheathed, no matter that I knew they were there. "I need not trouble myself with you, Quincy Harker. You will undoubtedly run afoul of someone with enough power to bring an end to your pitiful existence."

"Undoubtedly," I said, watching the faerie walk through the rubble and step through the giant hole in the wall before disappearing into the night.

"Good save," I said to Flynn, right before I passed out.

25

"I'm getting really tired of getting my ass kicked," I said when I woke up.

"Yeah, me too," Flynn replied, stepping into my field of view. "What kind of superhero gets beat up every single time they get into a little scrap? I'm starting to lose faith in you, Harker."

I sat up, wincing, but not nearly as much as I'd expected. Somebody must have poured some healing mojo over me while I slept. I looked around and saw the witch Miranda asleep with her face down at a nearby table and assumed that Flynn managed to convince her to patch me up a little. One thing about my girl—she's nothing if not persuasive. And sometimes persuasive translates into "armed and slightly psychotic."

"Well, if you've got to lose faith in anything, losing faith in my indestructibility is a good place to start," I said as I slid my feet down and got off the pair of tables they'd pushed together to make an impromptu operating table for me. The room didn't spin very much, so I managed to stand in one place and take a quick personal inventory.

My everything hurt. I mean, I had aches on top of pains in places I wasn't sure were really places, and I was pretty sure I'd bruised everything from my ego to my ass. But I was alive, and I could feel the well of power refilling within me, which allayed any worries that I'd burned out my magic channeling for the witch as she healed the demon.

Those are not words I ever expected to say when I was but a wee lad in merry old England. When your lifespan stretches across multiple centuries, you exceed even your wildest expectations on a regular basis.

The bar was a wreck, and I'm being a little insulting to wrecks to use that term. One wall was spiderwebbed out from a giant Harker-shaped hole that went straight to the cinderblock. Another wall was just *gone*, reduced to dust by Jo's hammer using some kind of magic I didn't think either of them possessed. The wall behind the bar was unharmed, surprisingly enough, so the mirror reflected the chaos that littered the rest of the room through the liquor bottles. At least we hadn't wrecked the booze. The tables that weren't shattered were ripped out of the floor, or in the case of the two that I'd just gotten off of, being used as beds. Most of the chairs were still intact, Mort having invested in solid metal chairs after my last visit.

There was blood and gore *everywhere*, from floor to ceiling in a lot of places. The ceiling fans were coated in blood, guts, and brain matter, and I really didn't want to be there the next time Mort turned them on. It wasn't that the walls were going to need a fresh coat of paint when we left, it was more likely to be cheaper and easier to just rip everything down to the studs and start over. In short, we had fucked Mort's bar *up*.

"Sorry about the bar, Mort. But they started it," I said to the nebbishy demon sipping Scotch at a table with Glory.

"I know, Harker," Mort replied. "You never start it. But your way of ending it often leans a little more toward the thermonuclear than I would prefer. But I suppose if you're still alive at the end of the week, I'll grant you Sanctuary here again."

"Yeah...speaking of that," I said. "I believe right before your scaled friend and I started our little dance, you said something about selling me out to the bad guys. How long ago did you make that call?"

"Oh, I haven't yet," Mort said. He laughed at my surprised look. "Not out of the goodness of this meat suit's heart, don't worry. No, your lapdog took my phone and said something about shoving a flaming sword in my taint and twisting until my nuts popped off if I even looked like I was trying to call someone."

"What do you care?" I asked. "It's not your body."

"No, but I feel everything that happens to it, and that sounded like it would really hurt. Besides, divine magic leaves scars on a demon's soul. You want to talk about cutting me deep? That would do it."

Well, that explained why Glory was sitting three feet away from the demon. She wanted to keep an eye on him. I sometimes forgot that when she wasn't giving me shit for my poor life choices, her whole job was to keep me safe. As much as I'd allow, anyway.

"Hmmm…Mort, I've got an idea," I said.

"Those are some of the most frightening words in any language," Flynn said, grinning over at me from the table she shared with Jo. The pair had empty beer bottles in front of them and fresh ones in their hands, and looked calm and relaxed, if a little worse for wear. Jo had a black eye that was quickly swelling almost shut, and Becks had a large bandage over one eye and her left wrist heavily wrapped. But I noticed that her right hand was resting on the butt of her service weapon and Jo's hammer might have been on the floor beside her chair, but the handle was in her fist. They were ready for whatever happened next. Which was good, because my plan had a healthy dose of crazy in it.

"I want you to call whoever offered to pay you a fuckton of money to hand me over to them." I held up a hand before all my friends could start to protest. "I swear this is less insane than it sounds. Because Mort is going to call them and tell them that I'm coming back here tomorrow night at midnight, and they should be here to ambush me."

Glory and Jo relaxed a little, but Flynn was still leaning forward in her chair. "And you want to get here even earlier so you can ambush them? Is that the plan?"

"Yup," I said. I was pretty proud of myself for coming up with a plan that had more steps than "find bad guys, fuck shit up."

Becks was somehow less enthused. "And we have to trust a demon for this plan to work? Harker, I swear to God, sometimes you're an idiot."

"Hey! Demons are perfectly trustworthy," Faustus protested. One withering glance from Flynn and he shut right up, though.

"Why don't I just get her here right now?" Mort asked, standing up.

"Because none of us can handle a fight right now," Glory said, yanking the demon hitchhiker back into his chair by his belt. "Harker is dead on his feet, I'm not much better, Jo and Flynn are beat to shit, and Faustus is still healing, so he's going to be even more useless in combat than normal. If you still want to kill Harker, then make the call. But remember, I won't die even if he does, and I'll be really unhappy with you." The look on her face was all the hint Mort needed as to what the outcome of Glory being unhappy with him would be.

"Okay, okay," Mort protested, raising his arms. "I won't call her until you tell me to. I promise. On my honor."

"You don't have any honor, fuckwit," I growled. "You said 'her.' Have you seen whoever's running this shitshow?"

"Yeah. So have you. At least, she told me you two had met. It's that bitch DEMON agent Walston that you met in Tennessee. What the fuck did you do to piss her off so bad, anyway?"

"I just talked to her," I protested.

"Yeah, that'll usually do it," Flynn said. I gave her a dirty look, and she held up her hands. "Don't shoot the messenger, Harker, but you're kind of a dick to authority figures. It's not a misogyny thing, I've seen you be a total asshat to men, too. You just take a great deal of pleasure in tweaking the nose of anyone who carries a badge."

I thought for a second about trying to defend myself, but the chorus of nodding heads around the bar told me it would be pointless. Apparently my charming anti-authority stance wasn't quite as charming as I thought. "Okay, I pissed her off. Big deal. That doesn't mean she needs to come all the way to Charlotte and fuck with my family. Besides, she was running that site in Tennessee while everything was going down here. Unless she can be two places at the same time, she can't be the boss."

"Oh, she's not," Mort said. "But I don't know shit about her boss. I just know Walston's here now, and she's the one hunting for you specifically."

"Great. She might not have been in charge of the Charlotte facility originally, but when I got under her skin in Tennessee…" I thought back to our conversation in the bunker on President's Island, just outside of Memphis. "She said something about Luke and Flynn then, too. I thought she was just trying to show me how much she knew, that the government had a thick file on me, but she meant more than that. She meant for me to know that they could get to the people I love. Oh yeah, I'm definitely killing this bitch."

"Get in line," Flynn said.

"I think Mama has dibs," Jo added.

"We can argue about who gets to kill her when we get Luke back," I said, while in the back of my mind I was totally thinking *but I'm killing her.* "For now, we need to rest, heal up as much as we can in the next twenty-four hours, and see what we can dig up on Special Agent Melissa Fucking Walston."

"You guys go back to base and get some rest," Glory said. "Mort and I will stay here and tidy up the place. I'm sure he knows some reasonably priced contractors that will come in on short notice."

"You don't have to stick around here, Glory," Mort said, a huge fake smile stretching across his face. "I can handle the cleanup."

"Oh no, Mortivoid," Glory replied, an equally large fake smile on her own face. "I wouldn't dream of leaving you to deal with the arrangements for tomorrow night and the cleanup on your own. Who knows what kind of details might get overlooked? I'll be right by your side, don't you worry."

Mort looked a little green as he realized he wasn't going to get a chance to betray me, but Glory just sat there beaming at him, her face pure innocence. "Okay, let's get out of here and get some rest. And some food. I'm fucking starved," I said.

"Before you go, Quincy Harker," Miranda's voice was raspy as she lifted her face from the table where she'd been sleeping, "there is the matter of payment for my services."

I patted my pockets. "Sorry, Miranda. I must have left my wallet in my other pants. Can I just owe you one?"

She smiled at me, and it was not the kind of smile that made me think of puppies and unicorns. No, this was the smile that made me think this must have been the last thing the canary saw before the cat went *chomp*. "That was exactly my intent, Quincy Harker. You shall owe me a favor of my choosing, to be called in at my discretion, at any time. I promise not to ask you to do anything patently evil, or anything that is certain to bring harm to you, any innocents, or any of your loved ones. But at some point in the future, I will call. And when I do, you will answer. Are we agreed?"

Her words had the weight of power in them. I had incurred a debt, and she was well within her rights to collect. This was as good a bargain as I was going to get on the rate, so I held out my hand to her. "We are agreed."

Quick as a hiccup, she whipped her hand out and slashed my palm, then her own, with a knife I didn't even see her holding. As blood welled up in the cut, she pressed our hands together, and I felt the magic wrap around my wrist, binding me to her. "It is done," she said, and released me.

I looked down at my hand, and the cut was completely healed. Nothing remained but a thin white scar to remind me that I'd just agreed to do a favor for a witch, no matter what, no matter when. *Oh well,* I thought. *If I die tomorrow, it doesn't matter what kind of shit I committed to for next month.*

"**D**o you think that was smart, leaving Mort on his own to set up this meeting with nobody to babysit him but Glory? She's awesome, but he's pretty goddamned sneaky, and she tries to see the best in everyone, even demons," Flynn asked as we walked through the door of our apartment.

I didn't break stride as I talked, heading straight for the bedroom and the laundry hamper. I stopped beside the dresser and started peeling off clothes. "I don't know what choice we have. I'm beat to shit, and it's going to be hours before I can call up enough magic to light a match, much less fight a rogue government agency. Everybody else is in the same shape, or worse. Faustus can stand, but only with something to hold on to. Pravesh can't walk yet. You and Jo aren't letting on, but I can feel every bruise you've got, and I think there's a cracked rib on your left side."

"Yeah, one of the human assholes in the bar caught me with a collapsible baton. I didn't see it in his hand until he smacked me with it. Jo's in better shape than I am, but that's mostly because they were all scared shitless of her pulling a Mjolnir on their asses."

"How *did* you bust through the wall? I've known that hammer for a long time, and I'm pretty sure it can't do that."

"Oh, it totally can't. But Detcord totally can, and I filched some from the SWAT boys." She saw the look on my face and broke out laughing. "Pravesh made some calls and got us a demolitions guy to come blow the wall. He was totally not interested in coming in and fighting monsters, but he was more than happy to make a big entrance for us."

"Okay, good. I really didn't want to think about how big a moron I'd be if I missed that ability on the hammer for all these years. Ow, fuck!" I hissed in pain as I peeled the t-shirt over my head. The blood-soaked fabric had dried to my skin and reopened a long slash down my side as it came free.

"That looks like it hurt. What happened there?"

"It does hurt, and I have no fucking idea. Probably the draco's claws. Or maybe that faerie motherfucker's sword. Or his other sword. Or a werewolf claw. Shit, I don't know. I've tussled with so many things today that wanted to kill me it's nice to be with somebody who only occasionally wants to rip my throat out."

She gave me a smile, and I felt my knees go a little weak. I swear, when that woman smiles, it's like the sun coming out from behind a cloud. Parts of me that have been dark for decades light up. I sat on the bed to take off my boots, then shimmied out of my jeans. I stared ruefully at the pile of clothes on the floor. "I should just burn them, shouldn't I?"

"I wouldn't go that far, but I'm pretty sure the only thing you can salvage is your underwear." Between the blood, the smoke, the dust, and the even more blood, she was right. My boots, socks, and boxer briefs could be saved, but my shirt, t-shirt, and jeans were toast. My leather duster was okay, but only because of the work I'd put in reinforcing it. The shielding spells were hanging on, but most of the time it was the Kevlar that did the heavy lifting on my coat. For a guy who fights monsters, there are a remarkable number of people that want to shoot me.

"Come on, Harker. Let's get you cleaned up and see about some food." Becks held out a hand and led me toward the bathroom.

"You gonna wash my back?" I tried to leer, but it turned into a yawn.

She smiled at me and unfastened her pants as she kicked off her shoes. "I am, but that's *all* I'm doing. I try to do anything else with you tonight and you're liable to break something."

"We can't have that," I said, sliding my boxer briefs down my legs and turning on the water in the shower to somewhere just shy of "surface of the sun."

"No, we can't." She stepped forward and wrapped her arms around me, pressing her face into my back. We stood there for a minute as the water warmed up, just enjoying each other's touch. "I missed this. I missed all the other stuff, too. But I really missed holding you."

"Me too. On the holding and on the other stuff."

She thumped me on my back. "Don't ever do that shit again, Harker."

I could *hear* the look on her face, and it was not a look I wanted to cross. "I won't. I promise."

"I mean it. I know you've looked after me for a long time, but we're together now, and that means we face the bad shit together. Side by side, no matter what."

"What about when we can't handle it? Because eventually that's going to happen, you know? One day something's going to come at me, and I won't be able to take it down."

"I know you're immortal, Harker, but fuck, do you want to live *forever?*" I felt her laugh into my shoulder. "We deal with it. Maybe we die. I'm a cop. A human one, who remembers when the man in the hat and badge came to tell her that her daddy was dead. I know what happens to cops. It happens to heroes, too. It's the deal. But not alone. Never alone. You got that?"

I turned around, and somehow she was pressed against me completely naked. I've never known how she could manage to get undressed without me knowing what was going on, but I wrapped my arms around her and pulled her in, pressed her right up against me, skin to skin. I kissed my way down the side of her face to her lips, then I grabbed on even tighter as we kissed.

"I got it. Never alone. Never again. I promise."

"Okay." She smiled up at me, and there it was again, sunlight beaming into more of my dark places. She made me a better man just by being in the same world. "Now get in the shower. You stink, and it's getting cold."

I kissed her again and did as I was told.

I woke up to sunlight streaming into my bedroom with no memory of even lying down. Becks sat on the edge of the bed, phone in her hand. "Yes, sir," she said. "We'll be right there. Yes, I'll bring him with me."

She swiped a finger across the screen and turned to me. "Good, you're awake. We've got a problem."

"What else is new?" I asked, throwing the covers back. I felt like I'd gone three rounds with Mike Tyson in his prime, but that was still a lot better than before I slept. "What's going on?"

"A crazy person with two curved swords sliced up three people in a Starbucks an hour ago. One of them was a cop."

"Fuck," I said.

Five minutes later we were dressed and in the elevator headed down to the parking garage. We'd left everyone else asleep in their apartments, except for Faustus and Cassie, who were in the "war room." I popped in to tell them what the plan was, and not to let anyone else follow us. Glory was still keeping an eye on Mort, Jo and Pravesh were too banged up, and too human, to be able to go up against this faerie, and Faustus couldn't even sit up, much less be any use in a fight. I didn't want Becks going with me, but one glance at her face told me exactly how much luck I was going to have getting her to stay behind.

I did pause long enough to grab the keys to Pravesh's Suburban. My car was still impounded, and there was no point in putting Flynn's personal car at risk when we had a perfectly good government-owned vehicle at our disposal, particularly one with a cache of weapons hidden in the floor of the cargo compartment.

Flynn pulled us up the ramp and out onto South Boulevard with lights and siren going full blare. It took less than five minutes to get to the Starbucks on East, which was surrounded by emergency vehicles. Becks just pulled up onto the curb, and we got out and walked over to a slim white man in an olive-green jacket.

"Must be nice being able to just park wherever the fuck you want," I grumbled. "Bet they don't tow your ride."

"I don't care if they do, Harker. It's not my car. They tow it, Pravesh gets to sort that shit out, not me."

"I love you more with every word that comes out of your mouth."

"That's sweet, Harker, but I still wouldn't shed a tear if the earth swallowed you whole," said the man in the green jacket. Captain Benjamin Herr was around forty, with a thin beard, longish brown hair, and a perpetually harried expression. I might have been a contributing factor to that last bit at times. He was a good cop and a decent human being by all accounts, but he often ran afoul of my deep-seated issues with authority.

"I missed you, too, Captain. What do we know?" I said, looking around the scene. I recognized a lot of the cops closest to the building, which meant that Herr was putting people near the action who had some clue about supernatural stuff. Good. That meant they were about five percent less likely to freeze up when shit inevitably went sideways.

"I know that some guy, or girl, reports aren't real clear on that part, followed a woman in off the sidewalk babbling some shit about mushroom rings and paths to the other side. The barista tried to convince the perp to leave, but they pulled out two weird swords and chopped him into little millennial chunks. Officer Daly was getting his morning half-caf bullshit and drew his weapon, but this asshole sliced through his vest like it was tissue."

"So it's swords? Not claws or anything like that?" I asked. "Sounds like a faerie knight. Their weapons are magical, and crazy sharp."

"Well, seconds later, most of Daly's insides were outside, and the suspect just walked out the back door, leaving one more corpse in the parking lot."

"Which way did they go?" I asked.

Herr pointed up East Boulevard toward downtown. "Up the hill, apparently. We've started canvassing the neighborhood, but we haven't seen any sign of them. What was that...what was it?"

"They're a faerie, and a very grumpy and well-armed one," I said.

"Is it a male or female?" Herr asked.

"I don't think those designations mean that much to the fae, and I don't really give a shit, so I figured I'd just hunt them down and make them all kinds of dead. That work for you?"

Herr scowled. "Normally I'd say no, that this suspect needs to be brought to justice. But..."

"But if this was something where your justice was effective, you wouldn't need me. Is that it, Captain?"

"Yeah, pretty much."

"Good, we have an understanding. Set up a perimeter with your officers and try to get eyes on the faerie, but don't engage. That's just going to get them dead. You handle surveillance and civilian control. Let me handle the justice."

"This time," Herr said.

"This time," I agreed.

Herr's radio crackled to life. "Captain, we have a sighting on the suspect entering Freedom Park."

"Good," I said. "Room to maneuver. Captain, get the civilians and your people out of there. I'll go take care of the rampaging faerie."

"God, I wish that was the weirdest thing I'd ever heard on this job," Herr said as I headed back out the front of the coffee shop in pursuit of a sword-wielding faerie.

27

I do not have great memories of Freedom Park. I don't have great memories of any place where I was almost barbecued the last time I set foot in it, and the last time I was in that park, I fought a tree elemental of some sort and learned that not all problems are solved by setting the bad guy on fire. Sometimes you just end up with a burning bad guy, and not a dead bad guy. That makes for a shitty afternoon.

This day wasn't shaping up to be much better. The weather was nice, but that was about the only positive thing I had to say. I listened in on my cell phone, which Flynn had tied into the CMPD radio somehow, as the police kept tabs on the faerie and worked to evacuate all the moms with strollers and random joggers. The only thing we had going for us was that it wasn't a weekend. That kept the bystanders to a minimum.

I came into the park from the north, turning into the main entrance by the soccer field and moving against a steady stream of pedestrians pouring out of the park toward their minivans and SUVs. There were a lot of people there for a weekday morning, and I raised an eyebrow at one of the patrolmen and gestured at all the people.

"Some kind of field trip," he said. "Bunch of parents and kids from

Myers Park High were doing some kind of exhibition at the softball fields. They were pretty pissed when we told them they had to leave, but they got a lot less pissed real fast when the psycho with swords showed up."

Fuck. "Was anybody hurt? Where's the psycho now?"

"No, and no idea. A couple other officers came in and tried to confront the suspect, but they were completely ignored. Last I saw, all three of them looked like they were headed for the lake. The other guys must have orders not to engage, because they're just following along with their guns out but not firing."

"Wouldn't do anything anyway," I said. "Your sword-slinging nut job is a faerie. They're pretty much bulletproof." I started off toward the lake, hoping I could get to them before the body count went any higher.

"If that thing is bulletproof, what are you gonna do?" the cop called after me.

I broke into a jog and called back, "I'm not going to use bullets." Then I was into the park and out of shouting distance. I followed the sidewalk around the perimeter of the park and saw a pair of cops standing by the bridge to the little island in the center of the park that holds the bandshell. "Let me guess, the faerie is on the bandshell and told you they'd gut you if you tried to follow them."

"Yeah," said one cop, a fit black man in his mid-thirties. He had his sidearm out, but it was down by his side. He stood with the relaxed posture of somebody who's seen some shit and isn't going to be fazed by some random headcase in the park.

"We've got eyes on the suspect. We can take him down at any time," said the other cop, a twitchy blond guy with freckles, muscles, and so much nervous energy he was almost vibrating. This was the guy I needed to keep an eye on, because if shit was going to go sideways, he'd be in the middle of it.

"I'm Harker," I said. "I think I'm the cavalry."

"Yeah, Captain Herr said you'd be coming. I'm Quentin Brooks, this is Marty Nus. We're supposed to contain the scene and prevent civilian casualties."

"Fuck that," the blond cop, Nus, said. "We get some backup in here, I'm taking that motherfucker down. He hurt Daly. He's going down for that."

I reached out and put my hand on the barrel of his gun, slowly pushing it down until he had the weapon pointed at the ground. "Marty," I said. "It is Marty, right?" He nodded. "Marty, if you do that, we can save the city a little money and just dig Daly's grave deeper. Then we can toss your dumb, dead ass into the hole on top of his and you two can ride out eternity together. Because if you get within ten feet of that faerie, they're going to carve you up into little bitty cop pieces."

"I don't have to get within ten feet, dumbass. That's what the gun is for. Now get your fucking hands off me so I can do my fucking job." The young cop's cheeks bloomed with splotches of red as his emotions took hold of his good sense and beat it into submission.

"You mean this gun?" I asked as I yanked his service weapon out of his hands. I heard the *crack* as his index finger broke when I did so, demonstrating the unspoken dangers of poor trigger discipline. I held up the pistol, ejected the magazine, popped the round out of the chamber, then pressed the button on each side of the slide and pulled it free. I put the slide in my back pocket and tossed the rest of the pistol to Brooks. "Hang onto this for your pal. He's a little too emotional to be trusted with a working firearm right now."

Then I turned my attention back to Nus. "I did that faster than you could even think about reacting, and I'm not half as fast as the son of a bitch standing on that island with your buddy's blood on their swords. If you'd drawn on them, you'd be staring at stumps where your hands used to be, and that's only if you were lucky enough to still have eyes. Now you stay back here with Brooks, who seems to be the smart one in this relationship, and let the grownups deal with the problem. *Capiche?*"

He was a persistent little bastard, I had to give him credit for that. He pulled his Taser, broken hand and all, and started to bring it up to zap me. Needless to say, I didn't let him. Faster than any human could move, I slapped the Taser out of his hand, tossed it over my shoulder into the lake, then spun Nus around and restrained him with his own handcuffs. I gave him a not-at-all gentle shove in the middle of his back while I hooked a foot around his ankles, sending him sprawling face-first into the grass, and I tossed the handcuff key to Brooks. "I'd leave him there for a little while until he cools down, but you do you, pal."

"What the fuck are you?" the stunned Brooks asked.

"I'm Quincy Harker," I said. "I'm the one you call when shit goes *really* sideways."

I left the pair of cops at the edge of the treeline and walked out to the bridge. It wasn't much of a bridge, because it wasn't much of a lake, mainly just a ten-foot moat surrounding the bandshell, which was a small stage with a roof over it, maybe twenty feet deep by forty feet wide, sitting on a man-made island. It hosted small concerts in the summer, but now it held one faerie standing in the middle of the stage, twirling around with swords in their hands. I watched for a few seconds, and something seemed oddly familiar about the patterns they were moving through, so I opened my Sight to see if anything was happening that couldn't be seen in the normal spectrum.

Sure enough, they were spell dancing. I'd heard of it, but never seen it done. Spell dancing was a way of using movement and sometimes music to manipulate energy, usually to change something about the world, like to affect weather, but sometimes it could be used to commune with the gods, or to travel between planes. The faerie was swirling together strands of magic in varying shades of blue, green, and yellow into a huge pulsing mass of energy in the center of the stage. I couldn't see what they were trying to create, but it looked a lot like a summoning circle or a Gate. The two are very similar, with the only difference being that a summoning circle only works one way, while a Gate allows for bidirectional travel between planes, dimensions, or even just places on the same plane. That's kind of a waste of a lot of effort, though, but I've known some practitioners who would will up a Gate to go to the grocery store, just to prove they could. I've known some real assholes with magic in my time.

"You calling up reinforcements, or trying to get home?" I asked, stepping onto the island.

"I wish to leave your ridiculous world, human. Ever since I have come here, I have either been bored or tortured. I enjoy neither of those, and frankly consider them to be nearly one and the same. Now I shall depart, and I am taking as many of my kind with me as would like to go." The faerie waved their hand, and I felt a pulse of magic go through me. It felt like the ringing of a chime, a vibration in my core. Looking at them with my Sight, I could see a beacon of power glowing in the sky directly overhead, a shining clarion call to any fae creature in the area.

"Do you wish to contest my departure? I did not come to this place with bloodlust in my heart, but I find that I would not mind one more minor test of my blades before I depart." A wicked grin flittered across their face, and I held up both my hands, palms out.

"All the nope," I said. "You want to leave, I'm not going to stop you. I just want to make sure the body count doesn't get any higher."

"Good. Then we shall await the arrival of my kin, and when they have assembled, we will depart your dismal world, hopefully never to return."

"Good enough for me," I said, lowering my hands.

"Not for me, asshole!" came a voice from behind me on the bridge, just before the flat *crack* of a pistol whipped through the air five times in quick succession. The faerie staggered back at the impact of the bullets, then drew their swords with a grin.

"You dare betray our trust?" the faerie said as they charged me.

I just had time to whip my head around and see Officer Nus standing on the bridge with a gun in his hands. It must have been Brooks's service weapon, since a key part of Nus's gun was still in my pocket, but who owned the gun didn't matter. All that mattered was the dumb son of a bitch had reopened the can of whoop-ass I'd barely managed to get a lid on.

"Get out of here, you fuckwit!" I shouted at the cop, before whirling around to the onrushing faerie and drawing my pistol. "These are cold iron bullets, asshole! Stop right there before I—ah, fuck it." I squeezed the trigger five times, and five times the faerie's blades intercepted the bullets and turned them aside. It was a lot like that scene in *Deadpool* when he blocks bullets with his swords, except this guy actually did it.

I tossed the gun aside and manifested my soulblade, grateful that I had enough magic restored to be able to even *create* the thing, then the faerie was on me and my shit well and truly hit the fan.

28

I called up a shield around my left forearm just in time to block the downstroke of the faerie's first blade, and somehow managed to block the other one with my soulblade, but I couldn't do a goddamn thing about the foot that crashed into the side of my knee and took me to the ground. I dropped to one knee and caught a kick right behind my ear, spinning me completely around until I lay flat on my back staring up at a cloudless blue sky. A sky that very quickly became full of blades as the faerie slashed down at my head. I rolled away, letting my sword and shield dissipate, then rolled again as the blades sliced long furrows into the concrete. Again and again the blade slammed down, ringing like bells as I barely kept ahead of the faerie's strikes.

After a few revolutions, I tumbled off the front edge of the stage and dropped a couple feet down to the grassy slope leading to the water. The faerie leapt over me to land between me and the moat, then raised their swords for another strike. I got my hands under me and spun my body to the left, swinging my legs up into the side of their knee and taking them down. Yup, I swept the leg.

With my opponent the one flat on their back for a change, I sprang to my feet and called power to my fists. When the faerie got to their feet a second later, I met them with a blast of force square in their chest. They flew backward into the moat, losing a sword in the process. Good, now I only had one blade to pay attention to.

At least that's what I thought until the faerie stood up and reached around behind their back, this time pulling a dagger from some kind of hidden sheath at the small of their back. If I didn't know better, I'd think they were literally pulling weapons out of their ass.

The faerie grinned a wicked grin and vaulted forward, leaping ten feet into the air and coming straight at me. I raised both hands and shouted, *"Liquifacio!"* sending a column of red energy streaming out to intercept my onrushing opponent. The faerie turned sideways and caught the spell on their remaining blade, and the magic just...winked out, like a snuffed candle.

"Well, shit," I muttered, gathering my legs under me and making a leap of my own, this one not quite as high in the air and backward. I landed in the middle of the stage and reached for my pistol. The pistol that was lying on the concrete some ten feet away. The faerie ran at me, but before we collided, Officer Nus's sidearm barked again, and several rounds from his Smith & Wesson .40 pistol slammed into the faerie's back. Several more of them *didn't* hit the faerie, including the one that smacked into my shoulder like a goddamned sledgehammer. I fell to the ground, injured by somewhat friendly fire, and thanked my lucky stars both that I'd put all that Kevlar into my duster and that Nus hadn't missed higher, because my face wasn't bulletproof.

As I clambered to my feet, I watched in horror as the faerie changed course and charged Nus. He didn't stand a chance.

"NO!" I shouted, but the faerie was neither listening to me nor obeying. They got to the cop, taking a few more rounds in the chest with zero effect, and shoved their sword through the cop's midsection just below his ribcage. I ran to help, but I hadn't taken more than three steps before the faerie spun around, lifting Nus over their head, and spiking him to the concrete like a deflated football.

Nus's head smacked into the stage with a wet *crack,* and his skull turned into pulp. The faerie planted a boot in the cop's chest and pulled their sword out with a sickening sound, then flicked the blade off to the side to clear the worst of the blood and gore from it.

"Shall we continue our dance?" they said, that wicked grin back on their face.

"Nah," I said. "I think I'm done dancing with you. *Glacio!*" This time when I pointed at the faerie, I held my hands straight out from my chest, palms down and fingers spread, with my thumbs touching directly in front of my nose. Freezing cold magic streaked from my fingertips, chilling the air between the faerie and me and freezing anything it touched. The faerie just smiled and leapt into the air, which was what I was counting on.

It's really important in a fight not to be too predictable. That's why sometimes highly trained combat veterans get killed by the village idiot. Because the idiot doesn't know what they're supposed to do, and the vet is behaving in a set pattern. This faerie had jumped into the air every chance they'd been given, so I figured they'd do the same thing this time. When they did, I aimed my hands lower, creating a strip of ice along the concrete between the spot I stood upon and the edge of the stage.

Then I took two big steps back, and when the faerie landed just in front of where I'd been standing, their feet went out from under them, and they landed right on their lethal faerie ass on the concrete. I don't know if you've ever fallen hard on your ass onto concrete, but it sucks. It jars everything in your body all the way up to your eyeballs, and generally takes a couple seconds to get your bearings. If you were in the middle of something particularly strenuous, it might even knock the wind out of you. In any case, you're going to be mostly defenseless for the next few seconds, giving anyone who wants it plenty of opportunity to step forward and kick your head almost clean off.

Which is exactly what I did. I planted my left foot, then threw all my weight behind my right as it smacked into the faerie's chin with every bit of force that I could muster, and not a small amount of magic that I wrapped my leg in for good measure. The faerie lifted all the way up to their feet, pinwheeling their arms to try to maintain their balance, but I used my momentum to spin left, dropping my right foot to the stage as I whipped my left up, slamming it into the side of the faerie's jaw. The remaining sword clattered to the stage as the faerie spun around, leaving its back to me completely exposed.

I am not nearly honorable enough not to take a shot at the exposed back of an enemy who's proven to be a much better fighter than me, not to mention one with the blood of at least four people, two of them cops, on their hands. So I took the shot. I called up my soulblade, wrapped both hands around the hilt of it, and took the motherfucker's head clean off. With two thumps, one louder than the other, the fight was over. I let my magical blade flicker out of existence and bent over, hands on my knees, as the exertion of the fight washed over me and threatened to put me back down for the count.

The applause started slow, and remained slow, in that kind of sarcastic slow clap that you just know isn't meant to be congratulatory but is really just somebody's way of being an asshole. I should know, I'm usually the one being the asshole. But not this time. No, this time that title was reserved for the faerie noble stepping out of the trunk of a tree just on the other side of the bridge to the bandshell island. She wasn't really *in* the tree, but her magical camouflage sure made it look like she was. I sighed, wondering if it was really too late to go back to Memphis. Or Hell.

"Hello, Ilandrane," I said.

"Hello, Quincy Harker," the Summer Court lady-in-waiting replied. "I am impressed," she said in a tone that indicated exactly how much she was *not* impressed. "You managed to best one of the Shadow Court assassins. That is no small feat, especially for one as weak in magic as yourself."

I didn't take the bait. She was right, compared to her, or any faerie, I *was* weak in magic. I mean, they're literally made of the stuff, so I'm losing that battle before the first punch is thrown. "What are you doing here, Ilandrane? I hope you haven't had second thoughts about my suitability as a mate, because my fiancée might object."

She laughed, a musical yet mocking thing that sounded somehow like water rippling across a sunlit stream and the sneering caw of a crow all at the same time. "No, Quincy Harker, I am now more convinced than ever that you are not suitable breeding material for one such as myself, although if I did want you, no mortal strumpet would be able to dissuade me. No, I am not here for you. I am here to go home. Did you not see the signal?"

She gestured to the sky, and I looked up, but saw nothing. Then I looked again, this time using my Sight, and saw that the beacon created by the now-dead faerie still shone brightly in the supernatural spectrum.

"Uh, sorry about that," I said. "I think I killed your ride home."

Ilandrane smiled at me, and it was the kind of sad, pitying smile that people use when the person they're talking to is brutally stupid. "Dear Quincy Harker, the Shadow courtier that you slew merely found the ideal location for a Gate. They did not possess the power to actually craft one. That is why they created the beacon—so that someone would open a doorway and allow us to travel home."

I felt a sick churning in my stomach. "Let me guess. You need someone to do the opening."

"Yes." She didn't even look like she cared about whether or not I could even open a Gate. She just wanted me to make it happen. Great, I love failing to meet the expectations of ultra-powerful faerie princesses.

"I don't know how."

"I will direct you through the ritual."

"I'm pretty injured. I may not have the energy."

"I and the other fae will lend you our strength."

"If you know how, and you have the power, why don't you just do it?"

She looked confused, as if the question itself didn't make any sense. "I don't want to stay here."

"Whoever opens the Gate has to stay on this side of it?"

"It certainly makes it more certain that everyone passing between the planes will survive the journey. You can travel through your own Gate, but there are risks inherent in that type of magic. You may not arrive where you intend, or you may not arrive anywhere. As I have a home that I wish to return to, I would very much prefer not to be hurled into the aether between worlds. Now, let us begin the ritual."

She produced a piece of chalk from somewhere and drew a circle on the stage, then lined it with symbols in a language older than almost any I'd ever seen. I didn't want to compare it too much with the Enochian I knew, because that was going to send me down a rabbit hole of trying to figure out what Heaven, Hell, and the land of Faerie really were, and Mecklenburg County doesn't allow booze in their parks on a Tuesday morning, so I was in a state of enforced sobriety.

It took her almost an hour to get everything drawn to her satisfaction, during which time I had to deal with a lot of cops who wanted something to shoot, a grumpy Captain Herr who wanted an explanation as to why this shit wasn't handled yet, and a Detective Flynn who wanted me to have exactly *nothing* to do with the faerie currently drawing symbols on the concrete in the middle of the bandstand.

As much as I agreed with her, I didn't have a whole lot of choice. As soon as Ilandrane was finished, I stepped into the circle with her and started casting. Flynn was working crowd control, and no one was more surprised than them when a dozen civilians stepped out of the gathering crowd, dropped the glamours they were wearing, and revealed themselves to be fae looking for a one-way ticket out of Humanland. With a nod from Ilandrane, they all came forward, crowding into the circle and making me really glad I'd put on the good deodorant that morning.

I called power, focused it into the circle in the pattern Ilandrane directed, and watched reality open up in front of me. The faeries bolted for home, leaving only Ilandrane standing beside me. "Remember, Quincy Harker. Wait for a count of ten after I pass through the Gate before you seal it behind me. Otherwise you may send me hurtling off into the Between." With that, she stepped forward and vanished, leaving me behind with a puzzled look on my face as I tried to remember where I'd heard the term "the Between" before.

I counted to ten and began to release my connection to the Gate just as I remember what the Between was. My eyes went wide at the same moment that I felt *something* push forward through the Gate. I severed my connection to the portal, but it was too late.

Something had come through. Something that should never, ever have been seen on Earth.

"**W**hat…the *fuck*…is that?" I asked, backing away from the vaguely man-shaped thing that was slowly rising from the stage.

"I don't know, but I don't think I like it," said a voice from my left shoulder. I turned to see Captain Herr standing beside me with a riot shotgun.

"You shouldn't be here. You can't kill that thing."

"Can you?" he asked without moving.

"Probably not."

"Then what the fuck are you gonna do?"

"I have no goddamn idea, but I'm not just going to run away and let it have my city."

"Me neither," I said.

"I didn't put on the badge to run away from trouble." His jaw was set, and I decided that even if I didn't like Flynn's boss, I had to respect the son of a bitch.

Are you okay? You feel…weird. Flynn's voice in my head sounded fuzzy, like something was interfering with our bond.

Get out of here, I said. *Get as far away from here as you can and get as many of those people out of here as possible. I don't know what this thing is, but it's wrong. It makes the whole world feel wrong just by being here.*

Got it. Be careful. I sensed her moving away as she herded the onlookers to safety, a task made all the more difficult by the overwhelming desire to stream the best footage to their social media accounts. If I didn't already hate technology, that would have pushed me over the edge.

"What do we do now?" Herr asked.

"The Gate is closed, and I don't know how to open one. I guess we fight," I said, trying to figure out how in the hell I was supposed to fight something that wasn't really quite there.

"Harker, I think the only thing you just said that I understood was 'fight,'" Herr replied.

"Count yourself lucky, Captain."

"I'll count myself lucky if everybody walks away from this shit. Whatever this is."

I looked back at what had come through the Gate and thought we weren't likely to be very lucky. The thing, whatever the fuck it was, looked like nothing more than a blank space in the air. It wasn't dark, it wasn't light, it just *wasn't*. It was like there was a vaguely man-shaped hole in the world, except it wasn't quite right to be called man-shaped, either. The legs were too long, and there were three arms instead of two. The neck was elongated, and the head was misshapen, like it had been stretched in a funhouse mirror.

It stood in the center of the circle, and I hoped for a moment that whatever energy Ilandrane had imbued the spell with would hold the thing captive, but that hope vanished like a leaf on the wind as the thing lurched forward, blurring toward us like a piece of film that was played back far too fast. One instant it was twenty feet away; the next it was right in front of me, swaying back and forth in a herky-jerky fashion, like something important inside it was broken.

It opened its mouth, I don't know how I could tell because it looked no more substantial than the instant before, and something both more and less than sound issued forth. It was a high-pitched keening, a shrill noise far above what even my enhanced hearing could really register, but I felt it in the marrow of my bones as much as I heard it. Every part of me vibrated in opposition to the sound, and a sense of revulsion crept over my entire body. I felt nauseous, terrified, and enraged all at the same time, cycling through emotions like a bored teenager switching TV channels.

One look at Herr told me he was even worse off than I was. He just stood stock-still, his shotgun pointed at the ground. His eyes were unfocused and flicking side to side wildly, like REM sleep, only his eyes were wide open. Sweat beaded his forehead, and as I watched, a blood vessel burst in his left eye, filling the white with crimson.

"Here, get out of here," I said, reaching out to shake him. When my hand touched his shoulder, his eyes snapped into focus, and a snarl of rage twisted his face.

"What are you?" he asked as he brought the shotgun up and fired at the creature, if that was even the right word for whatever it was.

The thing didn't try to dodge or block the shot; it just let the shot blow a hole clear through its midsection. Herr pumped round after round into the center of it, and it just stood there, viscous globs of ichor or ectoplasm or whatever the fuck this thing was made of just spraying across the stage behind it in a fountain. It didn't go down. It didn't even flinch. It just stood there, like it didn't even notice, and after a second or two, the globs of black slime just oozed back across the floor and reformed the creature like nothing ever happened.

Then it spoke, and if the odd whining sound it made was bad, its words were enough to drive a saint to mass murder. Its voice sounded like a dentist's drill in the base of my skull, while a jackhammer slammed into both temples at the same time. It was at the same time high pitched and thunderously low, with bass that rattled my ribcage and high frequencies that threatened to rupture my eyes in their sockets.

"Audacious monkey, you dare to strike me? It seems YHWH's grand experiment has forgotten there are things older than their pitiful god." Its breath was the stench of a thousand desecrated tombs, and my eyes watered from the acid it put into the air.

I saw the thing raise an arm and lash out at Herr, and I managed to shove him aside before it could touch him. The creature's fingers grazed the sleeve of my jacket, and I gasped as icy tendrils of agony wrapped around my forearm. The leather of my duster went from black to gray, then turned to dust at the thing's barest touch. I staggered back, shaking my arm through the air in an effort to make sure my flesh wasn't affected.

"You dare to interfere, half-breed? Then you can suffer his fate!" It thrust all three arms straight out at my midsection, and I managed to narrowly evade its grasp. I manifested my soulblade and brought the gleaming white sword down onto one of the thing's arms. Lightning shot through me as soon as my blade touched the creature, and I screamed as every nerve ending was lit on fire simultaneously. I fell to the ground, unable to do anything but twitch uncontrollably as agony coursed through every inch of my being, both physical and spiritual. I felt the pain down in my *soul*, much less what it was doing to my body. My soulblade winked out of existence, and I felt fairly certain I was about to do the same thing when a streak of white light flew in from out of nowhere and slammed into the center of the creature's amorphous mass.

"Get out of here!" Glory shouted as the thing flew back several feet, landed on its back, then immediately flowed upward into an upright stance again, not really standing up, just rearranging itself to be vertical instead of prone.

"Don't...think...I...can..." I gasped, my body still writhing like a snake on hot pavement on the concrete. I felt a pair of flaming daggers stab me under my arms, and I let out another scream. I could barely see through the stars in my vision, and I ran out of air to scream with before I ran out of agony.

"I'm sorry!" Herr cried, backing away from me. "I just wanted to help you get up!" It took me a second to figure out what he meant, then I understood. He was trying to help lift me, and my nerves were so fried that it felt like he was murdering me.

"It's...okay...just get out of here," I said, my breath finally starting to return. I looked to where Glory stood facing the...monster and was stunned to see another angel standing beside her. I knew there were other guardian angels around, I'd just never seen one. This one obviously lacked the good taste in television that Glory exhibited when she modeled herself after the villain from a later season of *Buffy the Vampire Slayer*, looking more like a dark-haired Chris Evans than anything else. The new angel called his soulblade and stood beside Glory. I couldn't hear what he was saying, but by the scowl he sent my way, he was totally blaming me for bringing whatever the fuck that thing was through to this world. I couldn't really argue with him, since I did anchor the Gate.

The angels slashed at the creature, which just flowed around their blades and reformed, then lashed out to catch both of them right in the chest with its arms. Glory flew back in one direction and Captain Angel-merica went in another, leaving the big bad standing directly in front of me with nothing to save me from being turned to dust from a touch. It blurred its way forward again and raise two arms overhead, preparing to rid the world of me once and for all.

This time it was a black streak that flew through the air and slammed into the thing, knocking it sprawling. I looked up to see Mort standing over me, but not Mort the hitchhiker demon in a nebbishy borrowed college professor body. No, this was Mortivoid the motherfucking *demon*, and he was there to kick ass. He held out his arm, and a black sword limned with purple flames blinked to life.

"What the fuck are you doing here?" Mort asked, and I had my mouth open before I realized he wasn't talking to me, but to the creature.

"I am here to reclaim what is mine—everything! You and your ilk have held sway upon this world for far too long, and now that the yoke of imprisonment has been thrown off, I shall raze this pitiful dimension to dust and wallow in the destruction of all you and your pitiful creator has made. Then I will free my brothers and sisters, and we will remake this plane in our own image. Prepare to suffer, Fallen One!"

"Well," I more croaked than said, "I gotta say, your plan sucks." I opened myself to the power flowing through the ground around me and channeled it into a beam of white light that slammed into the creature's chest. It took half a step back, which I considered pretty solid progress from a guy who still had to concentrate to stay upright. Then it took a full step forward, and I could almost feel it laughing at me.

"Harker, you are perhaps the stupidest human I have ever known. And that is a truly high bar," Mort said, stepping forward and slashing at the creature with his sword. The monster caught the blade in one hand and pulled Mort forward, sinking its hand into the demon's chest. Mort threw his head back and let out a scream of pure agony as he fell to his knees on the stage.

Glory charged in again with her angelic pal, and they struck at the creature with their soulblades. The monster let go of Mort, who collapsed for a moment before hauling himself to his feet and looking at me. No, he looked *past* me and yelled, "Get in here, you worthless fuckwits! If we don't help the angels, this shoggoth-spawned beast will destroy everything we've ever wanted to steal, fuck, or corrupt!"

I turned around, following Mort's gaze, and saw a dozen demons rushing at me, all with bloodlust in their eyes and blades of some type in their hands. And behind them, his hands aglow with purple magic I'd never seen him wield before, was Faustus.

"Quincy, could you please open that Gate again," the demon I'd last seen sitting on death's doorstep asked.

"Um, I'd love to, but I don't know the ritual," I said.

"I do," Glory called from across the stage. "Hold this fucker!" She flew to my side, picked me up, and flew us both over to Faustus. The other demons rushed past us as a dozen or more guardian angels swooped down from the sky, swords blazing.

She looked at Faustus. "You look like shit."

"I feel worse."

"Can you do this?"

"Do I have a choice?"

"Nope."

"Alright then."

I looked back and forth between them. "What the fuck is going on? And how are we killing that fucking thing?"

Glory stepped up and clasped hands with Faustus, facing the monster. "We aren't. We can't. Mort wasn't kidding when he called it shoggoth-spawn. It's not one of the Great Old Ones, but it's definitely from the time before, and it's some seriously old power."

"Time before what?" I asked, looking between Glory and Faustus. "And why are there a fuckton of demons and angels slugging it out side by side?"

"Before everything," Glory said.

"And there aren't many things that angels and demons agree on, but the return of the Old Ones and their subsequent destruction of Heaven, Hell, Earth, and everything in between them being a very fucking bad thing is one of them. If there's even a hint of them in the world, every divine and infernal being for miles around shows up to fight," Faustus said.

"Even you," I said. "No offense, but you're not the first one to rush into a scrap."

"I'm a lover, not a fighter," he replied. "But yeah, something this bad? Even I'll dust off my magic for this."

"How do we kill it?" I asked.

"Do you *ever* listen to her?" Faustus asked, gesturing to Glory, who shook her head in the negative. "We can't kill it. I'm pretty sure it can't die. All we can do is imprison it. You have to open up the Gate to the Between, so we can try to stick that asshole back in its cell."

"I don't even know how to open a Gate," I protested.

Glory reached out to me and pressed a finger to my left temple. Faustus did the same with my right, and as my eyes rolled back in my head and I almost collapsed to the concrete, they poured enough magical knowledge into my skull that I felt like spells were leaking out of my eyes.

"Now you know," Glory said.

And I did. It hurt like the blazes, but I knew how to open a Gate, how to anchor it at both ends, and how to unravel it. I also knew that Gate travel was fucking instantaneous, so that bitch Ilandrane was just making me hold it open in hopes that something nasty would come through and fuck with the world that made her a prisoner. I gave her props for creative vengeance but was still determined to bring her to a reckoning if I ever ran into her again.

I stepped forward, raising my hands over my head. I threw out tendrils of power to Glory and Faustus, feeling my raw nerves sing with pain again as their energy flowed into me. I chanted the Enochian words recently implanted into my skull, and channeled the divine and damned energy through me, filtering it with the power of this plane and charging the Gate. I used the memories I had of the Between when I met with Uriel and Lucifer there to anchor one side and tied it to this plane with my bond to Flynn.

Sorry, babe, this might hurt a little. You should sit down, I said over our mental link. I felt her surprise as magic started to flow back through her.

Oh yeah, I'm gonna need to not be standing for this.

I closed down most of our link to focus on the task before me, but I could feel Flynn drop to the ground and press her back to a tree. Good, it would be really inconvenient if my tether to this world fell down and gave herself a concussion in the middle of this shit.

"Move it toward the Gate!" Glory yelled, and the angels and demons redoubled their assault on the creature. It didn't budge, and in fact started to surge back toward us, tearing wings and limbs from their owners and hurling body parts through the air.

"They can't hold it," Faustus muttered.

"Mort!" I yelled. "A little help?" Mort clawed himself back to an upright position, only to drop like a stone from a casual backhand. The creature reached forward and pulped the skull of a demon, then felled Glory's guardian angel pal with the flick of a wrist.

"This is bad," Glory said, proving her grasp of the obvious remained unparalleled.

More demons charged in, and more demons fell. More angels joined the battle, and more angels dropped like stones. The creature devastated the divine and demonic with equal fervor, moving toward us inexorably, like the tides, until the entire stage shook with a resounding *BOOM* and a crack appeared, running jagged through the concrete.

I turned to see who was playing the savior and was stunned to see Jo Henry standing there, hammer buried in the floor. She lifted the head free of the concrete, and I saw the flames surrounding the weapon. It blazed with red and yellow fire, and as she slammed it into the ground again, I watched that fire run across the stage and stagger the Old One.

"What the fuck?" I whispered.

"Keep it open!" Glory snapped, and I whipped my focus back to the Gate, solidifying the flickering energy.

Jo walked forward, her steps measured and steady, her hammer swinging through the air like it weighed nothing. Flames wrapped the head and ran all the way down the handle, and those same fires were mirrored in Jo's eyes. Suddenly it all clicked. I'd seen those fires before. Not since I made it back from Hell, but I knew them.

"Michael," I said, and the Archangel riding shotgun in my friend turned to me and winked one of Jo's flaming eyes. Then they were upon the creature, and with a mighty hammer blow to the center of it, Jo/Michael sent the Old One flying through the air and straight through the Gate. I collapsed the spell, spinning the threads of the dimensional portal deep into the natural energy streams of the world.

I looked at Glory and Faustus, who both looked as exhausted as I felt. "Are we good to take the win, or are we going to have to fight all the demons now?" I asked.

"What demons?" Glory asked. "I don't see any demons. I just see concerned bystanders worried that there could be damage to the bandshell." I looked back at what had been a cluster of demons seconds before, and while the guardian angels had just vanished, the demons manifested their human disguises again, and were quickly dispersing.

"Now what the fuck do we do with a random Archangel?" I asked. "Again."

30

The answer was not "shave his belly with a rusty razor," or any of the other things you do with a drunken sailor. In this case the answer was "pretend you never saw him because he'll be gone by the time you walk over to your friend anyway."

"Jo?" I asked as I got to where she was standing, looking confused. "That you?"

She spun around, hammer coming up. I noticed that the weapon was no longer wrapped in mystical fire, which I took to mean that either the angel had left the building, or that Michael didn't think he needed all his power to swat me into oblivion. He was right, of course, but I hoped he was right and *gone*. My life was complicated enough without my friend being touched by an angel.

"Yeah," Jo said. "It's me. Michael bailed as soon as the Gate went down."

"You knew he was hitchhiking?" I asked.

"I gave him permission. He came to me back at the apartment and told me that he needed to borrow my hammer, and my body, for a little while to fight some ancient evil thing, and that he hoped to be able to return it unharmed. When I agreed, he kind of shunted my consciousness aside and took control. Pravesh drove us here, and well, you saw the rest. I was on board for the whole thing, but I had no control over my body. It was weird, and really uncomfortable, but I guess we won, right?"

"I guess," I said. "Whatever that thing was, it's gone now, sent back to wherever nightmares come from. And all the demons have put their human suits back on and vanished into the crowd, so I guess we can get back to our Prime Directive."

"Which one, Harker? Finding Luke or rounding up escaped monsters?" Jo asked.

"Finding Luke. When we were fighting that…whatever the fuck it was, it finally hit me that all this shit has been a smokescreen. All these attacks, all the freed cryptids, it's all been to hide the fact that they have Luke. As long as we're distracted by this other shit, they can take their time experimenting on him. Fuck that. It's time to rewrite the script. Time to get Luke back. Then we can concentrate on rounding up all the escapees and putting the dangerous ones away in Cryptid Gitmo."

"And what about the non-dangerous ones?" Pravesh said, walking up with Becks. The DHS director was moving a lot better than I expected her to be, given the damage she'd taken. The longer I was around her, the less I thought of her as "annoying federal agent" and the more I thought of her as "useful ally."

"I don't see any reason why we should lock up beings that don't want to hurt anybody. I mean, I'll admit a certain level of personal bias here, but if they don't start nothing, I don't see why there needs to be nothing," I said.

"That might possibly be the most bizarre sentence I've ever heard you speak, Harker, and you routinely yap about demons and magical beings. But I agree with you." Pravesh raised her voice to be heard by everyone near the stage. "Everyone listen to me! My name is Keya Pravesh, and I am the Regional Director for the Paranormal Division of the Department of Homeland Security. I hereby declare this to be a Cryptid Sanctuary City. Anyone seeking asylum shall apply for it at Mort's bar, and no case will be denied where the being doesn't want to start any trouble. We can live and let live."

There was a little grumbling from the crowd, but nothing that sounded dangerous. I watched a couple of "people," who I assumed were fae or cryptids of some flavor, slip out of the back of the crowd and disappear. I walked over to Pravesh and touched her arm.

"I don't think they're too inclined to believe any human with a badge right now," I said. "Since the last ones they encountered locked them up. And how are you moving around without crutches? I didn't expect you to walk for a month."

"I heal fast." She pointed over my shoulder. "Looks like somebody is trying to get your attention."

I followed her finger and saw Mort waving me over to him. He was trying to be subtle, which is almost impossible to do when you're eight feet tall with an alligator snout and more teeth than a Shar-Pei has wrinkles. I walked over to the giant demon. "Hey Mort. You going *au naturale* these days?"

"My true form has advantages over the ones I typically borrow. Besides, I needed to return the rental." Mort's true voice is a thing of nightmares. It's low enough that I could feel the bass in my chest, and there was a sibilance to it that made me think of a pit of poisonous vipers, which honestly wasn't too far off from what Mort was on his best day. "I got you a meeting with Walston."

"Seriously? She bought it? She agreed to meet with me?"

"She doesn't think it's a meeting. She thinks I'm luring you into a trap. I know how to manipulate humans, Harker. I've been giving them what I want them to think they want for millennia. Makes me very persuasive." I couldn't disagree. I'm not in the habit of disagreeing with eight-foot demons who could rip both my arms off and beat me to death with them. What the fuck am I saying? My whole *life* is disagreeing with demons that want to kill me and are more than capable of doing so, but this time Mort was right. He was persuasive as fuck, especially with all those teeth.

"When and where?" I asked.

"The Merchandise Mart. Tonight. Eight p.m.," he said. I raised an eyebrow at the change in time and location, and he shrugged. "She wouldn't come to my place. Said you had too many friends who might see shit go down and try to help. I told her you don't have any friends, but she wouldn't budge."

"Thanks for trying," I said, my tone dry as the Sahara.

"So she wants to meet you at the Mart at eight. She said for you to come alone, but we both know you're not going to."

"Nope. Not even close. This bitch knows where to find Luke, so I'm taking the whole damn cavalry. Shit, I might even recruit a couple strippers and homeless guys just to make it look like there are more of us. We'll get there around seven and be waiting when she shows up to ambush me. I appreciate this, Mort. What do I owe you?"

"A ride," he said, and the smile he gave me was chilling.

I decided to play dumb. "Sure, Mort. You're a little big for the seats in the Suburban, but the cargo area is pretty big. I'm sure we can get you in there. Where do you need to go?"

"You know better, Harker. I don't need transportation. My fee is one day, twenty-four hours, wearing the Quincy Harker meat suit. I promise not to hurt anyone you love, or even like, while I'm driving your body. But I get one day to be the Reaper."

Well, fuck.

I pulled the lead Suburban into the parking lot of the TV station just up the hill from the Merchandise Mart. It was closer to seven-thirty, but there was still plenty of sunlight, since it was early June in North Carolina. A TV station employee came out to shoo us off, but Pravesh badged her away. From here we had an unimpeded view of the main entrance to the building, but we were far enough away that we couldn't be observed without equipment that I really hoped DEMON didn't have on hand after they shut down their operations in the area.

"What did Mort charge you for this meetup?" Flynn asked.

"It wasn't cheap," I said.

"I'm sure it wasn't," Faustus chimed in from the back seat. "Mortivoid is widely considered one of the finest negotiators to ever climb out of a Pit. He has very rarely come out on the losing end of a bargain."

"Yeah," I said. "I noticed." I put the SUV in park and got out before they pressed more. I wasn't quite ready to unpack everything involved in promising a demon twenty-four hours riding around inside my head, and I needed to focus on the task at hand. Namely, convincing Walston to call off her vendetta against the cryptids of the world, release my uncle from captivity, and crawl back under whatever rock she came out from and play nice with the rest of the world.

Or I could just kill her. That would probably be the easiest thing, but I was *really* trying to stop killing humans. So when I walked around to the back of the SUV and opened the cargo bay, I only geared myself up with one pistol, my silver-edged short sword, and a pair of knives on my belt, one with a silver blade and the other one forged from cold iron. A couple extra magazines for the Glock, and I was good to go.

"You guys should wear vests," I said to Flynn and Pravesh.

"I'm good," Pravesh said, rapping her shirt. I heard the thick muffled sound of Kevlar and turned to Becks.

"Already on it," she said, reaching past me into the Suburban and strapping on a bulletproof vest with POLICE on the front and back in large white block letters. As she tightened the straps, I reached up and grabbed the Velcro rectangle and pulled the ID plate off with a loud *RRRIP*.

"What are you doing?" Flynn asked, staggering forward as I pulled. The Velcro didn't let go, and I didn't mind having her in my arms.

"Taking off the neon signs," I said, spinning her around and yanking off the POLICE label on her back. "If it's dark in there, those are a fucking beacon, and everyone who doesn't want to kill you knows you, so you don't need to identify yourself to us."

She thought about it for a few seconds, then nodded. "Yeah, if you guys don't have enough smarts to not shoot me by accident, then the world is pretty fucked."

"Do you have CNN?" Pravesh asked. "The world *is* pretty fucked. But that's our job—to unfuck it."

"That should be our motto," Faustus said. "Unfucking the world, one demon at a time."

"Catchy," I said. "Now button it. I don't think anyone ever expected me to come alone to this meetup, but there's no point broadcasting our flagrant disregard. I'll go in the main entrance. Faustus, you and Pravesh go in through the loading dock to the left-hand exhibit hall. Freedom, I think it's called. Flynn, you and Glory go in through the hall to the right. It's got easier access through the loading dock." I pointed out all the entrances on the floor plans I downloaded to my tablet. There's a lot to be said for holding a meet at a city-owned building, not the least of which is that you can probably get a shitload of information online.

"Sounds like a plan. Give us a couple of minutes to get into the building before you go barging in the front," Pravesh said.

I didn't respond to her disparaging my stealth. I just popped the transceiver into my left ear and clipped my radio to my belt. Now I could communicate with everyone, not just Flynn. The rest of the team did the same and headed off down the hill in opposite directions toward the huge low-slung building. It was a long walk down the hill and across the parking lot with the setting sun making long shadows of the few trees behind me. My boots on the pavement were the only sounds I could hear aside from the chatter of my team in my earpiece.

I didn't have high hopes for the meeting. I thought there was a microscopic chance that I could talk Walston into abandoning her crazy purge of supernatural creatures, but only the tiniest. I was really hoping to find a clue, some little shred of something that would lead me to where they were holding Luke, and maybe a hint as to who was behind this bullshit in the first place.

I opened the door and stepped into the lobby. The sun was low enough, and the building far enough downhill, that most of the light was cut off, and I stepped into deep shadows. I heard locks shatter and doors swing open through my earpiece as the others made their entry on either side of me, but there was no other sound. No other footsteps except for my people. Then I heard it, a creaking of rope on metal, the straining sound of something heavy swinging.

I knew that sound. This wasn't the first time I'd heard it, and it was never good. I pulled a flashlight from my pocket and shined it around the lobby, catching sight of the open door to the exhibit hall right in front of me. I walked forward, my Glock in one hand and my light in the other. Flynn and Glory came into the lobby, and I motioned them to hold their position. I did the same a second later with Pravesh and Faustus.

I stepped into the exhibition hall and reached over to flick on the lights. Huge banks of fluorescents flickered to life, throwing the massive empty room into harsh light. Except the room wasn't quite empty. There was one person there, and she was early for our meeting.

The body of Melissa Walston, Regional Director of DEMON, swung from the rafters with a rope tied around her neck. Our contact was dead, and I'd been set up. I didn't even need to hear the sirens to know what came next.

But I heard them anyway.

31

It had been a while since I'd felt the cold plastic of a Charlotte-Mecklenburg Police Department interrogation room chair under my ass, but I found my muscle memory coming back almost immediately. It took all of thirty seconds for me to assume a disaffected slouch, push the chair back from the table, prop my feet up, and rock back on the chair's rear legs. I closed my eyes, summoned power into myself, and whispered, *"Adflicto Affligo."* The red lights on the room's two surveillance cameras flickered once, then went out for good. A thin tendril of smoke came from the digital recorder sitting on the table in front of me, and I let a little smile creep across my face.

I'd spent many a night in these interrogation rooms, usually dodging uncomfortable questions from Becks. Back then she was just a young detective who didn't believe in any of my weird stories and was convinced that I was the worst thing she'd ever encountered. Nowadays I didn't even make her Top Ten list.

The door opened and a short man with a florid complexion and a dress shirt whose buttons were in a constant battle with his expansive belly bustled in. He extended a sweaty hand to me, then wiped it on his wrinkled khakis and held it out again. I just looked at him.

After a pause long enough to move all the way into "uncomfortable" territory, he let his hand drop and moved around to sit in the chair opposite me. "Hello, Mr. Harper. My name is Detective Joseph Borgan, and I'd like to ask you a few questions."

"Harker," I corrected.

"Excuse me?" He looked up from the manila folder in his hands, honest confusion on his round face. He pulled out a well-loved handkerchief from a pocket and mopped his brow. "Sorry. It's a gland thing. Makes me sweat."

"No, it's not," I said. "It's the bourbon, you jackass. Alcohol dilates the blood vessels and makes you warm. You're already fat, and you're wearing a long-sleeve dress shirt, undershirt, and a jacket in North Carolina the week after Memorial Day. Of course you're going to sweat like a whore in church. But you really ought to drink a less pungent liquor if you're gonna try to lie about it. I could smell the Wild Turkey the second you walked through the door."

His face flushed even more, and the joviality vanished from his expression. "I heard you were a fucking know-it-all. Guess the boys weren't lying."

"Did the boys happen to mention that I'm a fucking federal agent?" I asked, letting the chair fall forward. I leaned in, planting my elbows on the table and getting uncomfortably close to Detective Lardass. It was uncomfortable for him because I've been told I can be a little intimidating when I'm irritated, and it was uncomfortable for me because he smelled like a sausage fart in a distillery. "Now how about you get these cuffs off me and let me get on about my business because I've got shit to do that doesn't involve joining a CMPD circle jerk."

"How about you sit your ass right there and answer my questions about what you were doing with a dead, how did you put it, fucking federal agent? Because from where I'm standing, I've got probable cause to hold you and all your friends, search every piece of property you own, and generally shit all over anything you've got planned for the evening. How does that sound?"

"Like you're trying to whip 'em out and measure peckers, Detective. Well, let me be very fucking clear. I not only have a bigger dick than you, I've got more juice than you. Now get the fuck out of here, go get me somebody with at least two fucking stripes on their cuffs, and let the grownups sort this shit out. I let the patrol officers who responded to the scene haul me in here because they're the rank and file and were just doing their job, but you're a detective. You're supposed to know the goddamn score. Or did you think you got tossed in here with me because you were next up in the rotation?"

He looked more confused with every sentence, and finally I just shook my head and sighed. "You poor dumb bastard. You got this interview because the assholes on the other side of the glass know I didn't kill Walston, know that even if I did you couldn't touch me for it, and know that the only thing that's going to happen in here is I'm going to get pissed off and you're going to look fucking inept. But good news—I turned off the cameras and the recorder, so there's no permanent record of you not getting anything out of me."

"You did what?"

"I fried the recording equipment. It was a running thing I used to do to Flynn whenever she'd try to bust me. I bet your tech vendor has been real disappointed since I stopped burning out cameras on a weekly basis."

"Exactly how did you—"

"Magic."

"What?"

"Ma. Gic. You know, *poof?* Rabbits in hats, sawing women in half, making shit disappear? That stuff. Except what I do is a little different. A little more destructive. A little more fucking intense, which is exactly what I'm going to demonstrate in about ten seconds if somebody with enough stroke to cut me loose doesn't walk through that fucking door!" I aimed this last bit at the large window on the side of the room, or more specifically at the people I knew were watching through the two-way mirror.

I waited for a slow ten-count as Borgan stammered through some bullshit response about protocols and witness statements and other shit that didn't matter to me. When I reached ten, I looked back at the mirror. "Okay, assholes. You asked for it. But remember who's to blame when the bill for the new door comes due."

I stood up, paying just enough attention to Borgan drawing his sidearm to manifest a shield along my left arm, and called power into my right hand. I raised my fist over my head, energy coalescing into a crimson orb of lightning, and just as I was about to blast away the door and probably a couple of feet of wall on either side of it, a fifty-something man in a suit that actually fit walked in.

"Sit down, Mr. Harker, there's no need for theatrics. Borgan, you can go. Tell whoever is passing out bullshit assignments tonight that I'll be speaking with them before the end of the shift."

I let my magic dissipate, not without sending a little jolt to zap Borgan right in the sack, and sat down. I leaned back once more, propped my feet up, and laced my fingers behind my head. "Hi," I said. "I'm Quincy Harker. Who the fuck are you?"

"I'm Deputy Chief Christopher Kennedy, and I'm the guy who's going to get you out of here after you answer a few questions for me. I'm the new head of the CMPD Special Services Bureau. We handle anything that's out of the ordinary, and you, Mr. Harker, certainly qualify.

"I will be your liaison with the department moving forward, and I would appreciate it if you would keep us apprised of any operations you or your people are conducting within the city limits that may either need our support, or need us to stay out of your way. Detective Flynn has been reassigned from Homicide to Special Services, and I'm working with Deputy Chief Ridenhour to not only make her transition smooth, but to keep communication open between our divisions, so that he doesn't waste manpower and resources chasing down things that his people can't handle even if they catch them."

I looked him up and down. This was not an ordinary cop, and he had the look of someone who had walked through the fire more than once. He had the close-cropped haircut and upright bearing that screamed former military, but there was something disarming about him. His eyes definitely said he'd seen some shit, but I got no kind of deceptive vibe off him. By everything I could tell, he was straight up.

"Where did they find you, Chief?" I asked, wanting to get some background on this guy who I apparently was going to be dealing with a lot.

"I've been around a bit. Seen a few things. Spent some time near Cleveland, dealt with some vampires up there. Went out west, met this badass chick in Phoenix with a hammer and an attitude. Was heading up Homicide in Atlanta a couple years ago when some dick came through and wreaked all kinds of havoc downtown, and when I heard through the grapevine CMPD was looking for somebody to be their Mulder up here, I figured if even half the shit I heard about you was true, this was going to be the most exciting place on the East Coast."

There was something he wasn't telling me. Something behind his relaxed smile hinted at a deeper motivation, but if he was going to let me get out of the pokey and back on the hunt for Luke, I was willing to let it slide. For now.

"Okay, what's it going to take for me to get out of here?" I asked, dropping my chair down to all four feet.

"I need all the data you have on the monsters that are loose in my city. Then my men and I will round them up and get them the hell out of here."

I cocked my head to the side. "You've either got a low opinion of the cryptids or an inflated view of your men. I've spent some time with the CMPD, and they're good cops, but they aren't trained to handle this shit."

"My guys are. I've only been here three months, but the first thing I did was create a sub-team within SWAT stocked with men and women who are trained and ready to deal with supernatural threats. They aren't wizards, so nobody's throwing fireballs at the bad guys, but they roll out with silver, cold iron, holy water, and rock salt. They know that the monsters under the bed are real, and they've taken down a nest of vampires and a small pack of lycanthropes since we've formed them."

"Okay, but that's still nothing compared to some of these creatures. There was a fucking *medusa* in there, man. Your crew got a way to keep from getting turned to stone? Because I sure as hell didn't, and lemme tell you, it sucked. And even ignoring the power issue, some of these creatures just want to be left alone. I can't hand over a list to your guys and have them hunting down some dryad and burning her to death just because she isn't human. That's not right, either."

"Okay, then vet the list. Cull it down to the threatening creatures that you think a group of trained humans could take down, and don't put anything on the list that doesn't need to be shot on sight. We don't want to kill innocent beings, but there are a lot of monsters that just got turned loose on this city, and it's my job to stop them."

I thought about his plan. It wasn't the worst thing I'd heard. It wouldn't take me long to go over the data Jo culled from the DEMON computers and pick out the escaped cryptids that would almost certainly go on a rampage if given half a chance, then cherry pick the ones that Kennedy and his men could handle.

"Okay, fine," I said. "It'll be a couple days. I need to get home and go over the list, but I'll get you all the information we have on dangerous cryptids that your people should be able to handle without catastrophic loss of life." I stood up and stuck out my hand. "Deal?"

"Deal. Now, get out of here and get your uncle back." I shook his hand and walked out the door, part of me wondering who told him about my relationship with Luke, or that Luke was missing. I stepped out into the bullpen and Flynn, Pravesh, and Jo came over to me.

"Ready to roll?" Jo asked.

"They didn't try to hold any of you?" I replied.

"No, but we weren't found six feet away from a dead federal agent. And I have a badge," Becks said.

"Me too," said Pravesh. "And mine has a fancy title on it. No, we knew they were just jamming you up, so we let them have their fun for an hour or two until it became apparent to everyone what killed Walston."

"Which was?" I asked. I didn't like the look on Pravesh's face, but I hadn't gotten a good enough look at the DEMON Director's body to make a guess at cause of death.

"Exsanguination," she replied. "Her body was completely drained of blood."

"Fuck," I said. "If it's Luke, they've starved him until he drained her. If it's another vamp, then there's another vampire on the loose."

"Or there's some asshole in town making things look like vampire kills. Either way, we've got to find who or what killed her," Jo said. "I'm staying here to work with Chief Kennedy's computer techs for a couple hours. I can get them the beginnings of the list of cryptids they can go after, and I can use their resources to track where Walston's cell phone was today. That coupled with the computers we recovered from the first facility we found should give us some places to start looking."

"Sounds like a plan. When you get back to the condo, I can scry those places and see if anything looks like a place they could hold Luke," I said.

"There's something else we've got to figure out," Flynn said. We all looked at her. "We thought Walston was one of the leaders of this whole thing. If someone murdered her and strung her up as either a message to us or a feeble attempt to get Harker arrested, that means she was a lot less important than we thought, and that somebody else is really in charge."

"And exactly who the fuck is that? This Shaw we've heard a little about, or somebody higher up than her?" I asked. We were at the elevator, so I pushed the down button, and when the doors slid open, we piled in and headed down to the parking garage. Jo gave us a wave and headed off into the station to nerd out with the cops.

"I don't know, but maybe the Deputy Chief can do some more digging into DEMON's power structure. If Shaw isn't the one driving DEMON's new cryptid-hunting program, we need to find out who is. I'll call Washington from the car," Pravesh said as the elevator doors slid open.

I stepped out and felt my entire body tense up. It felt like every nerve ending was on fire, and out of the corner of my eye, I saw the others drop to the concrete. I fell to my knees, fighting against the pain.

"Hit him again," said a cold female voice. I turned to the side, and standing behind the six people in head to toe tactical gear was a woman dressed in a stark white pantsuit with hair so blond as to be almost translucent. I felt another shock as the kidnappers hit me with their stunsticks again, and I fell to the ground, blessedly unconscious before my face smacked the concrete.

32

The first thing I thought of when I regained consciousness was, "Well, this sucks."

Admittedly, that's my first thought on waking many mornings, especially if Becks isn't beside me, but it's always my first thought when I wake up hanging by my ankles with my hands just brushing the dirty floor below me. The blood pounded behind my eyes as I tried to focus on what I was seeing, which was mostly ankles. I think I counted four people in the room, three in combat boots, and one in men's dress shoes. None of the feet matched the white women's pantsuit that seemed to be in charge when I got zapped.

"Sir? He's awake," came a voice from above me. I couldn't tell which pair of feet spoke, but the dress shoes walked over to me and gave me a crisp kick to the collarbone. I tried to hold in the groan, but I didn't manage to play dead well enough.

"Indeed he is. Okay, flip him." His voice was crisp, accustomed to being obeyed, with an edge of a European accent. German, maybe? I watched a pair of boots walk over to a control panel, and I heard the click and whir of a motor engaging.

Something jerked my arms as I was stretched backward into a "U" shape, then another motor engaged and my feet started to lower. After a couple of minutes of lifting and lowering, I was upright, suspended by my wrists by a chain that went up into the darkness overhead and apparently attached to a motor up there somewhere.

I didn't say anything at first, just reveled in the relief of the blood flowing down from my skull. I heard a set of measured footsteps approach, then a trim man with an off-kilter smile and psychosis beaming from his eyes came into view. "Hello, Mr. Harker. I've heard a lot about you."

I tried to come up with a witty retort, but my mouth wasn't quite working yet, and I wasn't sure which of the two I should be addressing. I blinked a few times, and my double vision cleared up a bit. Not enough for me to feel like sniper school, but enough to figure out which of the wavering images of grinning asshole I should focus my eyes on.

"My apologies," the assclown said, still grinning. "It seems I have you at a disadvantage. Which is how I like it, but there's no need to be rude. My name is Wolfgang Gerhard, and I am your host for this part of your study."

"What am I studying?" I tried to ask, but it came out more like "whamastuding?" I ran my tongue around the inside of my mouth trying to generate enough spit to snark off to this dickhead properly, but it didn't help.

"Don't try to speak," Gerhard said. "It will be difficult, and I have no interest in your puerile attempts at bravado. You are alive only so long as I can glean useful information from you, after which you will be discarded like the gene-trash you are. So hold your tongue or I will have it removed. I assure you it is not required for what we wish to learn from you."

I didn't say anything, just kept my mouth shut and tried to keep a tight rein on my galloping thoughts. I'd heard that phrase "gene-trash" before, but I couldn't remember where. I wracked my brain for context, while at the same time trying to reach out and draw in magic. I got nowhere on both counts.

Gerhard chuckled, a dry, raspy thing with about as much humor in it as a skin graft. "I can see you trying to access your magic. It is no use. This facility is warded, you are bound with cuffs of cold iron and silver, and you are suspended within a circle of pure salt. You have no more access to magic than a normal human, Mr. Harker. Your devil-spawn gifts will not save you from my studies."

I glared at him, hoping to spur him into a monologue with dirty looks, but got nowhere. He just waved to one of the guards and said, "Begin with electricity. He has shown vulnerability to that."

The guard, one of three in the room, walked over to a table and picked up a pair of long metal probes with a cord attached to each one. There was a sponge attached to the ends of the probes, and I didn't like anything about where this was going. I liked it even less when the guard, who looked like his steroids took steroids, dipped the sponges in water and grinned at me.

"Hit it," he said. Another guard, still standing by the control panel that ran the motors suspending me from the ceiling, reached forward and flipped a switch. The probes twitched a little in Roid Rage's hands, and he brought them together in a shower of sparks. Then he took two steps forward and jammed the rods into my stomach. I let out a yelp as the electricity coursed through me, then realized I smelled smoke.

I glanced down and saw that the stupid fucks hadn't taken off my shirt, which was now smoldering under the high-voltage assault. The shirt scorched away, leaving my skin bare, but it took most of the water out of the sponges, too. This took a tiny bit of the conductivity out of the probes, but not enough to make them not hurt like a son of a bitch.

I screamed as best I could through my parched throat and jerked away from Roid-o. He just grinned a gap-toothed grin and stepped closer, which was exactly what I'd been hoping for. His foot brushed the circle of salt surrounding me, wiping a tiny portion of it away. It wasn't enough to breach the magical barrier, but I had hopes that if I could survive long enough, I could get these guys to make a mistake.

"Stop," Gerhard called. "Let him recover, then switch to the torch." Well, that didn't sound good. Electric shock was fucking terrible, but fire was worse. Most of the time when you're getting electrocuted, you can't smell your own flesh cooking. When you start wondering who's cooking pot roast, and *you're* the pot roast, it's a really bad day.

I hung there for most of an hour "recovering." There's not a lot of recovery going on when your entire body weight is hanging by magic-sucking handcuffs suspended from a chain, but as long as I wasn't being actively tortured, I had a moment to think. If Roid-o stepped on the salt line a couple more times, I might not be bound anymore, but I had to stay alive long enough for that to happen, and Gerhard had to not notice and not restore the circle. That was a fistful of things falling my way, and it hadn't been that kind of week so far.

The grinning dickwhistle had the right of it, though—I could no more touch the river of magic flowing through the world than a normal person, but he forgot one thing—I am a long way from a normal person. I twisted my hands around and gripped the chain, taking a little bit of the strain off my shoulders as I used my biceps to take some of my weight. Then I lifted with my right hand and pulled against the buckles on the cuff with my left, trying to strain the metal enough to pop the latch or weaken the links holding the cuffs together. I focused so tightly on pulling the cuffs apart that I missed Gerhard walking over behind me, moving slow to keep his footsteps soft.

Then a sharp *crack* split the air and a line of fire ran diagonally across my back from left shoulder to right kidney, followed by another that cut in the opposite direction, leaving an "X" of screaming pain across my back. I lost my grip on the chain and fell, feeling my shoulders come within a hair's breadth of yanking free from the sockets. I screamed as the whip fell twice more, leaving long bloody furrows down my back.

Gerhard stepped around in front of me, coiling the whip in his left hand. "Please do not try to escape, Mr. Harker. I have a great deal of experience in bringing someone to the very brink of death and pulling them back time and again before finally allowing them, after they have begged sufficiently, to flee their agony in a most permanent fashion."

"Fuck you, you verbose prick," I gasped. My throat was ragged from screaming, but I managed to get the words out pretty well.

"There is no need to be rude, Mr. Harker. Perhaps you are not as useful as the Director had thought. Perhaps you should just be cleansed, like the rest of the inferiors in this pathetic country. Sometimes I long for the Fatherland, for the world that should have been. The world that *would* have been, if not for the meddling of you and your parasite 'uncle.'" He turned and set the whip down on a wheeled metal table, then picked up something small.

When he turned back to me, I could see the scalpel in his hand. He held it like he knew what he was doing, which meant this was going to hurt. A lot. That's one of the things about scalpels—they can cut shallow or deep, depending on what an experienced wielder wants. If he wanted to just peel off pieces of me for hours, he could totally do that. If he wanted to slice clean through both carotid arteries and kill me in seconds, he could do that too. And with both hands and feet bound, there wasn't a goddamn thing I could do about it.

Gerhard stepped forward, that soul-chilling grin tickling my memories again, but any thoughts about where I'd first seen this asshole vanished as he drew a line of fire down my torso with the scalpel. He started just over my left clavicle, inside of the shoulder joint, and sliced a fine line straight down the length of me, only stopping when he got to my belt. There was no shirt to impede his progress, since his goon had burned it away with electricity an hour ago. There was just flesh, and blood. Lots of blood. He made a series of parallel cuts down my chest, none of them deep, all of them bleeding freely.

I watched his eyes the whole time, and they were as cold as any demon I'd ever seen. Gerhard had abandoned any sense of humanity long ago, and only the monster remained. A grinning monster with freckles and curly black hair falling almost over his right eye. He looked familiar, but every time I thought I had it figured out, the idea vanished in another spike of agony.

It went on for hours. He cut me, watched me heal, then cut me along the same place again. He tried to pour alcohol in the wounds to keep them from healing, but all that did was hurt. He poured salt in the open cuts along my arms and chest, but my flesh still knit closed in seconds. Agonizing seconds, but still just seconds. The lemon juice slowed the healing more than the salt, and both had a greater effect than the alcohol, but nothing worked quite as well as fire. He would peel three-inch strips of flesh from my stomach, running bands of pain outward starting at the center, then he put a blowtorch to the wound, scarring my flesh and making me scream until my voice broke again.

Then he used the motors to raise my feet until I was laying horizontal, and he gave me water. And by "gave me water," I mean he wrapped a towel around my face and poured water over it at varying speeds so I could never tell when it was safe to breathe and when I was going to come closer and closer to drowning. I screamed, I struggled, I tried to touch magic, reach out to Becks, anything.

I even prayed, and I hadn't done that since the flu took my brothers in 1918. I prayed, I bargained, and I begged, but nothing made the pain stop. And through it all, through every fucking second of it, Gerhard's voice haunted me. The silky accented voice that I knew and didn't know all at once. The voice I could swear I'd heard before but couldn't remember where. Then, in a flash, it hit me, and I was more terrified than ever.

I remembered where I'd heard that voice, and I knew who held me. That was when I thought I was going to die.

It was Argentina, 1975. I was working with a band of Nazi hunters chasing down escaped war criminals and bringing them to justice. There were several groups of people doing the same thing, most of which wanted to bring the monsters back to civilization and have them stand trial for the atrocities they committed in the camps. I wasn't working with one of those groups. The crew I was running with at the time preferred more permanent and less public solutions for the Nazis we found.

We'd managed to bag about half a dozen midlevel scum over the past two years. I worked multiple angles with the team. Sometimes I'd be in New York using contacts from Sister Lucia to research where to find the Nazis. Sometimes I'd be in the jungles searching for hidden compounds and villas bought with the gold the bastards stole out of the mouths of their victims. Sometimes, and these were the best times, I'd be the tip of the spear, the lead on an assault.

I was still working through a lot of shit, and Nazis brought out the very worst of it in me. Come to think of it, they still bring out the worst in me. I watched what those bastards did in the forties, and I've never gotten over it. Don't think I ever will. Any chance I get to kill a Nazi, it doesn't matter the risks—I'm in.

That was even more my attitude in 1975, and there was a lot more cocaine making me even more impetuous and convinced of my immortality. The day I remember best started off like most of my South American days—sweaty and traipsing through the jungle. This time I was in Argentina, close to the border with Paraguay, in a sweaty jungle nestled between the Paraná River and the tiny town of San Ignacio. Intel from Sister Lucia told us that there was a high-value Nazi target hiding in a small compound deep in the forest ever since the Mossad captured Eichmann nearly two decades before. Sister Lucia's sources couldn't give us a name, but there weren't many Nazis left out in the wild with anywhere near Eichmann's profile, so I was pretty sure I knew who we were after—The White Angel himself, Dr. Josef Mengele.

Mengele got out of Germany in the last days of the Reich, and Luke, the Council, and I had been looking for the bastard off and on for thirty years, ever since I came back to my senses. We would go months, sometimes even years, without any word about the chief architect of Hitler's "scientific" experiments, then we'd hear about a sighting in Brazil, or Uruguay, or Argentina. The last credible information we had placed him in Sao Paolo, Brazil, but Lucia's contact was certain the "scientist" of Auschwitz was holed up in a small collection of buildings set far back in the Argentinian wilderness.

Three of us went into the jungle on that mission: me, Adam, and a Brazilian Nazi-Hunter named Eaman. Eaman was a whip-thin man with a face like a hatchet and eyes like razor blades. His wits were as sharp as his tongue, and I thoroughly enjoyed drinking cheap beer and talking trash with him, but I trusted him completely when it came time for someone to have my back in a fight.

We left San Ignacio in a Jeep, but it was less than ten miles before we had to abandon the vehicle and make the rest of the way on foot. The undergrowth was thick, but here and there we saw signs of human traffic through the woods. A footprint in a muddy creek bed here, a branch snapped off a little too cleanly there. All these little clues told us we were on the right track.

"Why did you want to come on this hunt, Adam?" I asked the big man. He'd hunted down a few war criminals with me, but the cause didn't seem to have the same personal edge for him that it did with me.

He didn't answer me at first, just kept walking forward, slicing through vines and branches with his machete. After a silence long enough to make me doubt he was going to reply at all, he said, "If it is Mengele, he may have information useful to me."

I was a little stunned. "What kind of information, buddy? He was a horrible Nazi fuck who did all kinds of horrible experiments on people."

"Except for the title of Nazi, you have described my father perfectly. And given his views on the Jews and the Roma in Germany, I would not have been at all surprised to see him wearing a swastika had he lived long enough to see Hitler rise to power. But that is not the point. The point is that Mengele was a monster who experimented on human beings for some twisted type of scientific advancement. It is possible that he learned something that may be applicable to the way I was created, and he may have data on the extremes to which I can survive. Hitler was rumored to be fascinated by all things occult and magical, so if anyone was blurring the line between magic and science in a similar fashion to my father, Mengele is the most likely suspect."

"And you want to interrogate him?" I asked. This differed from my typical method of killing the bastards first and asking questions later, but I was willing to try new things.

"I am more interested in seeing any notes or notebooks he may have. If history has taught us anything about these monsters, it is that they are not terribly forthcoming with information, unless it is manufactured 'proof' of their genetic superiority to everyone else."

"You've got that right," I replied. "The fuckers love to pontificate about their brilliance, but they don't understand that if they were that fucking smart, we'd never find them in the first place."

We froze as Eaman held up a hand. He pointed ahead and to the right, and I stepped up beside him to see what he was pointing at. There were three buildings arranged in a triangle formation, with one about half again as tall as the others. The main building sat in front of the other two, a rectangle sticking up out of the jungle with narrow slits visible in the walls of the second story. They looked like arrow ports from old European castles, but I bet they would be pretty good places to shoot a rifle from, too.

I raised my M-16 to my shoulder and looked through the scope mounted to the carry handle. The upper level came into sharp focus, but the shooting windows were too narrow to see through. There was no visible movement on either the top level, which appeared to be just a large shooting/scouting platform, or in the lower level. Curtains blocked most of the view into the lower level, but there were a few gaps here and there. I swung the scope over to the left-hand rear building, a nondescript stone structure with no windows and a rickety roof. There was no way to see inside, so I shifted focus to the last building.

If the front building was a guard post, and the left building was a storage shed or pantry, then I assumed the last building would be the living quarters. The curtains on the front were pulled tight and seemed to be backed with blackout shades because I couldn't even get a peek inside from the treeline. The front door was slightly ajar, though, and swung in the light breeze that ruffled the jungle leaves.

I motioned to Eaman to stay behind, and I waved Adam forward with me. We approached the front building as quietly as we could, which wasn't anything approaching silently given Adam's size. I expected gunfire to erupt from above us with every broken branch, but nothing came. I motioned for him to push open the door to the guard building, and I stood back to cover him with the M-16. The door swung open with an ear-splitting shriek of wood, and a pair of small brown birds with yellow bellies flew out. I didn't shoot them, but it took a herculean act of will not to squeeze off a quick burst.

I stepped through the door first, swinging the rifle left and right across the room. The empty room. The whole building was one open room, with separate areas for eating and sleeping. It was deserted, just three bunk beds, a table with eight chairs, and a dark fireplace without even an ember glowing in its belly. I motioned for Adam and Eaman to come inside and walked over to the cabinets to see if there was anything there to tell me about the men who had lived here.

"Check the footlockers," I said as my companions entered the room. "Then Adam, you go upstairs and make sure there aren't any surprises overhead."

"What makes you think anyone up there wouldn't have shot us already?" he asked.

"Nothing, but I'd rather send you up a flight of stairs than be dead."

He didn't say anything in reply, just nodded and walked up the stairs along the back wall of the room. He came back down a few seconds later shaking his head.

"There is nothing there," he said. "But there do seem to be patches of disturbed ground and some rectangular mounds behind the other two buildings."

"Graves?" I asked.

"I would assume so, but I cannot say for sure without closer inspection."

"Well, we might as well inspect someplace else because there isn't shit here," I said. "Eaman, you find anything in those footlockers?"

"Couple of Brazilian *Playboy* magazines and some shoe polish, but nothing useful."

"Take the porn, leave the shoe polish," I said. Eaman smiled and patted his back pocket, which already had two folded glossy magazines sticking out of it. "Let's see what else we can find."

The storage building, if that's what it was, yielded even less useful material than the guard post. There were empty shelves, a moldy bag of flour, and a big sack of rice teeming with weevils. Nothing to indicate who had lived there or where they may have gone.

As we moved to what I was now thinking of as the "main house," I stopped for a closer investigation of the outside. There were indeed shades blacking out every window, on all four sides of the building. I concentrated hard but could hear no signs of life within. Either the place was empty or whoever was inside was preternaturally quiet. I wasn't ruling out exceptionally quiet supernatural creatures like vampires, but since it was mid-afternoon, I felt like we weren't in too much danger.

I pushed open the door myself this time, slamming it open and rushing through to sweep the room with my rifle. Once again, I saw nothing but a big empty room, this time with one small bed, chair, and fireplace along one wall and what looked like a laboratory dominating the other half of the place.

"Empty," I said to Adam.

"Of people, yes," he replied, walking over to the laboratory area. "But perhaps not devoid of useful information." Adam picked up a battered leather-bound journal and held it up to me, displaying the Swastika embossed on the cover. Even more than thirty years later, the sight of that symbol filled me with rage.

Adam flipped through the notebook and several others like it he found scattered around the lab while I searched the small dresser and poked around under the bed. In a compartment hidden underneath a rug, I found a set of identification papers for a Dr. Faustó Rindon, but the photograph attached to the passport was one I knew well—Josef Mengele, the Angel of Death.

"He was here," I said, flinging the passport to Adam. "He was here, and we lost him."

"We lost him, but we found his research," Adam replied. "And through that research, we can find him again."

But we didn't. We followed a paper trail back into San Ignacio, then to Buenos Aires, then to Rio, where we lost the scent. Then I got distracted by a fairy princess in New York, and the next thing I heard of the evil doctor, he was reported dead in South America. Which he obviously wasn't, since it was now forty years later, and he was alive and torturing the fuck out of me in North Carolina.

34

I came back to myself in a blast of white-hot agony, and my eyes snapped open as I screamed. I was hanging upside down again, and someone had unhooked my wrists from the chain that had suspended me from the ceiling. My wrists were still bound with thick metal cuffs, cold iron and silver if Gerhard, or Mengele, could be trusted. And why wouldn't I trust a Nazi who looks hardly a third his age? I mean, I look pretty good for a guy well over the century mark, but this guy couldn't have been much more than twenty years younger than me, but he looked forty at most.

He smiled when he saw my eyes open, then his smile stretched even further as something in my face told him I knew who he was. "Good," he said, his voice low and silky, like the velvet glove someone wraps around their iron fist before they beat the fuck out of you with it. "No need for any more pretense, then. You know who I am, and you know what I do."

"You're a Nazi fuckbag who conflates torture with science and has somehow managed to live long past his expiration date. Feel free to cut me down from here and I can help rectify that last part," I said with a snarl. Talking was easier, despite my throat being raw from screaming. Waterboarding is apparently good for hydration, if nothing else.

"And you are a mouthy little devilspawn whose death will barely provide enough genetic material to evoke mild interest, much less any real scientific advancement, and yet I sully my hands with you because of a limited pool of test subjects."

"By limited you mean one, you fuckburger. There's only one of me and you know it. And this one of me is about to fuck up this one of you." I'd been keeping an eye on his salt circle, knowing that it would be hard to keep that intact with all the water he'd been splashing all over me. Sure enough, as he strode over to me, scalpel in hand and cut a diagonal slash from my hipbone to my opposite shoulder, his foot erased the last little bit of salt sealing his circle.

Two things happened simultaneously: my chest erupted in new fire as blood began to cascade from the deep gash across my torso, and I was able to call up magic for the first time in hours. It wasn't anywhere near full strength, and I was a long way from home free, but I could touch power again, and I wrapped my hands around the energy and grabbed hold.

"*Discutio!*" I shouted, pouring all my focus into the cuffs at my wrists and ankles. The silver and cold iron resisted, being naturally magic-resistant metals, but I'm not a vampire, werewolf, or faerie, so the effectiveness of the bindings wasn't what it could be. The metal shattered, and either I put a little more *oomph* into the spell than I thought, or my magic had returned stronger than I expected, because not only did the bindings on my wrists explode, the shackles holding my ankles and the very chain itself shattered, dropping me onto my shoulders and slamming the wind out of me.

It was only sheer luck that Mengele was as startled as I was, and not nearly as motivated to get his shit together quickly. He took one step back and whipped his head from side to side, shouting for help. *BECKS!* I shouted through our mental link, scanning the area for any hint of where she was while I scrambled to my feet.

I'm here, Harker.

Are you hurt? A guard stepped up to me with his stunstick out. That didn't end well for him, as I took it from him and backhanded him unconscious before jamming his overclocked cattle prod into the crotch of the guard running in to help him out.

No...not much, anyway. Some bruises.

Where are you?

Small room. Looks like it was a supply closet. Must be close. I hear the commotion you're causing.

Sit tight. I've got— "Fuck!" I yelled aloud and in my thoughts as Mengele slammed a foot into my knee. I went down, but spun and came right back up, looking for the Nazi motherfucker. I might have missed him in Argentina, but he was not getting away from me this time.

"Get back here, you bastard!" I yelled at his retreating back, but the only answer I got was a couple of rounds from a revolver that he fired behind him as he ran. The shots went wide but distracted me long enough for the guard I zapped in the balls to tackle me.

I slammed to the concrete along one edge of the salt circle, gasping in pain as the salt rubbed into the cuts on my chest. The guard was heavy on my back, but he wasn't much of a fighter, throwing weak punches at the side of my head. He should have asked Flynn, she could have told him hitting me in the head was just going to hurt his hands. I swiveled my legs around, flipped my hips and rolled myself over, throwing salt up into the guard's eyes.

He pawed at his eyes and swatted at me, not being terribly effective at either one, and I slipped out from under him, slamming a knee into the side of his head. His eyes rolled back into his head and he slumped to the ground, out cold. I spared about half a second's concern for the concussion he was going to wake up with, then remembered he was working for a Nazi, so fuck him.

I took off after Mengele, and almost had him when he yanked open a door in the wall ahead of me and fired three shots into the supply closet. I heard a muffled scream, then a *thud* as something fell over in the closet.

Mengele turned to me with a grin on his face and said, "I don't know which one of them was yours, Harker, so I shot them both."

I reached for Flynn in my head, but there was nothing there. It wasn't like she was unconscious. She was just *gone*. I looked at the smoking gun in Mengele's hand, and I was standing in France again. It was 1943, and Anna lay dead in front of me. I felt that same yawning chasm of rage and pain swell up within me, and God help me, I dove right in.

I came to looking at the world through a haze of blood surrounded by screaming. My head hurt like the devil, and my ears were ringing like I was back standing beside the stage at the U2 concert in 2006. I was lying on something lumpy and warm, but I couldn't push myself upright because my hands were bound.

"What the hell?" I said, or tried to say, because my mouth was taped shut. I blinked a few times to clear the blood from my face and rubbed my eyes on the lumpy form beneath me. As my vision cleared, I realized I was rubbing my face on a person's thigh, and I pushed myself upright, trying to apologize, and froze when the lifeless eyes of Keya Pravesh stared back up at me. A neat round hole dominated her forehead, and the last few seconds came flooding back.

The skinny Nazi fucker yanked open the door to the closet where he had us hidden, aimed his pistol into the tiny room, and fired three times. The first shot went wild, the second drilled a hole in Pravesh's head, and the third must have grazed my skull, knocking me out and covering my face in a crimson mask.

My hands were bound with silver duct tape, but they were in front of me, so as soon as I was mostly coherent again, I ripped the tape off my mouth and starting tearing it off my wrists with my teeth. Seconds later, I had my feet free and was cursing the thoroughness of the guards who found and stripped me of the backup gun I had in my ankle holster. I couldn't tell what was going on outside the door, but it sounded real bad, and I would have felt a lot better about going out there with a gun in my hand.

Oh well, nothing for it, I guess, I thought, then stood up. I pressed an ear to the door but couldn't tell where the screams were coming from. It sounded like everywhere. I opened the door a crack to see what was going on, then let it swing free as I realized how fucked the situation really was.

The screams were coming from Harker. Not him, exactly. Not in the sense that he was screaming, but in the sense that he was causing them. There was a guard floating in midair, and he was surrounded by alternating rings of fire, ice, and lightning, each one taking turns tightening around the guard's body, then backing away after a few seconds. When the ring of fire touched him, his clothes caught fire, only to be extinguished as the ice ring shrank around him and bathed him in clouds of steam. Then lightning twined around every inch of his body before the rotation started again and he was bound by flame.

And it was all coming from Harker. My fiancé stood between the closet and the floating guard, and the air around him crackled with wild magic. Power leapt off him in little bursts of light and energy, like nothing I'd ever seen before.

I reached out to him through our link, but I couldn't feel him. My head hurt with the effort, and my vision blurred when I tried, meaning the bullet to the skull rattled my cage more than I thought. I took a step, but my feet were numb from being tied up, and I sprawled across the floor. I reached out to push myself upright and found my hand in something wet and disgusting.

I looked to where my left hand was, and when it registered what I was wrist-deep in, I flopped over on my butt and scooted back, horrified. There was a man there. Or there were parts of a man there, to be more specific. The skinny bastard who shot me and Pravesh was there. Well, his guts, chest, and head were. There were no arms, no legs, and the torso looked like it had been *pulled apart*.

"Jesus Christ, Harker, what the fuck did you do?" I whispered, horror filling my eyes as I scanned the room for the rest of the Nazi parts. I was happy to see him dead, but I did kinda want him in one piece. Or at least not all over my hand.

Another shriek from the guard snapped my attention back to where Harker stood, manipulating raw energy with the wave of his hand. I could feel the power in the air, could feel the magic making the hair on my arms stand up. I could feel it coursing through my veins, dancing along my nerves, and I realized that I wasn't feeling these things, I was feeling Harker feel them. I scrambled to my feet and started toward him.

"Harker!" I yelled. He turned to me, but there was no recognition in his eyes. There was nothing in his eyes but rage and pain, and I could see the magic dancing across his bare chest, see the purple, red, blue, and white streams of power flicker across the cuts in his rippling abs. I couldn't tell if the magic was coming from within him and tearing him apart to get out and destroy the guard and everything else nearby, or if it was coming from everywhere around him lashing at his flesh trying to consume him.

"HARKER!" I screamed at the top of my lungs, limping toward him as fast as my dizzy stumbling ass could manage. There was no reaction from him, just a maniacal grin on his face and bloodlust in his eyes. "HARKER!" I shouted again, closer this time, and still nothing but madness written on the face of the man I love. I was just a few feet away when I bellowed one more time. "QUINCY FUCKING HARKER!"

Nothing.

Fuck.

I took a deep breath and closed my eyes. I still couldn't lock onto him with my thoughts, so I did the only thing I could think of before he killed the guard and destroyed our last clue to where Luke was and who was behind this shit.

I took two steps forward, wrapped my arms around the burning, lightning-wreathed, bloody body of my fiancé, and kissed him.

35

Everything was blood. Everything was blood, and pain, and fury. Everything was rage, and I didn't care. I felt the flesh rending under my fingers as I pulled Mengele's body apart, and I smiled. I felt his blood splash hot and wet and coppery crimson across my face, and I laughed. I felt the power surge through every cell as I called up more magic than I had ever harnessed on my own and wrapped the guard in bands of fire, ice, and lightning, and I reveled in it. Everything was red and black and dark and burning, and I felt at home.

Everything was Hell, and I didn't care. My rage wasn't an emotion; it was an elemental force and I was just riding it. It was a tsunami of torment and death and I surfed it like it was a gentle swell at dawn. My anger and pain didn't consume me, they *became* me. I was my anger, and my anger was me, and there was nothing else. I was pure agony and hate and blind, murderous rage, and I laughed through it all. I felt the magic dance across my skin because even my body couldn't contain everything I drew in, and I couldn't blast it out of me as fast as I called it up, and every inch of my skin was burning and every nerve ending was screaming and all I did was laugh.

Everything was pain, and all I did was laugh. Laugh and kill and laugh and kill and laugh some more. I tore Mengele limb from limb and my only second of regret was when I realized I could only kill him once. I stabbed that guard with javelins of fire and daggers of ice and set his pain alight with forked lightning wrapped around his whole body, and I never wanted his suffering to end.

Because mine never would.

Everything was gone. Everything was pain and fury and blood and murder.

And then she kissed me, and it all went away.

One second I was torturing the guard with all the glee of Darth Vader mixed with Voldemort, and the next second Becks was in my arms, alive, with her lips pressed to mine, and all the power I'd drawn up just…faded away, like nothing had ever happened. The guard dropped to the floor, semi-conscious and writhing in agony, and I looked down at the woman in my arms. The very live woman in my arms.

"Rebecca?" My voice was a whisper. That was all I could manage between the screaming I'd done at the hands of my captor and the shouts of rage I'd cut loose with when I'd thought she was dead. "Is it really you? Or am I just that far gone?"

She pulled back from me and looked up into my eyes, and it was her. Our link was still gone, but there was no one else in the world who'd ever looked at me like that, with love, and exasperation, and humor, and snark, and acceptance. Even Anna hadn't looked at me like that. She'd always had a hint of fear behind her eyes. I don't think she even knew it, but she was a little bit afraid of me, what I meant, and the world I brought to her.

There was no fear in Rebecca Gail Flynn. Not of me, not of demons, not of Nazis that should have been dead decades ago, not of the world's most famous vampire. None of it scared her, and that was just one of the reasons she was amazing.

"Yeah, it's me, stupid. Who else is going to run in and kiss you while you're in full meltdown?" She reached up and touched my face, and the places where her fingers brushed my cheek were the only parts of my body that didn't hurt.

"Yeah, that's probably a short list," I agreed.

"I'd say one name is a short list alright."

"I thought you were dead. I couldn't, *can't*, feel you in my head."

"I think I've got a concussion. When your friend shot us, he grazed my skull. It bled like crazy, and hurts like a mother, but I'm fine. Fine for somebody who's seeing double and wants to puke herself inside out, that is."

"Pravesh?" I asked, but I knew from the look on Becks's face the answer I was going to get.

She didn't say anything, just shook her head.

"Motherfucker," I said, glancing back at the pieces of Mengele. "Now I really wish I could kill him all over again."

"I think that ship has sailed, Harker. You killed the shit out of that guy."

"He deserved it," I said. "You know who that son of a bitch was? Josef fucking Mengele."

"The Nazi? I thought he was dead. I mean, it's been almost seventy-five years, aren't they *all* dead?"

"The originals? Yeah, I thought so. But Mengele was Hitler's chief medical research guy. Maybe he figured something out. Or hell, maybe he found the Fountain of Youth somewhere in South America. But this was the real dude, and he was behind all the experiments on cryptids. I guess he got tired of humans and wanted to fuck with other species."

"You're saying all this is his fault?"

"I don't think all of it. I don't think he could have manipulated an entire government agency, not to this scale. But this little piece of it was his."

"Did he tell you where Luke was?"

I looked down. "I...wasn't in a good place to conduct an interrogation."

"You dismembered first and want to ask questions later? I don't think that's how it works, Harker. Unless you've got a necromancer in your pocket."

"Nah, I'm just happy to see you," I said, and just like that, we were back to our old sparring. I even felt a tickle of her amusement in my head, and then we both stared at each other.

"Did you—"

"Yeah," I cut her off. "I felt it, too."

I...guess...it's...coming back. This time, she spoke mind to mind. It was halting, like a child taking its first steps, but I heard her.

Yeah...thank God, I replied, and hugged her to me again. A groan from the floor cut short our reunion, and I looked down to the guard writhing in pain. "Well, maybe this asshole knows something."

"Sure," Flynn said. "And if he doesn't want to chat, you can always torture him. Oh wait, already done that."

I ignored her. Now that I knew she was alive, and I wasn't in any more of a murderous rage than normal, it was time to focus on getting Luke back. Mourning the fallen Pravesh and dealing with all the shitstorm that a dead government agent was going to bring could come later. I walked over and knelt down beside the guard, who scooted back from me and pressed his back to the nearest wall.

"Please don't hurt me anymore," he whimpered.

"I won't if you don't make me," I said, keeping my voice as reasonable as could be for someone who just came out of a complete fucking psychotic episode. I looked at the nameplate on his uniform. "Okay, Mr. Repode, where is Luke?"

"I don't know," the guard said, tears rolling down his cheeks. "Who's Luke? I don't know anybody named Luke."

"Your bosses might have called him Dracula," Flynn said from over my shoulder.

The guard's eyes widened, and he looked even more terrified, if that was even possible. "I can't. If I tell you where to find him, The Chancellor will have me killed. He'll have my mom killed, and my wife. I can't tell you anything."

Flynn and I shared a look. This was the first we'd heard of anyone calling themselves "The Chancellor." I reached out to pat the guy on the shoulder, but he screamed in pain at my touch. "My bad," I said, pulling my hand back. Turns out when you alternate between fire, ice, and electricity on a person's skin for a few minutes, they don't like being touched.

"Okay," I said, holding up my hands. "No touching. I promise, this Chancellor prick won't find out anything you tell us. We're federal agents; we can protect you from him."

The guard managed to look at me askance, even with his eyebrows burned off and in almost unspeakable amounts of fear. "Are you fucking kidding me? *I'm* a federal agent! Everybody here is a fucking federal agent. How much fucking good do you think that's going to do against the guy who took over DEMON?"

"I thought Director Shaw was running DEMON?" I didn't really care what he said, I just needed to keep the guy talking because as long as he was talking, he could slip up and give me something useful.

"That bitch? Nah, she's the figurehead, but The Chancellor runs things."

"Where is he?" Flynn asked. "Washington?"

"I don't know. Nobody does. Shaw's the only one who ever sees him. That's how she keeps the others in line, by keeping everyone away from the boss. And she's got a bunch of people all over the country working for her, or even pretending to *be* her, so nobody's ever really sure if they're dealing with the real Shaw or one of the fake Shaws. Some dude in Atlanta pretending to be a Shaw, some Asian guy in New York posing as a Shaw, another one in LA. There's fucking fake Shaws all over the country with different names, different faces, but they all report back to the real bitch." His eyes widened as he realized he'd been babbling for nearly a full minute. "Goddammit. I said too much. Just fucking kill me. If you do it quick, maybe he won't know I told you anything." His eyes kept flicking over my right shoulder, to a steel door with several heavy locks. He caught my eye and stared pointedly in that direction.

"We're not going to kill you," Flynn said, putting a hand on my shoulder and holding out a pair of handcuffs. "We're going to take you into custody, and we'll protect your family."

The guard shook his head violently, then reached for a knife at his side. He drew the blade and made a feeble stab at me. I twisted his wrist around behind him, plucked the knife from his grip, and pulled him away from the wall. I buried the little blade between two ribs and drew the guard in close.

I held him in a fierce hug as the knife pierced his heart, and as he died, I whispered in his ear, "We'll keep your family safe, and when I kill The Chancellor, I'll tell him you said hello."

The last breath rattled out of the guard's mouth and he slumped against my shoulder. I pushed him off me and stood up, my knees popping like firecrackers. Flynn was standing there with her arms folded over her chest, glaring at me.

"You didn't have to kill him."

"Yeah, I really did. If I didn't kill him, this Chancellor fucker was going to kill everybody he gave a shit about, so if you want to look for a good guy reason, it's a stretch, but I think you can make that enough. Or if you want to think of a bad guy reason, he was a corrupt piece of shit who helped imprison and torture sentient beings for no other reason than they existed. And he worked for the goddamn Angel of Death, Josef fucking Mengele. I'm not sure if that's a good guy reason to kill him or a bad guy reason to kill him, but it's my reason for killing him, and I won't lose a minute's sleep over Officer Fuckwit Repode. Now let's see what's behind Door Number Three."

I gestured toward the door Repode was eye-fucking in the last moments of his life, but Flynn wasn't paying me any attention. She was staring back over my shoulder at the supply closet where she'd been shot. I turned to follow her gaze and froze at the sight that greeted me there.

Director Keya Pravesh was walking toward us without a scratch on her, grinning like a cat with a canary in its clutches.

"What?" she asked as she reached us. "You think you're the only one who gets to come back from the dead?"

36

"P ravesh?" Flynn reached out to touch the other woman's shoulder, as if to confirm she was real. "You were dead. Bullet in the face and everything."

"Yeah," Pravesh said. "That sucked. But I'm a lot harder to kill than most people."

"Probably because you're not a people," I said. I held up both hands as she whipped her head over to me. "Hey, I'm not judging. I'm not human either, remember?"

"It's starting to feel like I might be the only person I know who isn't supernatural. Unless there's something about myself that you two want to tell me?" Flynn asked.

"Nah, you're human, babe. Trust me, I'd know if you weren't," I said. Then I looked at Pravesh. "Admittedly, up until two minutes ago I would have said that about her, so take anything I say with a grain of salt. Go ahead and spill it, Pravesh. What are you?"

"What makes you think I'm not a human with an extraordinary healing factor?"

"Because you look fucking nothing like Hugh Jackman, which pretty much takes Wolverine off the table," I said, opening my Sight to look at her in the magical spectrum. Nothing, just like every other time I'd used Sight around her. As far as everything I could determine told me, she was perfectly human.

"I'm a naga," she said. "No one in DHS knows. No one anywhere in the government knows, and I'd like it to stay that way if possible."

"I think if you want to keep it hush-hush that you're a supernatural being, maybe don't come back to life after taking a bullet to the face," I said. "How exactly did you manage that, by the way? I don't know a whole lot about nagas, but the last thing I heard y'all have snake tails. I don't remember anything about immortality."

"I'm not immortal," she said. "And in my natural form my lower body is in fact serpentine. As for how I kept from dying…I shed my skin."

"Did you shed your brain, too? Because that was a bullet hole in your skull, Pravesh. It wasn't a tattoo you wanted removed," Flynn said.

"It's complicated, but it boils down to this: in order to truly kill me, my heart and brain must both be destroyed. As long as either survives, my soul does too. And if my soul survives, I just need to shed the dead skin and manifest a new one. It's not enjoyable, it's very painful, and very messy, but it does in fact result in me surviving gunshots to the head. Or chest."

"But not both," I said.

"Right," she said with a nod.

"How do you know that?" Flynn asked. "That doesn't seem like the kind of thing that you can just randomly figure out."

"Oh it isn't, trust me. No, I found out the hard way. My uncle was hunted and killed for his scales in India many years ago. Most of my kind were hunted to extinction, in fact. But Uncle Vati was the only one I saw up close afterward. His head had been severed and his heart ripped out. Many hunters believed the rumors that we have fangs hidden in our mouths and poison glands, so they take our heads. And hearts, well, you know all the lore involved with eating the heart of something you kill."

"Yeah," I said. "How long ago was that? I haven't heard of any naga in decades."

Pravesh dropped her eyes. "It was a long time ago. Can we leave it at that?"

I nodded. "Yeah. It doesn't really matter, I guess. Are you good to go now that you're in your new suit of skin?"

"It will take a few hours for all the muscles to settle into place. I shouldn't try to shoot straight for a little while, but otherwise I'm fine. Better than you, probably." She ran her eyes up and down my front, and I suddenly remembered that I was standing there mostly naked and covered in gore.

"Most of the blood isn't mine," I said. Then I thought about what I'd just said. "That doesn't really make it sound much better, does it?"

"No, not really. But are you hurt? From what I can see of you, it looks like they worked on you with knives for quite a while."

"Knives, electrical shock, blowtorches, lemon juice, salt, scalpels, the whole nine yards," I replied. "The only thing they didn't try was bad karaoke."

"Good thing, too," Flynn said. "Nobody can stand up to that shit. Let's get this door open and get Luke back, then we can get out of here and you can get in the shower."

"You'd better steal a car to get home, Harker. There is no way you're getting in my Suburban with pieces of intestine in your hair," Pravesh said.

I plucked the offending Nazi chunk off my scalp and tossed it to the floor. "Let's find Luke, then we can worry about me getting an Uber while I look like an extra from a horror movie."

I walked over to the door the dead guard couldn't keep his eyes off of and pressed an ear against it. There was something moving on the other side, but I couldn't tell if it was one creature or more, and whatever was over there, they weren't talking. I knocked on the door. "Luke, you in there?"

The door shook in its frame as something massive slammed into the other side of it. The door was solid metal, in a reinforced frame, and I saw the concrete beside the door begin to buckle as whatever was on the other side battered the fuck out of the door trying to get out.

"I'm pretty sure that's not Luke," I said.

"I'm pretty sure that wall isn't going to hold much longer," Pravesh said.

One of us was right, as the door and frame broke free and slammed to the concrete. I was wrong, however, because the creature that sprawled on the door as it hit the floor was Luke, but it was a Luke I'd never seen before. His hair was wild, sticking up in all directions. His clothes, usually immaculate, were torn to rags and stained with blood and worse. His skin was even paler than normal, but the worst of it was his eyes.

His eyes, usually full of some variation on humor or disdain, rolled wildly in their sockets before finally focusing on the three of us standing there dumbstruck. There was only one thing left in those eyes, and it was no human emotion. No, the only thing the Luke that crouched before me knew was hunger, pure and simple.

"Fuck me, they've starved him," I said. I turned to Flynn. "Run!" I shouted.

Then Dracula charged at me and I had to fight my uncle for my life.

I've sparred with Luke before. Luke was the first person to really teach me how to fight and had a lot to do with the mixed brawling, combat, and martial arts style that my version of scrapping and ass-kicking developed into. We've gone at each other pretty hard over the years, but I've never thrown down with Luke when he wanted to *kill* me.

And I never want to again. It's fucking terrifying. The vampire that came at me in that warehouse wasn't the stern man who took on the role of a grandfather to me in the years when my father was learning how to deal with the fame that came from starring in Stoker's book. This wasn't the man I'd stayed up with through many nights debating theology and magical theory over many, many glasses of good wine, which despite rumors to the contrary, he very much drinks. This wasn't the man who had stood by my side in more fights than I could count.

No, this was the monster that inspired nightmares all over Europe for centuries. This was the monster from which all modern movie monsters were born. This was Dracula, the motherfucking King of the Vampires, and he wanted to rip my head off.

I was tired, in pain, barefoot, and unarmed, but that didn't matter. I had a bugshit crazy vampire coming at me, and for once, I didn't want to kill him. This was going to take a lot more thought than most of my fights, which usually boil down to "nuke it from orbit" as a strategy.

Luke came at me at a dead run, and I barely got out of the way of his outstretched claws. He was fully vamped out, with black eyes, fangs out, fingernails extended in long, hooked claws, and not a shred of sanity anywhere about him. That was my only edge—I was the slightest bit less insane than he was.

Get the fuck out of here! I shouted to Flynn. *Get behind Pravesh and get out of here. Close the door if you can.*

We can help.

No, you really can't. This is Luke at his worst. He's completely feral, and I don't know how I'm going to get him back. If he gets through me, he'll kill you both. Now go! I shut our link down to a trickle so I could concentrate on the task at hand.

That task was coming at me again, fangs out and ready to rip through my carotid. I called magic and blasted pure force into Luke's chest, but after everything I'd been through already, I didn't have enough power to stagger him, much less take him down. And it felt like there was still something interfering in my connection to the magic, like static on the line or something. I was outside the circle, but there was still something making it difficult to draw as much magic as normal, even taking into account my exhaustion and injuries. When I was berserk and thought Flynn was dead, I blew through whatever barrier existed, which only left me feeling even more raw and wrung out when she brought me back to myself.

I didn't have a lot of time to ponder it because Luke was on me again. This time he ducked below the energy blast I chucked at him and slammed a shoulder into my stomach. I fell to the floor, my back and head slamming into the concrete. Stars shot through my vision, and I retched a little. There was nothing to come up, and no time to puke, so I just spit bile out to the side and grabbed Luke by the hair.

I pulled his face back from me with my left hand and slammed my right fist into his temple. His eyes crossed momentarily, but he recovered in an instant to punch me in the chin and star my vision again. I twisted in his grip and slammed an elbow down onto the crown of his skull, stunning him just long enough to wriggle out from under him. I made it to one knee before he lunged at me again, just throwing himself along the floor with his legs, not even bothering to stand. I had the advantage of leverage, so I used his momentum to spin and fling him across the room.

He spun like a lanky frisbee and skittered across the floor before springing back to his feet and rushing at me again. This time I didn't bother to try to get out of his way; I just called up as big a shield as I could, and when he slammed into it, I bent the energy around him into a cage. I surrounded Luke with a cylinder of pure force, giving me a precious few seconds to catch my breath.

Concentrating on holding the shield in place, I stepped back from the raging vampire. "Luke!" I shouted, but no reaction. He just roared and slammed his fists into the walls of my impromptu cage hard enough to make the energy flicker and threaten to surge back into me.

"LUKE!" Nothing. "VLAD! GODDAMMIT, VLAD! WAKE THE FUCK UP!" This time I poured power into the walls of his prison, and when he slammed his fists into it again, he took a hefty jolt of electricity. It didn't faze him, but splitting my focus like that fucked up my concentration, and his hammer blow into the walls of the cage shattered the walls and sent magic arcing back into me.

I dropped to my knees as the backlash knocked me dizzy, and barely registered Luke leaping for me. In a moment of pure desperation, I latched onto the one idea that might bring him back to himself. As he came at me, I slid to the left, just enough to make him clip my shoulder and not knock me completely ass over teakettle. He hit me, I spun around, and as I did, I wrapped my right arm around his throat and leapt onto his back, riding him to the floor.

Luke pushed off with his hands as I slammed him to the concrete, and we both flipped over, me pinned beneath him. I wrapped my legs around his middle to hold him tight, and with a quick prayer that this was going to work, I jammed my free wrist across his mouth, pressing the veins into his teeth. I felt the sharp sting as his fangs pierced my flesh, then the world fell away in a feedback loop of magic, shared blood, and centuries-long possession as Luke tried to feed from me, and the demon that lived in both of us went absolutely apeshit.

37

I 've fed from Luke before, and it didn't have any kind of adverse effects. In fact, it saved my life on more than one occasion. But in all the years we've traveled together, Luke never needed to feed from me. Chalk that up to him being less impetuous and generally less likely to be near death than me, so we'd never had to see what would happen. But ever since learning that the source of Luke's, and by extension all, vampirism is a demon that lives partially inside Luke, I'd been wondering what would happen if we tried to go upstream, as it were.

I thought there were basically two options. Either the spark of demon that lived in me would join back with the piece that lives in Luke and I would be drained completely and left human, probably dying in the process, or the piece of the demon that lived in me for over a century would have developed some tiny chunk of sentience on its own, and would fight against being reabsorbed, and the chunks of demonic essence within each of us would fight like hell to defend their territory.

Fortunately, if anything in this shitshow could be called fortunate, the latter is what happened. When the infernal essence in me recognized the shard of demon soul living in Luke, each little piece of demon soul basically created a fuckton of magical antibodies, and our souls' hitchhikers fought each other for control of both bodies. But Luke was too starved to put up much of a fight, and I was too beat up and drained, so after we rolled around on the floor screaming for a minute or two, the demonic essences within us retreated to their little corners of our souls, and left Luke and I lying on our backs side by side, panting with exertion and pain.

I'd never been conscious of the demon that lived within me before, but now I could feel the little fucker, huddled in one of the many dark recesses of my psyche, licking its wounds and plotting, always plotting, to get me to do something terrible. Like I needed any fucking help doing awful shit. I had that shit pretty well covered without a demon's help.

After a few seconds of panting and staring at the ceiling, I managed to croak out a weak, "Well, that sucked."

"Quincy?" Luke's voice was thin and reedy, like it was barely strong enough to push past his lips.

"Yeah, it's me," I said, rolling up onto one elbow. Luke still hadn't moved, and he had that preternatural stillness that makes vampires creepy as fuck. "You gonna try to kill me again?"

"Did I?" Luke asked, turning his head. "I'm sorry, Quincy. I haven't been myself the last few days. Please accept my apology."

"Don't sweat it," I said, struggling to my feet. "We learned something from it, anyway."

"Yes, what was that?" Luke asked. "That even the strongest mind can be subverted by enough torture and starvation?" He struggled to rise, and with effort, made it to a sitting position.

"Nah, that's not it. We knew that already. I'm an expert on subverting one's mind. No, we learned that our demons have grown independent since part of your little devil started growing in me, and they don't want to go back together."

"Is that how you shook me free of the bloodlust?"

"Yeah," I said. "I had you feed from me. It didn't take. Hurt like a bitch. Snapped you out of your hunger, though."

"It may have brought me back to myself, but I am still well and truly starved, Quincy. I am too weak to even stand."

"That's okay," I said, standing up. "We've got a donor for you right over here." I pointed to the guard's corpse.

"He's dead," Luke said, holding up a hand.

I helped him to his feet, then walked him over to Repode. "Yeah, but just a few minutes ago. Everything should still be warm enough. Besides, this is the only human here that you can feed on. It's not exactly a buffet. This is the only option on the menu."

"Then let me down here, but I would ask a favor." I lowered Luke to his knees by the dead guard.

"Sure, anything," I said, taking a step back.

"I smell Rebecca and Director Pravesh. I assume they accompanied you here?"

I nodded.

"Please keep them away while I restore some of my strength. I would rather they not see me feed from a corpse like some type of scavenger."

I was surprised at the delicacy of Luke's self-image, but it made a kind of sense when I thought about it. He was royalty, then a gentleman, for centuries, and the appearance of decorum would be very important to him. He and I had seen each other at our best and worst over the years, but there was enough of either chivalry or chauvinist left in him to not want to show any weakness in front of the "ladies," despite their strength and capability. He probably wouldn't mind Pravesh seeing him feed if he knew she was a naga, but maybe he would. Hell, for all I knew he'd been aware of her nature all along.

"Not a problem," I said, walking toward a door in the far wall. I could sense Flynn on the other side of it, so I let her know I was coming through, and not to shoot me.

"Is he okay?" Becks asked as I pulled the door shut behind me.

"He will be. He's got to feed right now, and he asked that you two not watch. I think he wants to maintain an aura of invincibility or something like that."

"I get that," Flynn said. "He's a product of a different time, after all."

"Why don't I get that kind of consideration when I forget to put the toilet seat down?" I asked.

"Oh, I consider it," she replied. "That's just not going to stop me yelling at you when I sit down in cold water in the middle of the night."

I didn't have any response to that one, so I let it go. It just felt like the safest course of action.

A few minutes later, a much more hale and hearty Luke joined us. His color, what there ever was of it, was better, and he was walking much better. Which means he was walking at all. I looked him over, marveling at how much a little sustenance restored him. He still looked gaunt, and his clothes were torn in places, and his shoes were missing entirely, but given that he was taken while sleeping, he may not have been wearing any.

"Better?" I asked.

"Much, thank you. I appreciate your coming to my aid, but I fear there is something larger than me at stake here."

"Oh yeah," I said. "There totally is." We filled him in on DEMON, the facility we found, the cryptids we had dealt with throughout the city and the ones that were still on the loose, and finished up by telling him how we'd been kidnapped and brought here.

"And by the way," I added. "The crazy doctor? Josef Mengele. The real one."

"I thought he was dead," Luke said.

"He is now," I replied.

"A lot," Becks added.

"Was that..." Luke gestured over his shoulder to the mess in the other room.

"Yeah," I said. "I went a little nuts. It's been the day for it."

"Truer words, Quincy," Luke said, a shadow passing over his face. "Truer words..."

"Now what?" Pravesh asked. "The doors leading out of this room are locked, and all we have for weapons are a couple of handguns Detective Flynn and I retrieved from the guards." The room we were in was a storage room about twenty by forty. Much smaller than the massive warehouse where they had tortured me, but larger than where Luke was held, and a lot bigger than the supply closet where they'd kept Flynn and Pravesh.

"Locked doors aren't going to be much of a problem," I said. "I want out of this fucking building, and I'm going to *get* out of this fucking building. We've got Luke back, we took out the mad scientist, Walston is dead, so she's off the table, and most of the worst of the cryptids have been apprehended. I think we can call this a win."

"Except for one big thing," Flynn said.

"What's that?" I asked.

"Who killed Walston? And is that the same person that brought us here? Because there is no way those two guards and Mengele dropped all three of us, loaded us into a vehicle, and got us out of police headquarters without being seen. That took a lot more people than we've seen here."

I thought back to the abduction. "Yeah, you're right. There were at least six people, and there was a woman in charge."

"Did you recognize her?" Flynn asked.

"There was a woman giving orders the day they abducted me as well," Luke said.

"I'm gonna go out on a limb here and say the mystery woman is this Director Shaw we've been hearing about. Now we just need to know where she is, and where are the rest of the bad guys?" Pravesh asked.

"And what's fucking with my magic?" I added. When everyone looked at me, I explained. "There's something interfering with my magic. It's not like a circle, or if it is, it's not a very strong one. When Mengele and his goons were torturing me, they had me bound in a salt ring. That cut off all connection to magic. This isn't like that. I can still call power, but it's like there's interference. Something's trying to block me but can't quite manage it. Like a signal jammer, for lack of a better description."

"Do you feel anything?" Becks asked Pravesh.

"No. I do not use magic in the same way as Harker. I am *of* magic, but I cannot manipulate energy in that way."

"They know?" Luke asked. Pravesh nodded, and Luke said, "Good. It is always so confusing, trying to keep track of who knows what. Honesty really is the best policy, I find."

I didn't bother to correct the guy who literally spent centuries living under a false identity about his lack of honesty, I just started walking the room trying doors. They were all locked, except the door leading back the way we came. There were two doors that appeared to lead outside, if the red EXIT signs over them could be trusted, and one that looked as though it led into another part of the building. Maybe an office area.

"What do we want to do?" I asked the others. "Blow out the exit door and try to get home, with no real idea of where we are, what kind of resources we have for escape, or what will be after us as we try to get out of here? Or take Door Number Three and see if there's an office somewhere that can get us more information on who we're dealing with and how to neutralize them?"

As I gestured to it, the interior door, the one I'd dubbed Door Number Three, swung open and a small canister flew through to clatter at my feet. I recognized it for what it was and dove on the flash bang just before it went off, slamming an incredible amount of concussive force into my ribs and reminding me of every single second of torture I'd endured in the last two days.

I rolled over onto my back, a steady stream of profanity pouring from my lips as I watched a six-person tactical team pour through the door with their guns at the ready. They all froze as they realized that we weren't blinded and stunned by the flash bang, then a female voice yelled, "Kill them all!" from the other room, and everything went apeshit.

3 8

I yelled, "Try not to kill them!" then rolled back onto my hands and knees and pushed myself up. I looked up into the barrel of an MP-5 submachine gun, and dove forward, sprawling on my stomach on the floor and taking the DEMON agent in front of me down at the knees. I heard a *crack* from his left leg as we went down, and he screamed as he crashed to the floor. I crawled up his body and slammed an elbow into his jaw, knocking him silly for an instant.

"Stay the fuck down!" I yelled in his face, then pushed myself up to my feet. I reached down and snatched the gun away from him, pulling the sling over his head and arm. Then I punched him in the jaw again and spun around to the others, submachine gun in hand.

Luke was a blur of motion, disarming agents and slapping them to the ground. Flynn and Pravesh snatched up the discarded weapons and stood over the now empty-handed agents with their guns leveled at their heads. In less than a minute, all six DEMON agents were lying facedown on the floor with their hands bound behind them.

I pushed the end of a broken rib back into place with a sickening *crunch*, took a painful breath, and stumbled through the door into the room where I'd heard the woman's voice ordering the agents to kill us. She was gone, of course, but this was the first room that didn't look like an abandoned warehouse. This was a small office, with a desktop computer, a couple of chairs, and a picture of the President on the wall. I spared a second to look around but saw nothing immediately useful, like a rocket launcher or a Potion of Greater Healing. I headed through the far door, feeling a bit better now that my rib wasn't trying to poke its way out my back through my lung.

The next door opened into a lab much like the one where I'd met Tim and the doggos, only smaller. There were a couple of lab tables, three or four microscopes, and a large fridge with "SAMPLES" on the front in block letters. There was a door standing ajar in the opposite wall, and a closed door to my right. If this place was anything like the other testing facility, the open door led into a kennel for cryptids, and the wooden door to the right led into the hall. I looked from one to the other, trying to decide where the woman went, when I heard a crash of metal from the holding pens.

"Guess that answers that," I muttered, pushing the door all the way open and stepping into a darkened room, dimly illuminated by the glow from a pair of red LED exit signs. This was a big room, almost the size of the warehouse where I was tortured, dominated by rows of cages big enough to rightly be called cells. "Jesus Christ," I muttered. "How many of these fucking places do they have?"

I charged into the maze of cells as the smell of rot and waste assaulted my nose. Everywhere I looked, there were creatures dead in their cells. Some obviously tortured to death, some starved, some dead of no cause I could see. But they were all dead. I passed a dozen cages, giant constructs of steel and concrete, and everywhere I looked was another dead cryptid. Lycanthropes in mid-change, vampires so emaciated they made Nosferatu look like a Jenny Craig ad, faeries curled up as far as they could get from the cold iron surrounding them on all sides, just a lump of dead magic lying in the center of the cell. It was disgusting, it was heartbreaking, and it was enough to make a good man insane with rage.

I'm not all that good, so it made me downright *murderous*. It made me furious enough to be distracted, so when I came to the end of another row and saw a cage door standing open in front of me, I didn't think anything about it. Until the Sasquatch stepped through the open door and ran straight at me.

"Stop!" I yelled, reaching out to call power. My connection to the magic flickered again, but I managed to get a half-powered blast of energy thrown at the creature's chest before he slammed into me and lifted me up over his head. I looked down at the floor nearly ten feet away and tried to focus on the magic. I wrapped myself in a sphere of energy as the Sasquatch slammed me down, and the magic shielded me from being smeared across the concrete. I rolled away from the enraged creature and clambered to my feet, pulling myself up on the bars of a nearby cell.

"Hey!" I yelled. "Back the fuck off! I'm one of the good guys!" He either didn't hear me or was too far gone to give a shit because the Sasquatch just stepped forward and punched me in the chest with one giant fist.

I folded in on the punch, trying like hell to absorb some of the impact and keep him from rebreaking my ribs. The punch lifted me off my feet, and I flew back a couple yards before slamming into the concrete once more. I swear it was starting to feel like I should just save time and lay down at the beginning of every fight. I reached out to call power and create a shield, but whatever was interfering with my spellcasting kicked in again, and the disk of energy I surrounded my arm with flickered out after one punch. I ducked the next wild swing but caught a knee in the face as I dropped my head.

I staggered back, then dodged right as a massive fist pulverized the cinderblock where my skull had been a second before. I dashed away from the rampaging cryptid, looking down the rows of cells for the mystery woman who started this mess. I reached a door marked "EXIT," but it was locked tight. I leaned on the crash bar, but there was something jammed against the door from the outside, and it was more than I could move in my weakened state.

I felt the creature's presence behind me and spun around, knocking aside its fist and kicking the monster right in its oversized balls. It dropped to its knees, and I slammed my fist into its nose, sending streams of blood cascading down its hairy face. I punched the

Sasquatch again and again, trying to hit it just hard enough to inca-
pacitate it, but not do any lasting damage.

I shouldn't have worried about that because after my third
punch, the Sasquatch leapt to its feet again, grabbed me by the
tattered waistband of my jeans, and flung me down the corridor. I
smacked into the tiled floor and slid for a couple feet before I
managed to slow my flight and start clawing my way back to my
feet. I was running on fumes. Everything I'd been through in the
past twelve hours was catching up to me. The torture, the berserker
rage, the fight with Luke, the flashbang to the chest...all of it
combined with whatever was interfering with my magic to leave me
on my last legs.

But I was still standing, no matter how wobbly I was. I dragged
myself up and spit a gobbet of blood onto the floor. "Come at me,
motherfucker," I said, my voice ragged even to my own ears. "You
want to dance, let's fucking dance."

The Sasquatch grinned, then reared back and let out a howl of
challenge that made my ears ring all over again. It stalked toward me,
its eyes locked on mine and its fists opening and closing with every
step. It was just about five feet from me when I heard something from
the other side of the wall. Something completely unexpected, that
should really never be heard inside a building.

I heard a car engine, and it was getting louder as it approached. I
called up as much power as I could wrap my mystical fingers around
and enveloped myself in a shield just as the cinderblock wall erupted
in a shower of shattered bricks and dust. A black Suburban buried
itself in the building, driving a wedge between me and the Sasquatch.
I gaped at the obsidian face of Faustus grinning at me from the
passenger seat, then things got completely bizarre as I realized that
Jack Watson was driving.

I watched in shock as Watson rolled the driver's window down
and calmly leveled a pistol at the stunned cryptid standing beside his
car. He emptied the magazine into the Sasquatch, then gestured for
Faustus to roll his window down. Watson leaned forward and said,
"Sorry I'm late. Got held up in Customs. But your dark-skinned friend

here said he could find you, but couldn't get in. Looks like it really is better late than never, eh?"

I stared at the grinning Brit and just burst out laughing. The back doors of the Suburban opened, and Glory and Jo hopped out. Glory came over to me, concern on her face. "Are you okay? I lost contact with you when they brought you into the building, but something doesn't look right about you now."

"How could you lose contact? I thought that was the whole job?" I asked.

Glory looked chagrined. "Did you have any trouble using magic in here? And does it feel easier now?"

I reached out to call power, and it did feel better. My connection to the magic felt stronger, and my bond with Becks was clearer, too. "Yeah to both. What was the deal?"

"There was a trio of witches on the roof maintaining a circle. The entire building was ringed with salt, and the witches were chanting continuously," Glory said.

"Until Glory got here," Jo said. "Then they weren't chanting anymore. Your girl messed those witches *up*."

I cocked an eyebrow at the angel, who flushed slightly. "I take my job seriously, and I really don't like anyone interfering with that. I may have been a little overzealous in persuading them to stop what they were doing."

"Did you persuade any of them to death?" I asked.

"No!" she almost shouted. "That's beyond the pale, Harker. I don't kill humans if I can help it."

"Well then you're doing a lot better than me today," I said. "Although to be fair, killing a hundred-year-old Nazi doesn't really count. He was supposed to be dead a long time ago."

The looks they gave me were priceless, but I didn't have the strength to stand around jawing about it. "Did you see a woman running away from the building when you came in?" I asked.

"No, but the driver of the car that almost smashed into us in the parking lot might have been female," Watson said.

"Fuck," I muttered. "That means she got away, and I don't know a goddamn thing about her."

"I can probably help with that," Jo said. "I've found some very interesting documents using the CMPD computers to snoop around in DEMON's databases. But that can wait until we're home and you've had a chance to put on pants that cover more than a Speedo."

I looked down at the scraps of denim that used to be my jeans, and they looked a lot like what you'd expect pants to look like when the wearer had been tortured, attacked by a vampire, blown up, shot at, and beaten to a pulp by Bigfoot. In other words, it was a good thing I have nice legs.

"And let's get you into a shower, too," Glory said. "What the hell is that all over you?"

"Nazi parts," I said. "Nazi parts and concrete dust. I'm thinking about making it into a new cologne. I'm going to call it Eau de Kickass."

"It smells more like Eau de Asshole," Glory said. "Maybe we can find a hose before we try to get you into the car."

"We're gonna need another car, anyway. The four of us won't fit in there with you guys," I pointed out.

"Four?" Jo looked at me. "Did you find him?"

"Yes, Joanna." Luke's voice came from the end of the row of cells where we all stood. "They did indeed find me. Now can we please go home? I would very much like to never see the inside of this place again."

So home we went, but the whole drive I kept hearing the woman's voice ordering the DEMON agents to kill us all. Who was she, and was this the last we'd see of her? No way I could be that lucky.

EPILOGUE

Two hours later we were all showered, dressed in clean clothes, and gathered around the remnants of a huge delivery from Fuel Pizza, scattered all across the conference table. I popped the last garlic knot in my mouth and swigged a last mouthful of a NoDa Brewing Company Radio Haze Pale Ale. "Okay, now that I feel a little more like a human, what have you got, Jo?"

"All the relevant emails on Walston's phone seem to come from the same person, the infamous Director Adrienne MacDonald Shaw. It looks like she came to DEMON about a year and a half ago, and immediately shifted their role from a contain and observe policy to a hunt down a destroy policy. She reduced the research budget to all but zero and raised the weapons and containment facility budgets fivefold."

"Okay, this Director Shaw really didn't like cryptids. What else do we know? A home address, maybe?" Flynn asked.

"Nothing even close to that good," Jo said. "Director Pravesh's boss got me into DEMON's records, but every shred of personal information about Shaw has been scrubbed. We don't know where she came from, where she lives, we don't even know what office she worked out of, just that she wasn't based at headquarters in DC. She apparently roamed the country looking for hot spots and the most powerful creatures of legend, and either captured or killed them."

"Classy," I said.

"But risky," Luke chimed in. "If the majority of the creatures she hunted were near my power level, there was tremendous danger of getting her people killed."

"Fuck," I said. "Do we have anything useful?"

"Yes," Jo said, turning a laptop around to show me the screen. "This email exchange seems to be between Shaw and someone with an IP address in London, and it references a specific book of spells."

"I know that book," I said. "I think I *have* that book." I got up and hurried across the hall to my apartment and walked over to the book-case in the far corner of the den. I waved a hand over the front of it, dispelling the glamour on the books. The hardback Stephen King collection vanished, leaving the real spines of my arcane library visible. I found the book referenced in the email, pulled it down, and carried it back to my waiting friends.

"What spell is it?" I asked, setting the book down on the conference table.

"I didn't know you had a copy of Haynes' grimoire," Luke said.

"Picked it up on a case about ten years back. The former owner didn't need it anymore."

"Did you kill him, Harker?" Flynn asked. "Because I really don't want to know if you killed him."

"Don't worry," I said. "I totally didn't kill him."

"Good," she said, her shoulders relaxing.

"The hell wasps I summoned killed him." At her look, I said, "It doesn't take very many. You think regular yellowjackets are assholes? Imagine what a yellowjacket with the intelligence of a husky and more venom than a brown recluse can do."

"Goddammit, Harker," Becks said, putting her face in her hands. "Murder is bad, remember? We went over this."

"There's murder, and there's killing, babe," I said. "This totally fell into the latter category. The guy was into kiddie porn, and he was kidnapping little kids and selling them to cambion and demons for…

reasons. He was selling them for reasons, and we don't need to go into details about those reasons. But he's dead, and I'm not going to lose any sleep over it."

"Okay," Flynn said. "You can murder child molesters. That's okay."

"And Nazis," I said. "I get to murder any Nazis I find, right?"

"Yeah, fuck those guys," Flynn agreed.

"And—"

"Quit while you're ahead."

I shut up. I'd mention the need to rid the world of people who take up two parking spaces because they don't want their car to get scratched later. But they totally deserve it too. "Okay, Jo. What spell am I looking for?"

"The email doesn't say what the spell is, but it does give a page number. Three sixty-four."

I opened the book and flipped to the page she called out. "Oh, this isn't good," I said.

"How not good?" Becks asked.

"Pretty damn not good," I replied. "This is a spell to follow an entire bloodline to its end and eradicate any person sharing blood with the spell's target."

"Yeah," Faustus said. "That's pretty hardcore."

"It's more than that," Pravesh said. Everyone looked at her. "With the equipment in that laboratory, they were working on extracting DNA from cryptids. Once they had samples of each species' genetic material, it would only take a minor reworking of the spell to eliminate any creature sharing DNA with the spell's target."

"Wait a minute," I said. "That's not possible. You can't just…" My words trailed off as my brain caught up to my mouth and I thought the mechanics of it through. I reread the spell, and my stomach began to heave. I reached over to Flynn's glass of water and downed half of it in one gulp. Puking averted, I looked around the table. "She's right. You can change a couple of words in this spell, use the DNA as a focus, and one spell could destroy every cryptid that shares genes with the DNA sample."

"If you use Sasquatch DNA?" Jo asked.

I nodded. "No more Bigfoot sightings."

"What about vampires?" Flynn asked.

"I don't know. They aren't cryptids; they're magical creatures. Infernal, to be specific. So it might not work. Or it might, since all vampires are linked by Skyffrax, at least a tiny bit."

"Well, they got more than enough blood from Luke while they had him captive," Watson said.

"And me," I added. "If Luke's blood works, mine would too, and they got plenty of mine too."

"Fuck," Pravesh said. "We have to assume they have samples from every type of creature they had in any detainment center anywhere. What now? Are we going to start seeing mass extermination of magical beings any minute now?"

"No," I said. "There's more to the spell than just blood and words. There are components she'll need, and the spell must be cast by an inherently magical creature. A human can't cast it. Shaw will need to persuade or bribe a cryptid or a demon to cast it for her. That's a small blessing."

"Not really," Jo said, scrolling down on the laptop's trackpad. "Walston pointed that out to her in an email, and she tells her that part is handled."

"Does she have a magical creature on hand that is mad enough to commit genocide?" Luke asked.

"Not exactly," Jo said. "According to this email, Shaw can cast the spell herself because she's inherently magical."

"Seriously? What is she?" Flynn asked.

"Reading between the lines, I'd guess she's a succubus."

"Jesus Christ," I muttered. "The head of DEMON is a demon. That's so fucking apropos I can't stand it."

"Now what?" Flynn asked. "We have no idea where she went, and we have no idea what kind of resources she has at her disposal."

"But we know what she's looking for," I said. "Because there aren't many copies of this book out there, and Shaw didn't have a whole lot of time to grab library books when she ran out of her lair last night. So someone needs to go secure any magical texts in that building, and the rest of us need to get started finding the components for this spell and making sure Shaw doesn't get her hands on them."

"Sounds like we're off on a scavenger hunt," Faustus said.

"Yeah," I agreed. "One where entire species' lives are at stake. Let's get some rest tonight, gang. Tomorrow we have to save the world. Again."

TO BE CONTINUED

If you enjoyed this book, please leave a review on Amazon, Goodreads, or wherever you like.

To make sure you don't miss any of the ongoing Quincy Harker adventures, please join my mailing list at https://www.subscribepage.com/g8d0a9.

You can get some free short stories just for signing up, and whenever a book gets 50 reviews, the author gets a unicorn. I need another unicorn. The ones I have are getting lonely. So please leave a review and get me another unicorn!

ACKNOWLEDGMENTS

Thanks as always to Melissa McArthur for all her help, and for trying in vain to teach me where the commas go.

The following people help me bring this work to you by their Patreon-age. You can join them at Patreon.com/johnhartness.

Sean Fitzpatrick
Missy Walston
Vikki Harraden
Amanda Justice
Mark Ferber
Andy Bartalone
Sharon Moore
Wendy Taylor
Sheelagh Semper
Charlotte Henley Babb
Tommy Acuff
Larry Morgan
Delia Houghland
Sarah Ashburn
Noah Sturdevant

Arthur Raisfeld

Jo Good

Andreas Brücher

Sheryl R. Hayes

Amaranth Dawe

Butch Howard

Larry Nash

Travis & Casey Schilling

Michelle E. Botwinick

Leonard Rosenthol

Lisa Hodges

Patrick Dugan

Michelle Kaylan

Patricia Reilley

Diane Jackson

Chris Kidd

Mark Wilson

Kimberly Richardson

Matthew Granville

Candice Carpenter

Theresa Glover

Salem Macknee

Pat Hayes

Jared Pierce

Elizabeth Donald

Andrea Judy

Leland Crawford

Vikki Perry

Valentine Wolfe

Noella Handley

Don Lynch

Jeremy Willhoit

D.R. Perry

Anthony D. Hudson

John A. McColley

Dennis Bolton
Shiloh Walker/J.C. Daniels
Andrew Torn
Sue Lambert
Emilia Agrafojo
Tracy Syrstad
Samantha Dunaway Bryant
Steven R Yanacsek
Rebecca Ledford
David Hess
Ray Spitz
Lars Klander

ABOUT THE AUTHOR

John G. Hartness is a teller of tales, a righter of wrong, defender of ladies' virtues, and some people call him Maurice, for he speaks of the pompatus of love. He is also the best-selling author of EPIC-Award-winning series *The Black Knight Chronicles* from Bell Bridge Books, a comedic urban fantasy series that answers the eternal question "Why aren't there more fat vampires?" In July of 2016. John was honored with the Manly Wade Wellman Award by the NC Speculative Fiction Foundation for Best Novel by a North Carolina writer in 2015 for the first Quincy Harker novella, *Raising Hell.*

In 2016, John teamed up with a pair of other publishing industry ne'er-do-wells and founded Falstaff Books, a publishing company dedicated to pushing the boundaries of literature and entertainment.

In his copious free time John enjoys long walks on the beach, rescuing kittens from trees and getting caught in the rain. An avid *Magic: the Gathering* player, John is strong in his nerd-fu and has sometimes been referred to as "the Kevin Smith of Charlotte, NC." And not just for his girth.

Find out more about John online
www.johnhartness.com

ALSO BY JOHN G. HARTNESS

THE BLACK KNIGHT CHRONICLES
The Black Knight Chronicles - Omnibus Edition
The Black Knight Chronicles Continues - Omnibus #2
All Knight Long - Black Knight Chronicles #7

BUBBA THE MONSTER HUNTER
Scattered, Smothered, & Chunked - Bubba the Monster Hunter Season One
Grits, Guns, & Glory - Bubba Season Two
Wine, Women, & Song - Bubba Season Three
Monsters, Magic, & Mayhem - Bubba Season Four
Born to Be Wild
Shinepunk: A Beauregard the Monster Hunter Collection

QUINCY HARKER, DEMON HUNTER
Year One: A Quincy Harker, Demon Hunter Collection
The Cambion Cycle - Quincy Harker, Year Two
Damnation - Quincy Harker Year Three
Salvation - Quincy Harker Year Four
Carl Perkins' Cadillac - A Quincy Harker, Demon Hunter Novel
Histories: A Quincy Harker, Demon Hunter Collection

SHINGLES
Zombies Ate My Homework: Shingles Book 5
Slow Ride: Shingles Book 12
Carnival of Psychos: Shingles Book 19
Jingle My Balls: Shingles Book 24

OTHER WORK

Queen of Kats

Fireheart

Amazing Grace: A Dead Old Ladies Detective Agency Mystery

From the Stone

The Chosen

Hazard Pay and Other Tales

FALSTAFF BOOKS

**Want to know what's new
And coming soon from
Falstaff Books?**

Try This Free Ebook Sampler

https://www.instafreebie.com/free/bsZnl

**Follow the link.
Download the file.
Transfer to your e-reader, phone, tablet, watch, computer,
whatever.
Enjoy.**

Made in United States
North Haven, CT
26 December 2021

13718731R00162